Ra… …es:

"Gleeful, c… …he tension between L… …nagical assailants, he… …r meddling mother, and… …eatening in a well-crafted, rollicking mystery." —*Publishers Weekly*

"Fans of Charlaine Harris's Sookie Stackhouse series will appreciate this series' lively heroine and the appealing combination of humor, mystery, and romance." —*Library Journal*

"Seasoned by a good measure of humor, this fantasy mystery is a genuine treat for readers of any genre."
—*SF Chronicle*

"With a wry, tongue-in-cheek style reminiscent of Janet Evanovich, this entertaining tale pokes fun at the deadly serious urban fantasy subgenre while drawing the reader into a fairly well-plotted mystery. The larger-than-life characters are apropos to the theatrical setting, and Esther's charming, self-deprecating voice makes her an appealingly quirky heroine. The chemistry between Esther and Lopez sizzles, while scenes of slapstick comedy will have will have the reader laughing out loud and eager for further tales of Esther's adventures." —*Romantic Times*

"Plenty of fun for readers." —*Locus*

"A delightful mélange of amateur sleuth mystery, romance, and urban fantasy."
—*The Barnes and Noble Review*

"A paranormal screwball comedy adventure. Light, happy, fantastically funny!"
—Jennifer Crusie,
New York Times bestselling author

Also by Laura Resnick:

DISAPPEARING NIGHTLY
DOPPELGANGSTER
UNSYMPATHETIC MAGIC
VAMPARAZZI
POLTERHEIST
THE MISFORTUNE COOKIE

LAURA RESNICK

The Misfortune Cookie

An Esther Diamond Novel

DAW BOOKS, INC.
DONALD A. WOLLHEIM, FOUNDER
375 Hudson Street, New York, NY 10014
ELIZABETH R. WOLLHEIM
SHEILA E. GILBERT
PUBLISHERS
www.dawbooks.com

Cover art by Daniel Dos Santos.

Cover design by G-Force Design.

DAW Book Collectors No. 1636.

DAW Books are distributed by Penguin Group (USA).

First Printing, November 2013
1 2 3 4 5 6 7 8 9

DAW TRADEMARK REGISTERED
U.S. PAT. AND TM. OFF. AND FOREIGN COUNTRIES
—MARCA REGISTRADA
HECHO EN U.S.A.

PRINTED IN THE U.S.A.

To my dear friend Cindy Chivatero Person, who was a good sport about wading through ankle-deep slush with me in New York's Chinatown during the Lunar New Year.

多福多壽

Much happiness and long life.

Prologue

鬼佬

Ghost Man

Sometimes in his dreams he still saw her, though she had been dead for more than a century. He saw again the grace of her tapered fingers as she poured tea, the warm smile that could unexpectedly brighten her serious face, and the intent way she listened when others spoke. Her dark eyes, so direct in their shrewdness, could be so bright with anger and so rich with tenderness. He remembered her unflinching courage, the delicate strength of her wrists as she wielded a weapon, the discipline and artistry of her body in combat . . . Her hair, when unbound and unwound, flowed like black silk . . .

And sometimes in his nightmares, he again saw her battered, blood-drenched corpse.

A world away and several lifetimes later, his memories of her were still as sharp as a blade.

"Gwai lo," she had called him when they met. *Ghost man,* referring to his white skin.

It was how the Chinese referred to Westerners, and it had come to signify "foreign devil." It was a phrase more commonly used in Canton, where her mother's family was from, far south of where he and she met. Unfriendly at first, the phrase later became her affectionate nickname for him.

Well, he hoped it was affectionate. Li Xiuying was not a woman who readily showed her emotions, after all, and the two of them came from such different worlds. But he knew that trust, respect, even friendship had developed between them. And after her death—after it was too late—he wondered if there could have been more . . .

They knew each other so briefly, though, in that tumultuous era which crushed all tenderness in its bloody fist. And apart from the rifts of language, culture, and society that lay between them, there was also an age difference of more than two hundred years. That alone might have prevented him from ever speaking his heart to her—or even opening it wide enough to look inside it himself—if she had lived.

Even so, he thought that if he had ever known a last love, a final blossoming of that all-too-human yearning, it had been she.

Li Xiuying . . . Beautiful Flower.

Brave, gallant, talented . . . Proud, defiant, principled. Stubborn, impatient, a little sharp-tempered.

He remembered his first sight of her, her delicate skin flushed with exertion, her eyes alight with pleasure as she worked with her students. She later told him that her fighting art was called Wing Chun and had been developed by a woman in the south of China. Li Xiuying's late mother had learned Wing Chun there many years ago before coming north with her new husband, now also deceased. She had taught it to her daughter, who now taught it to others.

He first arrived at her remote compound on a bright summer day with his one-man entourage—who was an incompetent interpreter and an even worse guide. They had been wandering in circles for days, and they had apparently broken the law in the last town they passed through. Two days ago, they had also narrowly escaped stumbling straight into a skirmish with the Boxers—the European name for the Society of Righteous and Harmonious Fists, whose rebellion against the corruption of both foreign powers and the crumbling Manchu dynasty was sweeping violently across northern China.

Upon being presented with her visitor, Li Xiuying said tersely to his interpreter, "If you and this *gwai lo* are looking for the Christian mission, then you're very lost."

He had learned enough of the language on his previous two visits to China to understand her words, and he made a gesture to silence his interpreter, who was translating this ungracious greeting into slow and stumbling English.

"I am Dr. Maximillian Zadok," he said in careful Mandarin, talking over the interpreter, who refused to give up. "The Magnum Collegium sent me. I thought I was expected."

The only change in his beautiful hostess' expression was a slight pursing of the lips. After a moment, she said, "Yes. You were expected some time ago. By now, I had ceased expecting you."

"I'm afraid my departure was delayed, and the journey took longer than expected," Max replied apologetically. "And I have met with further delays since I arrived in China. I assume you are aware of the Boxer Rebellion?" Rather than struggling to pronounce the Chinese phrase for the current hostilities, he used the English words.

Li Xiuying glanced at Max's interpreter, who just stared blankly at him.

Max made little punching motions as he clarified, "The Harmonious Fists. There's fighting all over this region."

"Yes, I know. I thought perhaps they had killed you," Li Xiuying said dispassionately. "They are not pleased with the presence of *gwai lo* in China."

"I understand. But *I* have not come to steal land,

kill Chinese, convert people to my religion, or feed opium to children," Max pointed out.

"The Harmonious Fists will not ask you *why* you are—"

"I have come to consult a respected sorceress about the mystery of my long life and slow aging, in hopes that I might unlock its secret and share that knowledge with my colleagues." He added, "I was given to understand that the sorceress was also keen to explore this mystery."

She said, with a change in her tone, "Your Mandarin is not good."

"I apologize."

"No need. Very few *gwai lo* bother to learn our language. I appreciate your courtesy in speaking it . . . a little."

Max realized she was amused. He smiled ruefully. "It is a very challenging language."

"Are you English?" she asked.

"No."

Li Xiuying gestured to his interpreter as she said, "But that is the language he uses with you, is it not? I recognize it from the missionaries."

"I speak English, but it is not my native tongue. I was born near Prague."

She frowned. "Where?"

"It's a city in Austria-Hungary." Seeing her perplexed expression, he added, "That's a kingdom in Europe."

"Oh."

"I have a certain ability with languages, but I found it very difficult to learn some Mandarin during my previous visits to China."

"When were you here?" she asked.

"My last visit was almost 50 years ago."

Max had arrived in 1853, early in the long and bloody Taiping Rebellion, in which millions perished. The Manchu dynasty, which had conquered China in 1644, had presided over centuries of violent internal unrest, and it had succumbed decades ago to domination and humiliation by foreign powers. Its severely weakened government was now divided into bickering factions. Some favored siding with the Boxers, while others favored relying on the foreign powers, whose destructive influence in China was chief among the Boxers' grievances.

China really *wasn't* the best place for a *gwai lo* to be in 1900, least of all one who specialized in mystical Evil rather than mundane warfare and civil unrest. Max regretted giving in to the Collegium's exhortations to make one more effort to unlock the secret of his longevity. He vowed that this was the last time. He had been blessed (or cursed) with an unusually long life, and after this, he would not waste any more of it in trying to determine exactly what alchemical formula had *made* it so long.

The sorceress whom he had come all this way to

consult was studying him curiously. "And when was your first visit to China?"

"Oh, a long time ago," Max replied.

"I would say the Taiping Rebellion was a long time ago," she pointed out.

"Ah. Yes." The longer he lived, the less easily he recognized how different his own sense of time was from everyone else's. "My first visit was more than a century ago." After a moment, he added, "The roads have improved."

"May I ask when you were born?"

"Of course." He knew that most people who met him now assumed he was in his early fifties, but his true age was nearly two hundred years older than that. Upon noticing that his interpreter couldn't convey the date he named, Max elaborated, "My birth was approximately twelve years after the Manchus came to power in China." Seeing how startled Li Xiuying looked, he said, "I thought this information was shared with you by the Magnum Collegium."

"Oh, I am not the sorceress you seek," she said.

"No?" He was surprised. Although young by his own standards, she appeared to be a mature woman and in authority here, and she had an air of gravitas that suggested power. "I beg your pardon. Who am I seeking?"

"My grandmother," said Li Xiuying. "But I regret to inform you that she died four months ago."

"Four months?" he repeated in dismay. Before he had even set out for China.

There were numerous ways, Max reflected wearily, in which the twentieth century was proving to be much like its predecessors.

"Grandmother looked forward to your visit. But she was very old and could not linger any longer."

"I am sorry to hear this sad news." Out of habit, Max added in Latin, "May God have mercy on her soul."

Li Xiuying and the guide exchanged a puzzled glance.

Then his hostess said decisively, "You have had a long journey, and you are my grandmother's eagerly awaited guest. You are most welcome."

"Thank you," said Max. "With your permission, we shall pass the night here."

"Of course."

"And in the morning, we will begin our return journey," he added to his guide, who reacted with undisguised horror.

It was fortunate that Max spoke adequate Mandarin, since his unenthusiastic guide and interpreter fled during the night. It was even more fortunate that the loss of his escort delayed Max's departure; the following day, Li Xiuying received word that the Dowager Empress had declared war against all foreign powers in China, and the foreign quarter of Peking was under siege. Max agreed to stay here while they awaited further news, rather than travel across the countryside in these circumstances, conspicuously European as he was.

The next information they received was that the Boxers, as well as government troops and authorities, were murdering foreigners throughout the region, including women and children.

Realizing what this meant, Li Xiuying rode out with a small retinue of armed warriors to protect the local Christian mission. She didn't approve of their converting Chinese to their foreign religion, but she approved even less of wanton murder. Max, who agreed with her, insisted on accompanying her.

They arrived too late to prevent the slaughter, so they took the survivors back to Li Xiuying's compound. This courageous act of compassion became known, as was bound to happen, and it sealed her fate. When the crisis came, thirteen days after that defiant rescue, Max honored her wishes by protecting the innocents in her care, and he accepted her decision to fight rather than flee when her home was attacked. But he knew when he saw her lifeless body that her honor had come at much too high a price. Too high, at least, for him.

Yet even now, in his dreams, sometimes she lived anew, still brave, stubborn, skilled, and beautiful, still vibrant in the bloody twilight of a decrepit and doomed dynasty that had fallen more than a century ago. And the ghost of this last love shadowed his heart.

1

不幸

Misfortune, adversity

Detective Connor Lopez slept with me and then didn't call.

What else is there to say about a man after you've said that? I mean, doesn't that just say it *all?*

Except that I can add one more thing: After he did that, then he *arrested* me.

Yes, Lopez deserved to die for that. He really did.

But the heart is fickle, so when I realized someone was trying to kill him, I got upset and was determined to save his life. No, I have no rational explanation for this.

Well, okay, I suppose there was the usual "precious value of human life" and "in order for Evil to triumph, all that is necessary is for a struggling actress to do nothing" stuff. But any noble motives I may have had were pretty mixed up with the other kind—such as feeling that if anyone had a right to kill Lopez, that person was me. So when a murderer got in line ahead of me, I had to do something about it.

And, of course, the fact that the killer was targeting and taking out *other* people, too, was also a crucial factor. Sure, I try to mind my own business and abide by a live-and-let-live philosophy. You have to, if you want to stay sane and out of prison when living in the Big Apple, where people from every walk of life are all crammed together and living on top of each other in the city that never sleeps (or even takes a little nap).

But when someone starts, oh, *killing* my fellow New Yorkers—even the ones I don't like and can't honestly mourn—I take exception to that. Because sooner or later (usually sooner), a killer's victims and targets include the innocent—in which group I number myself, my friends, my colleagues, and (as long as they pay me) my various employers. I used to include Lopez in that group, too, until he slept with me and then *didn't call*—not even after I left him a message *asking* him to call.

God, how I regretted leaving that message. I regretted sleeping with him even *more,* obviously. But that message certainly ranked second on the list of things I fervently wished I had never done.

At the time, it seemed a perfectly normal thing to do. You sleep late after a long night of hot, passionate sex with a man whom you've fantasized about too many times—a man who, in the flesh, exceeded your steamiest imaginings. And when you wake up alone, because he had to leave for work at dawn, you feel sated, glowing, and giddy, and you can't stop thinking about him. So you phone him, and when he doesn't answer, you leave a slightly gushing message on his voicemail. Of course you do. It's perfectly natural.

Or so it had seemed the morning after.

Now, a week later, I felt dizzy with humiliation every time I thought of Lopez listening to that message and deciding *not* to call me. Ever again, apparently . . .

Where was I?

Oh, right. People getting killed.

When murder is mystical in nature, I know from personal experience how important it is to nip that in the bud. Because if you fail to step up to the plate as soon as you realize Evil is rearing its ugly head again, then the next thing you know, a voracious demon summoned forth from some hell dimension will wind up eating half of Midtown during a lunar eclipse. (Don't even get me started. It was this whole big thing.)

So that's my excuse for going to great lengths—wholly unappreciated, I might add—to save Lopez's life in Chinatown when he damn well didn't deserve such consideration from me.

Also, I really needed the work. I got a role in an indie film after the holidays, and there was no *way* I was going to let Evil mess that up for me. Especially not when, thanks to Lopez, I had no other way to pay my rent.

Not after the night he arrested me, exactly one week after he'd slept with me.

FADE IN: New Year's Eve in Little Italy . . .

Esther Diamond, a grumpy, depressed actress, twenty-seven years old, is waiting tables at Bella Stella, a notorious mob hangout and tourist trap on Mulberry Street, where she works as a singing waitress when she's "resting." About five foot six, with an average build, fair skin, brown eyes, and shoulder-length brown hair, her cheekbones are generally considered her best feature. Her looks are versatile enough for a variety of stage roles, including romantic leads, and she's done a little television work, but she's not Hollywood gorgeous.

Which is *not* to say that she's so unattractive that it naturally follows that a man who spent half the night making love to her a week ago would be so horrified by the sight of her first thing in the morning that he'd decide never to call her again. Not even after she's left a message asking him to call! Where does a man get the *nerve*, the stinking gall, to treat a woman that way? A man who pursued a woman to her apartment that night! A man who told her he wanted to get back together . . . Or together for the first time, I guess, since they'd never really been . . . That is to say, we'd always . . . But we never . . . Oh, forget it.

Where was I?

Oh, right, working at Bella Stella on New Year's Eve.

The restaurant, which did good business even in lean times, had been a gift to Stella Butera, its owner, from her lover Handsome Joey Gambello. This generous gesture may not have been wholly disinterested, since Bella Stella was rumored to launder money for the Gambello crime family. I had never met Handsome Joey, who got whacked right there in the restaurant a few years before Stella hired me.

Stella Butera was a fair employer, and since she wanted servers who had performance skills, she accepted that our acting careers were more important to us than waiting tables. Prior to becoming a semi-regular staffer at Bella Stella a couple of years ago, I had been fired from several demeaning, poorly paid jobs by managers who were unwilling to accommodate my occasional scheduling requests so I could go to an audition, or who were enraged when I wanted to spend two days acting in a guest role on a television show more than I wanted to work the underpaid shifts they refused to let me have off. Stella, by contrast, was accommodating about that sort of thing. She also understood that actors come and go from day jobs, depending on whether or not we've got acting work. So I was able to rotate in and out of the staff at Stella's pretty comfortably.

Most of the time, that was. By the time the limited run had ended for *The Vampyre,* an Off-Broadway play I was working in through late November, Stella's staff was so packed with musical theater majors coming home from college for the holidays that she had very little work for me in December. And one or two shifts per week wasn't going to cover my rent—especially not in Manhattan. I live in a rent-controlled apartment that's rapidly surrendering to entropy and located in the seedier part of the West Thirties; but in New York, that just means it's very expensive rather than catastrophically ruinous.

So, facing the cold and harsh reality of my living expenses, I had taken a job in December playing Santa's Jewish elf at Fenster & Co., a famous old department store in Midtown. Depending on your point of view, this was either a blessing or a curse, since it meant I was around to foil a deviously demented and deadly scheme to destroy the store, the Fenster family, and (incidentally) much of New York City.

Despite my role in saving the volatile Fenster family (and a large swath of Manhattan's retail industry) from annihilation, I felt certain the Fensters would never want me back in their employ, even if they still had a retail empire next Christmas—which was by no means certain, now that one of their own family members had been exposed as a key culprit in the series of high-profile heists which had wrecked the season of love, joy, and shopping this year. And, in fact, I was perfectly comfortable with no longer being wanted at Fenster & Co. (whereas no longer being wanted by the arresting officer in that mess was making me a little crazy these days), since I was still undecided about which experience had been more horrifying: working the sales floor of Fenster's as an elf during the holidays, or confronting a voracious solstice demon rising from a hell dimension there.

In any case, elf season was now over—much like my train wreck of a love life—and no one really hires new staff between Christmas and New Year's, never mind holding auditions. (In fact, with the business so dead at this time of year, my agent was in Wisconsin until early January, reluctantly visiting his family and probably drinking a little human blood. But that's another story.) However, on the day I realized that my food supply had dwindled down to one box of bargain-brand pasta and some nonfat yogurt, I finally caught a break.

Stella called me to say that a couple of the college kids who'd signed up for tonight's lucrative New Year's Eve shift had just informed her, at three o'clock this afternoon, that they'd decided to go to a party out on Long Island instead. They also asked her to mail them their final paychecks for the holiday season. Stella told me she was thinking of having the checks personally delivered by a Gambello enforcer who'd explain the meaning of responsibility to them.

I, on the other hand, wanted to send a thank you card to those brats. I was very pleased to get called in for tonight's shift. Wiseguys tip well, and tourists in town for New Year's Eve usually do, too. By the time I finished the shift, I'd have a nice wad of cash in my pocket, which was a profound relief to me. Although I had scraped together enough to pay my January rent, I had no money left over for food or utilities. And within the next few days, the extra holiday staff would be going back to school, so Stella should have plenty of shifts available for me after this. At least I'd be able to eat this month—and start saving for next month's rent.

Working at the restaurant tonight would also get me out of my apartment, and it was high time for that. I'd been wallowing for several days, and I had no plans for tonight, having been too grumpy and depressed to make any. So I welcomed the obligation, as a singing server, to focus on something other than my empty bank account and my humiliation (as well as my raging hurt) over being dumped right after sex.

One other guy had done this to me. Back in college. That kind of treatment is mortifying when you're nineteen, and it had taken me a long time to get over it. But that jerk did the same thing to other girls, too, as I later learned. Whereas Lopez had never seemed like that kind of guy to me. Whatever else I may have thought of him from time to time (rigid, cranky, critical, cynical, arrogant, and, believe me, I could go on and on), I'd always thought he was a good man, and a sincere one. And I was . . . fond of him. Or had been. Until I realized he wasn't going to call. So this was even *more* mortifying than my previous experience had been with this kind of insensitive, inexcusable, dipshit behavior.

It was also painful because our—let's call it "friendship"—had been complicated from the start. When that guy in college had dumped me right after getting me into bed, I had wondered obsessively if he hadn't liked my body or had found me sexually boring. But Lopez's uninhibited enthusiasm that night, and the following morning as he was getting ready to leave for work, ensured I had no insecurities about his views on that score . . . so I was obsessing over a lot of other possibilities. Did he think I was too flaky? Too much trouble? Not someone he really wanted to get serious with, after all, despite some of the things he'd recently said to me about this?

Or was he just such a *guy* that it didn't occur to him I might expect to hear from him—and to see him again—after he'd spent the night in my bed? What sort of person *doesn't call* after that? For a *week?*

Yes, I really needed to get out of the apartment and focus on something else.

So it was a relief, in more ways than one, to be serving food and drink to notorious criminals at Bella Stella as midnight approached on New Year's Eve. In fact, *pretending* to be in a festive mood was making me feel better. I'm a professional, after all, so I had my game face on from the moment I started my shift. I gave good service, I was friendly to visitors and cheerfully firm with the wiseguys (who could be a little grabby), and I threw my heart into every song I sang for the crowd.

There are various schools of impassioned thought in my craft about whether it's better to work from the inside out or the outside in. Method acting versus technical acting. Do you produce real tears onstage because you dredge up your inner emotions eight shows per week, or because you reproduce the facial expressions and respiratory patterns that physiologically precede crying? I'm not a passionate proponent of one school over the other, because I've always found that if I work from both outside and inside, the two processes meet somewhere in the middle and produce a result that's convincing and sincere. And sometimes one side works faster than the other. When I played Miss Jane Aubrey in *The Vampyre*, for example, working on the accent, posture, and body language of a genteel Englishwoman in the early nineteenth century helped me understand some of Jane's more obtuse choices in that play (such as her submissive thralldom to the notorious Lord Ruthven, the vampire who marries her and then eats her—and not in a nice way).

So pretending to be in a good mood that night at Bella Stella helped me focus on thoughts and feelings that supported this pretense, and I started actually having a good time and enjoying myself.

True, the façade was fragile enough that if anyone asked me to sing a ballad, let alone a torch song, there was a real risk I wouldn't get through it without choking up. But since it was New Year's Eve and everyone was in party mode, all the requests I got were for upbeat numbers: *Fly Me To the Moon*, *Mack the Knife* (boy, do gangsters love that song), *Beyond the Sea*, *That's Amore,* and, of course, *New York, New York.*

Jimmy "Legs" Brabancaccio, a Gambello soldier who actually had quite a good voice, rose from his dinner table to wow the crowd with his rendition of *My Way.* Then, at the insistence of our customers, a waiter named Ned sang *Mack the Knife* (I mean, they *really* love that song). Then Ronnie Romano, also from the Gambello crew, sang a traditional Italian ditty that was unfamiliar to me, but that our accordionist knew. Ronnie had a reedy, off-key voice, but he sang with heart.

Ronnie and Jimmy Legs were sitting at a table in my station, at their insistence. I was sort of a favorite with the Gambello crime family, since my friend Max and I had inadvertently wound up helping them out a couple of times. Victor Gambello, the Shy Don, had made it clear in public that he considered us friends of the family. He had also tried to help us when Max and I were recently held prisoner for about eighteen hours by Fenster & Co. (Call it a misunderstanding. We'd had a slight arson mishap while confronting Evil.)

Despite Stella Butera's connection to the family, I found it a little odd that wiseguys hung out regularly at the restaurant, since three Gambellos had been murdered here in recent years. First there was Handsome Joey Gambello, who was shot to death. Two or three years later, Frankie Mastiglione got fatally knifed here while he was only halfway through his dinner. Then just seven months ago, Chubby Charlie Chiccante was shot while I was waiting on his table. I was an eyewitness, which had led to my becoming more familiar with the NYPD's Organized Crime Control Bureau (OCCB) than I'd ever expected to be.

Of course, all the shooting and stabbing probably made it a little odd that *I* hung out here, too. But between Stella's management style and the good tips I earned, it was the best non-acting job I'd ever had, despite the mortality rate.

"Hey, Esther! Another round!" Jimmy Legs shouted at me, trying to be heard above the cheerful din of the crowd and the soaring tones of Ned giving his all to *Feeling Good.*

"Not for me," said Lucky Battistuzzi.

"Aw, come on, Lucky!" Ronnie urged.

"Nah, you get to be my age," said Lucky, "and you gotta pace yourself. Besides, the boss said he might want to see me later."

I knew that references to "the boss" meant Don Victor Gambello, who was in his eighties, chronically ill, and seldom left his Forest Hills house, out in Queens. He also seemed to be an insomniac, since it wasn't unusual for him to summon Lucky in the middle of the night.

"Tonight?" I said. "But Lucky, it's New Year's Eve."

The old hit man shrugged philosophically. "We don't really get days off in Our Thing, kid." He added, "Just like you, huh?"

Due to the way that facing off against Evil encourages the most unlikely people to become bedfellows, so to speak, Alberto "Lucky Bastard" Battistuzzi, who'd gotten his nickname by surviving various attempts on his life, was someone I considered a trusted friend. Somewhere in his sixties, with short gray hair, an expressive, heavily lined face, and shrewd brown eyes, he wasn't inclined to share any "professional" secrets with me, and I wasn't rash enough to encourage him to do so. But I had seen enough to know that Lucky, a semi-retired Gambello *capo*, was someone on whom the Shy Don relied.

"And I'm *glad* to be working New Year's Eve," I assured Lucky. "No income, no eating."

"So get your *boyfriend* to take you out for dinner," Ronnie said darkly. "Cops get regular salaries, don't they?"

Ronnie had never approved of my dating a police officer—let alone one who was a detective in the OCCB.

"He's not my boyfriend," I said. "We have nothing to do with each other."

"How's that?" Lucky looked puzzled. "When we was investigatin' that polterheisty demon business at Fenster's last week, I thought it kinda seemed like you and NYPD's Boy Wonder were getting ready to start choosing china patterns."

"No, you imagined it," I said tersely, feeling my stomach sink. "So that's another round for Jimmy and Ronnie, but nothing for you?"

"I'll have a cup of coffee," Lucky said. "What's wrong with these young guys? The way the good detective looked at you, especially when he thought you was about to go down for the dirt nap, I thought for sure—"

"Are you guys done with these dessert plates?" I asked loudly. "Why hasn't the bus boy removed these yet? Ralph! This table needs clearing!"

"Coming!"

"If Esther's not interested in that guy," Ronnie

said censoriously to Lucky, "that's for the best, case closed, and you shouldn't poke your nose in."

"Thank you, Ronnie," I said.

"A girl like Esther with a *cop?*" Ronnie shook his head. "It ain't right. It was never right. It's good that it's over."

"It never got started," I said firmly, as Ralph the bus boy started clearing their table. "We went on a few dates. That's all. There was nothing else between us."

"Oh, if I were gulling-bull enough to believe that," Lucky said, "you really think I woulda survived this long in *my* line of work?"

I frowned. "I think you mean gullible."

Ralph, who was moving with more rapidity than grace, knocked over an empty wine glass while clearing the dishes.

"Careful!" I grabbed it before it could roll off the table, then I wiped up the spot where a few remaining drops of red wine had spilled.

"Oops! Sorry," Ralph said anxiously. "Did it spill on you?" He almost tipped over another glass as he gestured at Jimmy.

"Watch out," I said, moving this other glass out of Ralph's reach before he wound up knocking it into Lucky's lap.

"Sorry!" Ralph said again, agitated now. "Are you okay?"

"We're fine, kid," Lucky said to the bus boy. "But do us a favor and back away slowly with your hands in plain sight."

Coming from a notorious Gambello hitter, the comment, though intended as a joke, obviously made Ralph nervous. I thought he probably didn't have the temperament for working at Stella's. Or the coordination to work in a crowded restaurant.

Jimmy Legs confirmed that impression, after Ralph headed toward the kitchen with his load of dirty dishes, by saying, "That kid nearly scalded me last week when he was topping up my coffee. He's a menace to society."

"They shouldn't oughta let guys that dangerous circulate freely," Ronnie said with a disapproving frown.

Going straight back to the topic that I had hoped was finished now, Lucky squinted at me and said dubiously, "So you and Mr. NYPD really ain't together?"

I didn't have to answer, since Ronnie jumped in: "Jesus, give it a rest, would you? The cop's out of her life. She said so. Let's not go diggin' up that corpse."

I winced at the imagery.

Jimmy Legs added, "Ronnie's right, Lucky. If Esther broke the engagement—"

"We were never engaged," I said.

"—then you should leave it alone. She can do a lot better than that guy." Jimmy continued, "Good riddance to him. He don't know how much he's lost, letting go of a girl like her. Someday he'll regret it. But there it is. Whaddya gonna do?"

Oh, great, now I felt like crying again.

"I'll go get your drinks," I said quickly. "We're getting close to midnight. The bar is swamped, but I'll try to make it quick."

When I returned to their table a few minutes later, Lucky had decided to accept the drab news about my love life. "I gotta admit I'm surprised," he said, "but I guess it's just as well you're not dating the detective."

"This is what I been saying!" Ronnie clinked glasses with Jimmy.

"Because, lemme tell you," Lucky said with feeling, "that guy is giving me *such* a pain in my . . . you know where." He didn't like to use crude language in front of a lady.

"Uh-huh," I said, setting down his coffee.

"The boss' lawyer has been on the phone every day this week with the DA's office. And with OCCB, too, so he's talked to your boyfriend a bunch of times."

Well, that's *probably making Lopez's holidays merry,* I thought with grim satisfaction. "He's not my boyfriend."

"The boss is protestin' their outrageous intrusions into his family's perfectly legitimate business interests."

"I see."

"I swear, by now those mooks at OCCB probably know how many times the boss gets up at night to use the john." Lucky shook his head. "Victor Gambello don't need this kind of aggravation at his age."

I tactfully refrained from pointing out that the Shy Don could have avoided all this by choosing a different career.

"You figure that's why the boss might want to see you later?" Jimmy Legs asked Lucky. "*More* trouble with OCCB? And on New Year's Eve, for the love of God!"

"Probably," Lucky said gloomily.

"The *nerve* of those guys," Ronnie fumed. "Ruining the boss' holidays. There oughta be a law."

Jimmy grunted in agreement.

Lucky said to me, "So it's not like I'd be dancing at your wedding to Detective Lopez, kid."

"We weren't engaged," I said wearily. In fact, the closest Lopez and I had ever even gotten to a dinner date was when he bought me a chili dog in the park a couple of nights before Christmas.

"Hey, Esther, we need another song!" Freddie the Hermit called from his table. He was here tonight with a date—and his companion wasn't Mrs. Freddie. In any other setting, I'd have thought she was a hooker, based on her big hair and tiny clothing; but among wiseguys, very few of whom practiced monogamy, her look was fairly standard for girlfriends and mistresses.

"As soon as the ball drops," I promised Freddie over my shoulder. Midnight was only minutes away, and Stella had turned on the TV so we could watch the annual countdown ritual in Times Square, about fifty blocks north of here.

"A duet!" shouted Tommy Two Toes. "Esther and Ed should do a duet!"

"Ned," said Ned. "My name is Ned."

"Whatever. We want you should do a duet with Esther."

"As soon as the ball drops," I repeated.

Brushing past me on his way to the bar, Ned muttered, "Anything but *Mack the Knife* again."

"Agreed."

"I swear, I hear that song in my sleep ever since I started working here."

"I'm glad you weren't as serious with Lopez as I thought," Lucky said to me, still riffing on his theme. "Because it really burns me up that he ain't helping us at all."

"That bum!" said Jimmy Legs.

"Well, he is an OCCB detective," I pointed out, though I had no interest in defending Lopez. "Helping the Gambello family isn't anywhere in his job description. Just the opposite, in fact."

"But he *knows* we wasn't involved in the Fenster hijackings!" Lucky said in outrage. "He knows that better than anybody, since he's the one who arrested the real culprits. And now who's suffering for the crimes committed by a couple of rotten kids with too much time on their hands? *We* are. How is *that* fair? But is your boyfriend standing up for us? No!"

"He ain't her boyfriend," said Jimmy Legs.

"Good riddance," said Ronnie, clinking his glass again with Jimmy's.

After several heavily loaded Fenster trucks were hijacked during the Christmas shopping season, the NYPD came under heavy pressure from the media to solve the crimes. Consequently, OCCB came under heavy pressure from the Police Commissioner, because the Gambello crime family, who had a history of hijacking Fenster trucks, were the obvious suspects. But, actually, the heists were the brainchild of a vengeful Santa and a demented Fenster who used mystical means to recruit unwitting accomplices for the robberies. (According to news accounts this week, the NYPD vaguely attributed the couple's control of their unwilling accomplices to drugs and "psychological conditioning." None of the dupes could remember anything about those events, there was no evidence against them, and the two villains who had manipulated them were pleading guilty. So it looked like the case file was closing quickly on that one.)

Nonetheless, the initial erroneous assumption

that the Gambellos were involved in the heists meant that OCCB—which "had to show juice," as Lucky had put it, due to all the media scrutiny—brought a whole new meaning to the phrase "thorough investigation," digging deep into the Gambellos' lives in their search for evidence. And this was still proving to be extremely uncomfortable for the Gambellos, though they were cleared in the Fenster hijackings when the arrests were made a week ago.

That was the same night Lopez came to my apartment and had his way with me, then left a few hours later for his shift on Christmas morning. And never looked back.

That bum.

"Here we go!" Tommy Two Toes shouted, startling me.

Stella Butera, wearing tight leopard-print clothing covered in sequins, appeared next to me and bellowed, "Ten! Nine! Eight!"

I blinked and realized the old year was ending. The big ball was descending in Times Square. The crowd on the TV screen, like the crowd inside Bella Stella, was counting down to a fresh start. A new beginning. A chance to get it right this time.

I joined in. "Three! Two! One! Happy New Year!"

Everyone in the restaurant started cheering and embracing. Stella gave me a bone-crushing hug, then allowed Jimmy Legs to kiss her. I gave Lucky a hug and kissed his weathered cheek. Ralph the bus boy tried to hug me and somehow wound up nearly poking my eye out. In a way, this was a relief, since it gave me a convenient excuse to let a few tears trickle out of my eyes. I was feeling emotional now.

That year is over, the year when I met Lopez. It's done. I swear *I'm going to move on. He's in the past now.*

I stumbled toward the bar with one hand pressed gingerly over my eye while a mortified Ralph apologized to my retreating back. Amidst all the cheering and hugging, the accordionist began playing *Auld Lang Syne.* Everyone in the restaurant started singing. Everyone but me; I was elbowing my way through the crowd so I could get some ice from the bartender for my throbbing eye.

I leaned quietly against a wall for a few minutes, trying to keep out of the way as I soothed my eye with a couple of ice cubes wrapped in a linen napkin.

I'd met Lopez in the spring, and for the rest of the year, I'd had a lot of highs and lows because of him. The highs, though few and far between, kept making up for the lows . . . Until this past week. Now that I was out of the apartment and working again, now that it was a new year, a fresh start, time to shake off old troubles and bad habits . . . I realized just *how* low I had been in recent days because of him, and I was determined not to go back there. So I made my New Year's resolution while huddled in the corner of a crowded mob hangout with a cold, wet napkin pressed to my teary eye.

From this moment on, I vowed to myself, *I am getting over him. From this moment on, I'm only going forward and upward.*

Feeling better, I dropped my melting ice cubes into the sink behind the bar, dropped my damp napkin into the laundry, and checked in with the kitchen, where I was expecting an order to be ready for a couple of late diners.

"Table seventeen?" said the cook. "Yeah, we just sent that out a second ago, Esther. That kid Ralph took it for you. He felt real bad about blinding you, or something?"

"Okay, thanks," I said, grabbing some parmesan and heading for my table to make sure they had everything they needed.

Since Ralph was loaded down with plates of food and I wasn't, I nearly caught up to him. A few more steps, and I could have prevented what happened next. As it was, though, I was only close enough to shout a warning when Ralph stumbled, his hand tilted, and a big serving of lasagna flew straight at Lucky's head. Thanks to the reflexes that had probably saved his life on several occasions, Lucky sprang out of his chair when he heard me shout and saw the pasta flying straight at his face. But he wasn't quite quick enough to escape contact, and it hit him squarely in the chest. A huge mound of gooey cheese and steaming tomato sauce clung to him lovingly for a moment, as if temporarily immune to the laws of gravity, then tumbled to the floor with a messy splatter that flecked his shoes and trousers with glistening red spots of savory sauce.

After a collective gasp, the whole restaurant fell silent, staring in awkward anticipation at the notorious old mobster who was now a sullied mess. Ralph looked white as a sheet, and I feared he might faint from sheer terror as Lucky scowled at him.

"You know," Lucky said slowly, "I never whacked anyone for personal reasons. Not even once." He looked down at his ruined shirt, then back at Ralph. "But I could make an exception."

Ronnie and Jimmy guffawed. Ralph started hyperventilating. Stella grabbed the bus boy's arm and dragged him away before he could pass out or vomit, either of which seemed possible. I snatched up the discarded linen napkins lying on Lucky's table and started dabbing at the mess on his chest. Our accordionist began playing again, and the rest of the customers went back to their revels.

"That's not gonna do any good," Lucky said to me as I blotted and smeared. "What a *mess.*"

"Come on," I said briskly, taking his arm. "We need a sink."

"That kid needs to find another line of work," Lucky grumbled as I led him through the restaurant.

"Something where he ain't endangering life and limb. And lasagna."

"He's going back to school in a couple of days," I said soothingly.

"Christ, I hope he ain't studying surgery or something like that."

When we got to the door of the ladies room, which was my destination, Lucky balked. "I can't go in there!"

"All right." I pulled him across the narrow hall at the back of the restaurant and pushed open the other door. "Men's room, then."

"Hey!" A man inside exclaimed when he saw me entering.

"Oops."

"Sorry!" Lucky dragged me back out of the room. "She's *sorry.*"

Realizing the man was standing at the urinal with his fly unzipped, I closed my eyes until after Lucky had shut the door.

"You can't go in *there.*" The old hit man was scandalized. "What's the matter with you?"

"Sorry," I said. "Very distracted tonight."

For God's sake, get him out of your head, would you? It's a brand new year. Move on, *already.*

"Give me those." Lucky said in exasperation as he snatched the napkins out of my hand. "I can deal with this myself. You go . . . do things."

"Maybe you should take off your shirt and soak it for a few minutes," I said.

"Oh, and *then* what am I gonna wear?"

"I'll check the staff room and see if we've got any extra—"

"Never mind. I'll figure out something. You just move along," Lucky said to me. "That guy you interrupted in the john won't want to see *you* standing here when he comes through this door."

True enough. I nodded and went back out into the restaurant, leaving Lucky to try to clean about a pint of Bella Stella's special sauce off his clothes.

As I passed Lucky's table, Jimmy asked me, "Has Lucky killed the kid?"

"No, but I think he'll be in the bathroom for a while," I replied.

"We should have a name for that dish," said Ronnie. "How about Lucky Lasagna?"

"With extra sauce!" Jimmy added.

While they enjoyed their laugh, Freddie the Hermit insisted it was time for the duet that Ned and I had promised.

"All right," I said as Ned finished wiping a table and nodded his agreement.

"Mack the Knife!" Tommy Two Toes shouted.

"Yeah, give us Mackie again!" Ronnie said.

"That does it," Ned said to me, losing all will to live. "I'm going to go drown myself in the kitchen sink."

"Wait, wait." I grabbed his arm as he turned to go. "I'm not taking requests for this one, fellas. It's dealer's choice."

"Fair enough," said Freddie. "Let the lady decide!"

The accordionist asked me, "What'll it be, Esther?"

I thought of my New Year's resolution. *"From This Moment On."*

"I'm not sure I remember all the words," Ned warned me.

"Just follow me," I said with determination.

He did, and although we'd never worked together before, we performed well as a duo. So well that the customers demanded another song and we promptly complied. The crowd was jubilant, the joint was jumping, and by the time we were on our third song, *The Best Is Yet To Come* (in keeping with my personal New Year's theme), the two of us were literally dancing on tabletops.

Ned leapt from Tommy's table to Freddie's while singing about what a ripe plum he had plucked from the tree of life.

Ronnie and Jimmy were swaying and singing along as I danced atop their table. Giving Ned a flirtatious look, I raised the hem of my black skirt to show him a modest flash of stocking-clad thigh as I sang that he ain't seen nothin' yet. This went over well, and our audience gave a boisterous cheer as I inched my hem a little higher and kept singing, smiling at Ned.

At that exact moment, Detective Connor Lopez entered the restaurant, wearing a dark blue vest with "NYPD" printed on it and his badge prominently displayed as he shouted, "Police! Nobody move!"

2

陰陽

Yin-yang

Complementary yet contradictory forces, often represented as female and male.

More than a dozen cops barreled into the restaurant right behind Lopez, all of them wearing NYPD vests or jackets, all of them armed and shouting.

One of them was saying into a megaphone, "NYPD! Stay seated! This is the police! Do not move! Stay where you are!"

Holy shit.

"It's a raid!" Ronnie screamed as he leapt to his feet. "Police raid! Run! *Run!*"

"Are you *nuts?*" Jimmy stayed seated and tried to tug Ronnie back down into his chair.

Frightened diners were already screaming. Some jumped out of their seats and were strongly (and *loudly)* encouraged to sit right back down. Other people were sliding out of their chairs to hide under their tables. The accordion squealed atonally as the staggering musician got squeezed between the panicking people and the cops who were ordering them to stay calm.

A confused customer bumped hard against the table Ned was still standing on. The actor lost his balance as the table rocked; he flailed briefly, then flew headfirst into a pair of cops. The impact carried all three of them to the floor, shouting and groaning, while startled diners around them shrieked in alarm.

"What the *hell . . . ?"* I glanced around frantically, unable to form a coherent thought. My heart was pounding, my breath coming in little pants. I looked at Lopez, who was standing in front of my table, staring up at me in apparent shock, his jaw hanging open, his eyes wide with horror.

Not exactly the expression a woman hopes to see on a man's face the first time they meet again after spending a passionate night together.

"It's a *raid!"* Ronnie screamed while being strong-armed by the police *and* Jimmy Legs. "Save yourself!"

"Will you calm down?" Jimmy shouted at his colleague. "They'll put a bullet in you if you keep this up!"

"He's right!" confirmed a grimacing, redheaded cop who was trying to subdue the panicking mobster. "You're tempting me, Ronnie!"

"You can't shoot him!" Jimmy turned on the cop in outrage. "I want my lawyer!"

"Viva la revolución!" someone in the kitchen screamed. *"Viva la libertad!"*

Everyone paused for a moment to look in that direction.

Then Ralph dropped a whole tub of dishes. It fell to the floor with an earsplitting crash of shattering ceramic and glassware, and everyone started screaming again.

"Sorry!" Ralph wailed. "Sorry about that!"

Still on top of my table, I gaped down at Lopez. "What's going on? What are you *doing?"*

He blinked, as if surprised to hear me speak. Then he frowned thunderously. "What are *you* doing?"

"Working!"

"No, what are you doing *here?"* He was scowling up at me as if my very existence offended him.

"Working!" I repeated, staring down at him while people all around us continued screeching, shouting, and bounding around the restaurant in agitation.

Stella was bellowing, "What the hell do you think you're doing? I got rights! I'll *sue!* Get out of my restaurant!"

I looked away from Lopez long enough to see a couple of cops shove Stella up against the wall next to Ronnie, Jimmy, Tommy Two Toes, and Freddie the Hermit. They were all being frisked, along with four or five other Gambello wiseguys. A policewoman started searching Stella, who continued shouting threats and questions despite being ordered to pipe down.

Lopez said something to me.

"What?" I looked down at him again, unable to hear him above the roar of the crowd.

"You're not supposed to be here!" he shouted, as if accusing me of breaking a promise.

And then it hit me.

You bastard! *You slept with me and then didn't call!*

"You weren't supposed to start working until next week!" he shouted up at me.

"Hey, Lopez, some *help* over here?" hollered the redheaded cop who was handling Ronnie and Jimmy.

He ignored that and continued shouting at me, "You told me you weren't getting any shifts here until after the holidays!"

Lopez's rich blue eyes, fringed with thick dark lashes, were bloodshot and shadowed by dark circles. His straight, shiny black hair was rumpled. His strong face, exotically good-looking, appeared drawn and tired, and his golden-dark skin looked a little sallow tonight—at least in this light. The vest he was wearing added some bulk (I vaguely realized it was one of those bulletproof things), but under it, he had a slim, lithe, athletic build. And now that he was here in the flesh, the last person I had expected to see tonight, looking almost edibly gorgeous despite his apparent fatigue and furious scowl . . .

I wanted to *kill* him.

I wanted it so much, my hands bunched into tight fists, clutching the fabric of my skirt, and my shoulders started creeping upward in vengeful wrath as my chest swelled with righteous indignation.

"You can lower your skirt any time now, Esther," he added irritably. "I think the wiseguys are getting enough excitement for one night."

"What?" I looked down and realized that I was still holding my skirt hiked up to display a flash of thigh. In fact, in my agitation, I had tugged my hem up almost to my panty line and was displaying a lot more than I'd realized. "Oh!"

I dropped my skirt and smoothed it over my legs.

"What the hell were you thinking?" Lopez demanded. "Lifting your skirt for these guys!"

"Don't talk to me like that!" I snapped.

Jimmy Legs roared, "I want my phone call! I want my lawyer!"

"I will sue you bums into the next century!" Stella bellowed.

"Everyone calm *down!*" the megaphone cop ordered the agitated diners. "You'll all be able to leave as soon as an officer collects your information."

"But I don't *have* information!" a sweating man wailed. "I don't have *any* information!"

"As soon as an offer gets your personal details," the cop amended.

"You're not getting *my* details!" Freddie the Hermit's date insisted, now clustered with the regular diners.

The cop said doggedly, "Please wait quietly in your seats until—"

"This is still a free country, buddy!" someone cried. "You can't hold us prisoner here!"

"No one here is a prisoner," said the cop, clearly growing exasperated.

"Does that mean I can go now?" Tommy Two Toes called across the restaurant. "I know you already got *my* details."

"No, you're a prisoner," the cop said to Tommy while fiddling with the volume on his megaphone.

An outraged diner rose from his seat. "So we *are* prisoners! By what right—"

"EVERYONE CALM DOWN AND STAY SEATED!" The officer had turned up the volume so loud, the walls reverberated. Seeing the way everyone flinched, he added, "Sorry."

"So are we prisoners or not?"

"Yeah!" said Tommy. "Inquiring minds want to know!"

The cop said, "*Most* of you will be able to leave as soon as an officer collects your information. *Some* of you . . ." He looked across the restaurant at Stella and the Gambello crew. ". . . will be taken into custody, read your rights, and allowed to make your phone call, see your attorney, and use the toilet. This is New York City, not Soviet Russia."

From the kitchen, we heard, *"Viva la revolución! Vivan los trabajadores!"*

"WILL SOMEONE SHUT THAT GUY UP?" After a moment, the cop added to everyone else, "Sorry."

The restaurant remained noisy and the crowd was still anxious, but the panic died down as some semblance of order took shape. Gambello wiseguys were separated from everyone else and obviously being prepared for a mass arrest. More cops entered the restaurant, and four of them headed straight for the stairs that led up to Stella's office on the second floor. Another detective presented her with a search warrant. Stella tore it up and stuffed some of the pieces into her mouth before Jimmy Legs advised her not to bother trying that.

Money laundering, I thought suddenly.

Ever since I had started working here, I'd heard the rumors that Bella Stella washed dirty money for the Gambellos. But I'd always vaguely supposed that if it were true, then Stella would be arrested and the restaurant would be shut down.

As the policewoman placed Stella under arrest and recited her rights to her, I realized that OCCB's intense investigation of the Gambello family in recent weeks must have uncovered evidence confirming the rumors.

My startled gaze flashed back to Lopez, who was glaring up at me again.

Before I could blurt out the questions forming in my mind, he demanded, "What are you doing here? You weren't supposed to be here tonight. What the hell happened?"

My lips moved in speechless outrage. I hardly knew where to start. If he had bothered to *speak* to me since leaving my bed a week ago, I'd probably have told him that I was working tonight. I tried to think of words scathing enough for the stinging response he deserved.

Still glaring at me, Lopez added, "And get off the damn table, would you?"

He reached up a hand to help me down.

I slapped it away. "Don't *touch* me!"

He looked surprised. "What?"

"Miss, do *not* behave violently toward a police officer!" a male voice said sharply on my left.

I looked in that direction and flinched when I recognized Detective Peter Napoli. "You!" I said in horror.

Napoli froze when he recognized me. "Oh, God help us, it's *you* again."

Detective Napoli, who had seniority over Lopez, had questioned me in connection with Chubby Charlie's death here in the spring. That interview had not gone well. In fact, it had gone so badly that Napoli had wanted to take me into custody, and he suspected me of being involved with Gambello business. So he was someone I'd really hoped never to meet again. Judging by the expression on his face now, the feeling was mutual.

Napoli said accusingly to Lopez, "Did you know about this?"

"That *she'd* be here?" Lopez reacted with apparent revulsion. "No!"

Infuriated, I said, "How could he possibly know I'd be here? He'd have to *talk* to me for that!"

Napoli said to Lopez, "I don't want her causing any trouble."

"Trouble?" I said in outrage.

"She won't," Lopez assured him.

"Trouble?" I repeated.

Lopez said darkly, "Not now, Esther."

"Who steamrolled in here without warning in the middle of the party, scaring everyone half to death and nearly starting a riot?"

"You tell 'em, Esther!" shouted Freddie the Hermit.

"Thatta girl!"

I continued, "*That's* trouble, and it sure wasn't *me* who caused it, you sorry bast—"

"Please come down from there now," Lopez interrupted, reaching up to grab my hand.

I slapped him away again. "Don't you *dare*—"

"Miss Diamond," Napoli said sharply, "this is your last warning about striking a police officer."

"What? Are you *kidding* me, you moronic jack—"

"I'll deal with this," Lopez said loudly to Napoli. "Leave her to me."

" 'Leave her to me?' " I repeated, appalled.

"Sort out your problems with your girlfriend on your own time," Napoli said tersely. "We're working."

"She ain't his girlfriend!" Jimmy Legs said.

The redheaded cop smacked him on the back of the head. "Shut up, Jimmy."

"I'm not his girlfriend," I insisted from my tabletop, looking down at Napoli.

"All right, everyone take a deep breath," said Lopez. "Let's calm down and—"

"Shut up," Napoli and I said to him in unison, which made him blink.

Napoli looked up at me. "What*ever* you call your thing with Detective Lopez, I won't have it interfering with this bust. Is that clear?"

"I don't have a 'thing' with him," I said, swamped with anger and humiliation. "There is nothing between us. *Nothing.*"

Lopez looked sharply up at me. "What?"

I glanced down at him and saw his startled expression. "What do you mean, 'What?' "

Napoli said to Lopez, "Get her over there with the rest of the staff and get her details."

Lopez said to me, "What do *you* mean?"

Napoli said, "Or have you already got her details?"

He got a lot more than my details.

"Did I miss something?" Lopez asked me.

"Oh, my *God.*" Realization dawned as I stared down at my ex-almost-boyfriend.

Since I still didn't want Lopez touching me, I leaned down to put my hand on Napoli's shoulder—ignoring the way the detective flinched and tried to move away from me—and used him for balance as I hopped off the table.

I stood in front of Lopez, eye to eye. (Well, nearly. He's almost six inches taller than I am.) I gaped at him for a long moment before I spoke. "You thought I'd sleep with you again?"

"Well . . ." He looked bemused. "Yeah."

Ronnie Romano started chuckling. "Oh, this is gonna be good."

The redheaded cop said, "Shut up, Ronnie."

I was incredulous. "You thought I'd *sleep* with you again?"

Now Lopez was annoyed. "Yes."

"As in, maybe some day in the distant future, if we're the last two people left on the whole planet after a global disaster?"

"No, I was thinking it would be sooner than that," he said in exasperation.

"We don't have time for this," said Napoli.

"How could you possibly think I'd ever let you near me again?" I shouted.

"I really did miss something, didn't I?" said Lopez.

"Oh, my God! I can't believe what a jerk you are!"

"Er, detectives?" called another cop. "I hate to interrupt, but we're sort of in the middle of a big bust over here and could use some help."

"No, no, take your time," said Tommy Two Toes. "No rush."

"Shut up, Tommy," said Napoli.

"What are they doing?" Stella shrieked as cops started coming down the steps from her office with boxes full of her business files. "That's my stuff! Put that back!"

The policewoman said, "It's all covered by the search warrant you tried to *eat* a few minutes ago, Miss Butera."

"Oh, shut the fuck up."

"Why won't you sleep with me again?" Lopez asked, looking bewildered. "What happened?"

"What *happened?*" I repeated. "*Why?*"

"Oh, this is almost worth getting arrested for," said Ronnie.

"Lopez," said Napoli, "we actually *are* in the middle of a big bust, so—"

"Yeah, *why?*" he said to me.

"Because you slept with me and then didn't call!" I raged.

"Whoa! Really?" said Jimmy.

"The bum!" said Stella.

Ronnie burst out laughing.

Napoli looked at Lopez. "Is that true?"

"It's been a week!" I added.

"Yikes," said the redheaded cop.

Tommy added, "What a jerk!"

"A *week?*" said Napoli.

"Yes!" I said.

"No, of course it hasn't been a week," Lopez said dismissively.

"Christmas Eve!" I shrieked, enraged beyond all measure. "We had sex on Christmas Eve! *Twice!*"

"Stamina," Tommy said judiciously.

"Young guys," Freddie said with envy.

"Oh, that explains why you were late for work Christmas morning," said Napoli.

"And I haven't heard from you since then!" I shouted. "A *week!*"

"What a mook," Freddie said in disgust.

Lopez shook his head. "No, Esther, it was only . . . only . . ." He paused. "Oh."

"The penny drops," said Ronnie.

Lopez squinted at me. "It's been a week?"

"Yes."

"Christmas Eve . . . New Year's Eve . . ." We all waited in taut silence while he thought it over. "You're right. I guess it's been a week."

"You *guess?*" A moment ago, I hadn't thought it

was possible to get any angrier. Now I realized how wrong I'd been.

"God, even for a *cop,* this is pathetic," said Ronnie.

"Put a sock in it, Ronnie," said Napoli.

"That ain't no way to treat a lady," said Jimmy Legs, shaking his head as the redheaded cop handcuffed him.

Apparently thinking he had a good argument at hand, Lopez said to me, "You could have called me if you wanted to talk t—"

"I did call you! I left you a message!"

"Oh . . ." He looked dazed. "That's right. I forgot . . ."

"You didn't call her back?" blurted the policewoman who was cuffing Stella. She met my eyes. *"Men."*

"Hey, we ain't all like that," protested Freddie—who was here tonight with his mistress while Mrs. Freddie was probably at home alone.

"Men," I repeated.

"Jesus, Lopez," Napoli said in exasperation. "After Chubby Charlie got whacked, why did I have to go around and around and *around* with you about this woman, if you were just going to wind up dumping her? You could've saved me a lot of antacids if you'd just—"

"Don't you have a big bust to supervise?" Lopez said to him.

"You're the one who insisted on doing this to-

night," Napoli shot back. "*I* wanted to wait a couple of days, when we'd have more staff available for this and it would be easier to find a sober judge. But noooo, you pushed and pushed until—"

"Fine, this is all my fault," Lopez snapped. "*Everything* is my fault. Okay?"

"Well, *there's* something we can agree on," I said.

"But as long as we're here now," Lopez prodded Napoli, "maybe you'd like to go arrest someone." He nodded toward the wiseguys who were lined up next to Stella.

"No, that's all right, we can wait," said Tommy. "Don't put yourself out."

"Shut up," Lopez and Napoli said in unison.

Then Napoli glared at Lopez, gave a disgusted shake of his head, and turned to the arresting officers, whom he urged to stop gaping at us and get this bust back on track. He crossed the floor and started assisting them.

Lopez looked around uncomfortably at the crowd for whom we had been providing a free floor show. "Look, can we talk about this later?" he said to me.

"No, there's nothing left to talk about!" Immediately contradicting myself, I said, "How could you do that? What kind of a person *are* you?"

"He's a loser, that's what kind!" said Freddie as he was being escorted out of the restaurant by two cops, his hands cuffed behind his back.

Napoli told Freddie to mind his own business.

"What were you *thinking?*" I raged at Lopez, getting it all off my chest now. "You insensitive, self-centered, callous—"

"I was busy!"

I was so furious I could barely speak, but I forced the words out. "You were . . . *busy?*"

Lopez lost the last shreds of self-control. "*Yes,* goddamn it!"

So did I. "*BUSY?*"

"Lame," said Jimmy.

"Priceless." Ronnie was laughing again.

"And so were *you,* it turns out," Lopez shouted.

"What does *that* mean?" I demanded.

"It means I got here, at the end of a week made in *hell*—"

"Oh, now you remember it's been a week!"

"—to find you *dancing on tabletops!* Having the time of your life—*and* giving a bunch of wiseguys a good long look under your skirt!" He was beside himself now. "So don't pretend you've been sitting around waiting for me to call!"

Since that was *exactly* what I had been doing, this was too much. Just *too much.* Before I knew it, my hand was whipping across his cheek in a loud, stinging slap. Lopez fell back a step, startled. So did I. I'd hit him so hard my hand burned, and a white palm print stood out sharply against his dark skin for a moment.

Stella and the Gambello crew were cheering.

"Way to go, Esther!"

"Good for you!"

"That'll teach the bum!"

Lopez and I stared at each other, both caught off guard by what I'd just done. I heard harsh, rasping breaths—and realized they were my own.

"That does it," said Napoli. "Put your hands behind your back, Miss Diamond."

"What?" I said distractedly. It seemed a peculiar request.

"Pete, no," Lopez said suddenly. *"Don't."*

"I warned her," Napoli said. "Hands behind your back *now,* Miss Diamond."

"Huh?" I said in confusion.

Lopez stepped close to us and said to his colleague in a low voice, "Come on, don't do this."

"You know I can't let it go," Napoli replied, also in a low voice, as he pulled out his handcuffs. "Slugging a cop during a bust?"

"Wait a minute," I said, realizing what was happening as Napoli snapped a cuff around my right wrist. "No!"

"Hitting an officer in front of witnesses," Napoli continued to Lopez. "And in front of *these* witnesses. I can't give her a pass on this one."

"Oh, come on, Pete, you *know* why she hit me."

"Ow! That's pinching!" I tried to wriggle out of Napoli's grasp.

"Hold still," he said tersely to me. "Don't make things worse for yourself."

Lopez persisted, "It had nothing to do the bust. Or with me being a cop."

"Believe me," said Napoli, "I sympathize with Miss Diamond's motives and understand her actions."

"Then let me go," I urged as he pulled my arms behind my back and snapped the other cuff on my left wrist.

"But she picked the wrong time and place. I gave her two warnings in a row about violent behavior to a police officer—"

"You can't be serious!" I said.

"—and she did it, anyhow." Napoli added, "In the middle of a high-profile bust, while arguing with the cop in question. You know I can't let it go."

Lopez rubbed his forehead and said, "I'd really like to wake up now. Please, God, let me wake up."

"You're going to let him *arrest* me?" I demanded of Lopez. "You're really letting this happen?"

"Shut up," he said without looking at me. "I'm trying to think."

"This is no time for thinking," I insisted, feeling the cold weight of police metal encircling my wrists. "*Do* something."

"Esther Diamond," said Napoli, "I'm arresting you for—"

"Wait!" Lopez was apparently done thinking. "I've got it. I'll do it."

Napoli and I both stared at him.

"I'll book her," he clarified.

"What?" I blurted.

"No, I've got this," said Napoli. "You don't . . . *Oh.* I see."

"*You're* going to arrest me?" I said incredulously.

"Yeah, I'm going to arrest you," Lopez said with resignation.

"*That's* your bright idea?" I said. "Swapping places with Detective Charm?"

Napoli asked him, "Are you sure you want to do this? It won't look good."

"It *already* doesn't look good," I said. "How *dare* you two arrest me, when he had the nerve, the *gall—*"

"You'll catch some shit for this," Napoli warned him.

"You *bet* he will," I confirmed.

"I'll deal with it," Lopez said.

"Stop!" I said as Lopez took a step toward me. "I don't want to be arrested by *you.* I want someone else! Haven't you done enough to me already?"

Ronnie, who was being led to the door in cuffs, burst out laughing again. "Oh, buddy," he said to Lopez, "your love life is deader than a thirty-year-old corpse in a Jersey landfill."

"Yeah, I'm sensing that," Lopez said tersely as he brushed Napoli aside and put his hand on my shoulder.

"Don't *touch* me!" I jerked reflexively away from him—and, in doing so, accidentally banged the back of my head into Napoli's nose.

"Agh!" the detective staggered backward, clutching his face.

The Gambellos who were still inside the restaurant cheered again. So did some of the diners who were still waiting to be allowed to leave.

"Whoa! Esther clips two of New York's finest inside of five minutes!"

"Go, Esther!" said Stella. "Do them all! The bums!"

Napoli's eyes were tearing as he snatched up a dirty napkin from a nearby table to dab at his nose, which was bright red now. "Arrest her, goddamn it!" he said to Lopez. "And get her the hell out of my sight!"

"Honor is due, Esther," Jimmy Legs said as the redheaded cop led him past me and out the door. "You are one fine dame."

"She's about to become a dame with an assault record," muttered Napoli.

Looking very sad that he had ever met any of us, Lopez gave a heavy sigh and said, "Esther Diamond, I am placing you under arrest."

3

八仙

The Eight Immortals

These legendary figures embody the various conditions of human life—poverty and wealth, youth and age, male and female. Born human, they achieved immortality through their deeds.

It turned out that being arrested for assaulting a police officer put me at the pinnacle of the criminal pantheon inside the women's holding cells. Even Stella ranked below me. I would have thought that laundering money for the mob was a more impressive deed than slapping your former almost-boyfriend. But slugging a cop evidently imbued me with legendary status among the hookers, crack addicts, and shoplifters sharing this illustrious space with me in the wee hours of New Year's morning.

Also, I don't think any of them had the faintest

idea what money laundering *was*, and Stella and I were both too agitated to explain it well.

I settled into my demoralizing situation—starting off the New Year in jail—by trying to distract myself and use the time productively. In pursuit of my craft, I attempted to study my fellow prisoners, who represented diverse conditions of human existence.

I was initially interested in the prostitutes, since I had played one recently—a guest role on the cable TV cult hit, *The Dirty Thirty*—and might play one again someday. But apart from their enthusiasm over my having hit a cop, they just seemed sleepy and bored, providing me with very little material.

Still trying to be conscientious—and still trying not to think about my immediate future, which I wasn't ready to face—I focused next on three Ivy League coeds who were also locked up in here tonight. I didn't know what they were charged with, but the extent of their inebriation suggested several possibilities. They were obviously from wealthy backgrounds, and just as obviously not used to surroundings like this. I decided to observe how these three young women reacted to the gravity of their situation and to being in close quarters with streetwalkers, thieves, addicts, and a furious restaurateur.

But this was pretty dull, too. One of the girls promptly fell asleep and was snoring away peacefully. Another had vomited twice and was rocking back and forth now with her arms folded over her stomach. And the third one kept hitting on me. As a waitress who'd clobbered a cop in a mob joint, I evidently represented exciting erotic possibilities for a bisexual society girl who was briefly enthralled with the idea of rough trade. After I got tired of telling her to leave me alone, which didn't work, I yanked so hard on her hair that she retreated sulkily to a corner, glaring at me in resentful silence thereafter.

Stella was pacing back and forth, muttering to herself, still dressed in her sequined, leopard-print outfit. I thought any random stranger who passed this area would assume she was the hookers' boss, rather than mine. Compared to all my companions here, I almost looked like a nun in my server's outfit of white blouse, knee-length black skirt, support hose, and sensible shoes.

By now, I was sitting hunched over on a wooden bench, my chin in my hands. It had been a couple of hours since I'd been locked up in here with the scum of the earth (I refer, of course, to the privileged young drunks who'd never had to look for work or worry about rent money), and I stared at the floor as I morosely forced myself to confront my situation.

On the plus side, I would have legal representation. True, my attorney would be a notorious mouthpiece for the mob, but he was very experienced and I wouldn't have to pay for him. Since I was a friend of the family and had been scooped up in a sweep of the Gambellos, Stella assured me that "the boss" was going to take care of me—which included securing and paying for my counsel. Although I realized that requesting a public defender might better demonstrate law-abiding propriety on my part, I decided I'd prefer to stick with the Shy Don's lawyer. He routinely kept killers and extortionists out of prison, after all, so I hoped my case would be a cakewalk for him.

But even with my legal fees covered by Victor Gambello, I was really worried about money. The cops had raided Stella's at the height of the evening, before the customers, many of whom had been camped at their tables all night, had paid their checks and left. So I had only collected tips from the early crowd, the people who ate dinner and then left Bella Stella to attend festivities elsewhere. Which meant that when Lopez—that *bastard!*—arrested me and put me in the back of the police van with all the Gambello prisoners, I only had about one-third of the earnings I was counting on for the night. The rest would have rolled in later, around two o'clock in the morning, if the place hadn't been busted.

I wondered how long I could last on the quantity of cash that I estimated had been in my server's pouch at midnight. And when would Bella Stella reopen for business? Not soon, I suspected—not with its owner facing indictment. OCCB wouldn't have staged such a big bust tonight if they didn't have a strong case.

With Bella Stella off the menu, so to speak, I wondered how soon I could get another job—and collect my first earnings from it. In fact, *could* I get another job, now that I had a recent arrest on my record? What if, despite the Shy Don's lawyer defending me, this arrest turned into a conviction?

Damn Lopez.

If I got out of jail for assaulting him, the first thing I was going to do was kill him. He deserved it.

"Hey, handsome," one of the hookers suddenly said in a sultry voice. "You lookin' for a party?"

"No, I'm looking for my assailant."

My head jerked up the second I recognized Lopez's voice. I saw him standing outside our cage, looking even more exhausted than he had during the bust, as if he was by now running only on the *memory* of fumes.

Serves him right.

He had replaced his bulletproof vest with a navy blue pullover sweater. I resented this, since that was a good color for him. It brought out the blue of his eyes, flattered his olive complexion, and made his coal-black hair look even darker. The fact that it was a ratty-looking old wool sweater with unraveling cuffs didn't seem to mute its effect on me.

I had a sudden, unbidden memory of clumsily helping him pull a different sweater over his head exactly a week ago. It fell to the floor of my apartment, quickly followed by the rest of his clothes—

which he was frantically shedding as we clung and kissed and embraced, feverish and uninhibited with each other, his ravenous mouth on mine, his hands all over my naked body . . .

I sat bolt upright and started choking on a sort of shocked hiccup, appalled by where my thoughts had just wandered based on one quick look at the tired, shabbily-dressed cop who had *arrested* me to-night.

"Are you all right, Esther?" he asked.

Our gazes locked. I swallowed, cleared my throat, and composed myself.

"What do *you* want, detective?" I asked coldly.

"Oh, I get it," said the hooker who had greeted him. "You're the cop she decked?"

"I'm the one," Lopez said wearily.

Most of my fellow prisoners perked up, looking at him with interest now.

"Oooh, honey," the same woman said to Lopez. "What ever did you do to make her wanna wallop such a pretty face?"

"He slept with me and then never called," I said tersely, rising from my bench.

"Seriously?" She looked at Lopez with a much less flattering expression now. "That is so tacky!"

"I think there are still some people in the tri-state area who haven't heard," Lopez said to me. "Do you want to alert the media? It would save time."

"God, men are all the same," said another of the prostitutes. "Don't you just hate them?"

"You're a bum!" Stella told Lopez.

"I'm going to be sick!" said the drunk coed with the weak stomach.

"Again?"

We all took a few steps back.

She burped, then said, "Never mind. False alarm."

The society girl who'd been hitting on me earlier stood up, pointed at me, and said to Lopez, "She assaulted me, too! I want to press charges. Against her *and* against the department—for putting this *animal* in here with me!"

"What did you do *now?*" Lopez asked me.

"I defended my virtue," I said crankily.

He lifted a brow. "Surely it's a little late for that?"

"Oh, don't you *dare*—"

"Kidding," he said. "Kidding."

"You are in no position to kid me," I reminded him.

"I guess not," he admitted.

"Where's my lawyer?" Stella asked, seething with impatience. "Isn't he here yet?"

"Yeah, he got here about twenty minutes ago. He's meeting first with Ronnie and Jimmy and Tommy and . . . oh, all the rest of them," Lopez replied. "He'll see you after he's done with them."

"How long will *that* take?" she demanded.

"I'm guessing you could make a dent in *War and Peace* while you're waiting."

"I ain't got all night!"

"Actually, you do," Lopez pointed out.

"Why, you rotten, lousy, stinking—"

"Hey, *I'm* not the guy who sent only one lawyer here to represent all of you," he said. "Take it up with Victor Gambello if you're not happy."

"Hmph."

Turning away from Stella, Lopez nodded to the uniformed policewoman who stood nearby. She unlocked our cell as he said, "Come on, Esther. Let's go."

"Huh?"

As the cell door opened, Stella stepped protectively in front of me and eyed Lopez. "Where are you taking her?"

"Relax, Stella. We're letting her go."

"You are?" I said in surprise.

"Yeah." He gestured for me to exit the cell. "Come on."

I looked doubtfully at Stella, not wanting to leave her here. When she realized why I was hesitating, she shook her head and patted my arm. "Don't worry about me, kid. I'll be outta here pronto. I just gotta wait for my lawyer."

"And for a judge," Lopez said.

"Oh, shit," she said in disgust. "I forgot. It's New Year's Day."

Stella sighed, rolled her eyes, and sat down on a

bench, settling in for a long wait. I asked if she wanted me to bring anything here for her, now that I was evidently being set free; but she said her assistant was taking care of that. So I gave her a quick hug, wished the other inmates the best of luck with the legal system, and exited my cell.

I felt a rush of relief as I followed Lopez down the hall and left the holding area. I was out of there! And apparently not going to appear before a judge, after all, let alone face being convicted of assaulting a police officer.

Lopez didn't stop walking until we reached the window where I could reclaim my possessions from the NYPD. He gave them my name and verified my release.

A moment later, a man appeared at the end of the hall. "Has anybody seen—Oh, there he is. Lopez!"

As my companion turned to look at him, I recognized the redheaded cop who'd participated in the bust at Bella Stella.

He recognized me, too. His face split in a grin. "Miss Diamond! Delighted see you again."

I shrewdly sensed that the wiseguys weren't the only people who'd found certain events at the restaurant vastly amusing.

Lopez asked him, "What do you want?"

"We need to finish the—"

"Yeah, I know. I'll be there in a few minutes," Lopez replied. "I just need to wrap this up."

"Do you need any . . . Oh, *right.* Never mind." The cop grinned again. "I just love a happy ending." He was chuckling as he turned and went back the way he had come.

"God, will this shift never end?" Lopez muttered in despair.

I searched my soul for some compassion but didn't find any. Go figure.

While we waited for someone to retrieve my stuff, I asked him, "What's going to happen to Stella?"

"In the long run, we'll see," he said. "Meanwhile, she's right—she'll be released on bail after she's arraigned."

"What about the restaurant?"

"It won't be reopening for a while, Esther." It was clear from his tone that he knew this was bad news for me. "Maybe not ever—not as Stella's place, anyhow."

"Oh." I wasn't surprised, but my heart sank, even so.

He was avoiding my eyes as he said, "You'll have to find another job."

"Uh-huh." After a moment I asked, "Am I all done here? I mean, what happened to my arrest for . . . ? You know." I made an awkward gesture indicating the cheek I had slapped.

"We're dropping the charges."

"Good!" I said with relief. Then: "Um, why? Napoli seemed to think that *hanging* would be too good for me."

"I screwed up the arrest," said Lopez, looking through the clerk's window to check on progress. "This could take a few minutes. They're under-staffed tonight."

I frowned. "What do you mean, you screwed it up?"

"Oh, I charged you with the wrong thing." He sounded as tired as he looked. "I didn't read you your rights. I filled out the report wrong. And so on."

I hadn't even noticed any of this. I'd been too up-set to be aware of the whole ordeal as anything other than a surreal nightmare.

Lopez added, "I thought about sexually harassing you in front of witnesses, but that seemed like over-kill. And I'll have enough explaining to do, as it is."

I stared at him as I realized what he was saying. "You mean you screwed up on *purpose?*"

"Of *course* it was on purpose," he said a little tes-tily. "Although you might not believe it, based on tonight, I'm not actually a raging incompetent."

"I don't understand," I said. "Why did you screw up?"

Now he was annoyed. "Because seeing you at the restaurant—where you *weren't supposed to be,* Esther—right in the middle of my bust . . . Well, it threw me off my game. I got rattled. And then you and I devolved into some kind of insane tabloid brawl. Which I *still* don't really know how . . . Wait. *No.* I swore I wouldn't go there again. Not here and now." Lopez took a deep breath and regrouped. "I'm just saying, I'm normally a lot better at my job than that."

"Um, no, I meant, why did you screw up my arrest?"

"Oh." He blinked. "That?"

"Yes," I said, clinging to my patience. "That."

He scrubbed a hand over his face before answering, as if trying to wake himself up. "Well, I saw there was no way Napoli would let you go. Not in those circumstances. He was going to bring you in tonight, no matter what." Lopez shrugged. "So I made sure that we can't keep you."

Now I thought I understood. "By handling this so sloppily that you have to drop the charges?"

He nodded. "You'd have to be a much more important collar for the prosecutor to stick with this and try to press charges after the mess I've made of your arrest. So we're cutting you loose."

I remembered Napoli's comments in the restaurant when Lopez decided to take over arresting me. "Detective Charm knew you were going to do this, didn't he?"

"Yeah." He looked through the window again. "Oh, good, they've got your stuff."

"I don't get it. Napoli is such a jerk. Why—"

"He's not the easiest guy in the world to get along with," Lopez admitted, "but he's a good cop, and he's fair. We've learned how to work with each other. Though you probably couldn't tell, based on tonight's performance."

"But he can't stand me," I said. "So why did he let you go ahead and do this?"

"Because it's a fair compromise all around," Lopez said dryly. "You got to slap me, which Napoli thought I deserved. He got to make his point in front of the Gambellos about hitting a cop. And me . . . well, I guess I won't have to explain to anyone why you've got a criminal record." As he handed my stuff to me, he concluded, "See? Everyone walks away a winner."

"Some victory," I muttered. "No money, no job . . ." *No boyfriend.*

"You'll find another job," he said firmly. "You can do better than a mob joint that's full of wiseguys hitting on you."

"I liked it there," I said grumpily.

His shoulders slumped. "I know." His voice was soft, and he was avoiding my eyes again.

"So I guess this thing happened because of the way OCCB has been putting the Gambellos under a microscope ever since the Fenster heists first hit the news?" I said.

Lopez nodded, then said, "Now check to make

sure this is everything that you had with you when you were brought in, then sign for it."

"Miss Diamond," said the clerk. "Here's the rest of your belongings."

"The rest?" I said with a puzzled frown. My server's pouch was the only possession I'd been arrested with (and as far as I could tell, all the cash was still inside it). Then I saw what he was handing over to Lopez. "Oh! Well, that's good, at least."

It turned out that shortly after I was arrested, it had occurred to Ned to get my daypack and my coat from the staff room and give them to the cops, so I could be reunited with these things upon eventually being released. Lopez set my daypack on the floor and held my coat slung over one arm while telling me this. I was relieved, since this meant I wouldn't have to go back to Little Italy and try to convince the cops to let me into the restaurant so I could remove my stuff.

It also meant I had the keys to my apartment now, so I could go straight home and collapse. I suddenly realized how exhausted I was. Without thinking, I grabbed Lopez's wrist and looked at his watch. It was nearly five o'clock in the morning.

"Oh. No wonder I feel like a pumpkin," I said, still holding his wrist.

"Uh-huh."

"It's almost morning," I said.

But suddenly I wasn't thinking about the time.

"I know," he murmured.

My thoughts had shifted to how sturdy his arm felt. I hadn't touched him in a week—except to slap him tonight.

"I wanted to release you sooner, but um . . ." His voice was a little breathless now. "But it takes some time to . . . uh . . ." He trailed off.

I looked up into his face and our eyes met. I had stepped closer to him to look at his watch. Now I realized *how* close. I could feel his body heat. With our gazes locked, I saw the fatigue in his dark-lashed eyes replaced by a spark of something else. Something I'd seen there before. His gaze drifted down to my lips and his breathing changed.

Everything inside me quickened and my hand tightened on his wrist. Touching him for a moment, even with his wooly sweater between my fingers and his flesh, reminded me of what it was like to touch him elsewhere . . . Everywhere . . . *Really* touch him. Anywhere I wanted, as much as I wanted . . .

NO. Stop right there.

I dropped his wrist like a hot rock and stepped away so quickly I stumbled.

"Careful." He reached for me.

"Don't," I snapped, staggering away from his outstretched hand.

"Huh?"

I balanced myself against the nearby wall, aware

that I was breathing too hard for someone who'd simply been standing around for the past few minutes.

"Esther?" he prodded.

"Don't *do* that," I said. "You are not allowed to do that."

"Okay," he said quickly.

"Just *don't.*"

"I won't," he promised.

"Good."

After a pause, he said, "Just so I know . . . What are we talking about?"

I stared at him incredulously. "I never cease to be amazed," I said in disgust, "at what a *guy* you can be."

"And here we go," he muttered.

"No, here we *don't,*" I said. "I'm leaving. Right now."

He nodded, apparently perceiving the unwisdom of saying anything more just now. My coat was still slung over his arm. He shook it out now and held it open for me.

That date-like gesture upset me, all things considered, so I snatched the garment away from him and slipped into it by myself. It was a heavy, knee-length wool coat with a hood. I'd found it at a thrift shop two years ago. It had a ragged hem and a dark stain on one side, and its profusion of buttons and zippers always took a while to fasten and unfasten. But it was really warm and very good at keeping out the icy winter winds that hurtled down the urban canyons created by the city's tall buildings.

While I zipped and buttoned, feeling self-conscious as Lopez watched me, I said, "I need to go home and get some sleep. Because then I have to go look for a new job now that *you've* closed down my place of employment."

"I was doing *my* job," he shot back. "And if Stella didn't want her restaurant to be shut down, then she shouldn't have . . . Um . . . never mind."

Apparently my expression had made him recognize the folly of justifying tonight's events to me at this particular moment.

Lopez sighed and, in an apparent attempt to placate me, said, "Look, maybe some acting work will turn up soon. You'll get some auditions and . . . and . . ." After taking a good long look at my face, he said in defeat, "I probably just shouldn't speak, huh?"

"No. And that shouldn't be a problem for you." I picked up my daypack. "As I've learned this past week, you're really good at *not speaking* to me."

I turned away and stalked toward the exit, eager to get out of here—and away from him, before I either hit him again or else burst into tears.

"Esther! Wait!"

I heard his footsteps behind me, but I didn't slow down, let alone turn around. I had a dark feeling that tears might triumph in a few more seconds, and

I didn't want him to see that. Being around him kept reminding me of the night we'd spent together, which made it that much harder for me to bear everything that had happened since then.

"Esther, *stop,*" he said, right behind me now.

When I felt his hand on my arm, trying to halt me, I tried to jerk away from him. "Leave me alone!"

He tightened his grip, pulled me to a sudden stop, and turned me around to face him.

"Don't!" I yanked myself out of his grasp.

"Sorry, sorry." He raised his hands, palms out, and took a step back. "Sorry, but this is important. There's something . . ." He looked uncomfortable. "Something I . . ."

Against my will, I felt a little flutter of hope unfurl inside me. "Something you want to say?" I prodded.

"Yes." He nodded. "Something I want to say."

I hesitated only a moment. "Okay. I'll listen."

"Good." He took a breath . . . but seemed to have trouble getting started. "Um . . ."

I waited, running his lines for him in my head: *I'm sorry. I should have called. I'm a toad, a worm, a dung beetle. But I'll do anything in the world to make it up to you. Can you ever forgive me?*

That would be a good beginning. I waited for him to start there.

"There's something I keep thinking about . . ." he said tentatively.

I can never apologize enough for the way I've treated

you. I don't deserve it, but even so, I'm begging you for another chance.

I liked that. He could riff on that for a while. And then he'd need to explain what the hell had happened. Since it was obvious his tongue hadn't been cut out by marauding bandits, I tried to think of some other acceptable excuse for his failure to call me. Maybe . . .

As soon as I left your apartment, I was abducted by aliens and taken to the mother ship. They didn't release me until tonight. Nothing less than that would have made me go a whole week without calling you after what happened between us.

Hmm. Maybe not.

I frowned as I tried to think of a more plausible reason that would be equally acceptable.

Nothing came to me. I started feeling vexed with him again.

A week! A whole *week.*

"Well?" I prodded, thinking this had better be good. *Really* good. "What are you trying to say?"

"Are you still taking the pill?" he asked in a rush.

I blinked. "What?"

"We didn't use anything that night. You know—protection. And, uh, I didn't ask at the time . . ." When I didn't respond, he added, "It's something we should talk about."

"Oh, *now* you want to talk," I said, feeling fresh outrage rush through me. "All week, you couldn't be bothered to speak to me! But now that you've *arrested* me, you're feeling chatty."

"Could we please stick to the subject?" he said irritably. "Just for a *minute?*"

"I *am* on the subject!"

"Are you still taking the pill?" His voice was getting louder. "That's all I want to know!"

A man being led past us in handcuffs looked at us with interest. So did the cop who was escorting him.

Lopez noticed and made an exasperated sound. "Great. We're the floor show again."

I waited until those two men were out of earshot, then I demanded, "How did you even know I was taking birth control pills?" We had never discussed it.

"I saw them in your bathroom a few months ago."

"You've got no right to search my bathroom!"

"I *didn't.* You left them lying out," he said. "I noticed them when I was, you know, using the bathroom."

"Well, you shouldn't have noticed," I sputtered, too angry to care how lame that sounded. "It's none of your business."

"It is *now,*" he pointed out.

"So this is what you've been thinking about?" I demanded.

"Yes."

"*This* is what you wanted to say to me?"

"Yes."

I thought about hitting him again.

When I didn't answer him, he said in exasperation, "*Fine.* Let me put this another way. Could you be pregnant now?"

There was a roaring in my ears for a moment, and then everything went silent. I stared blankly at Lopez, suddenly feeling drained and empty. The combination of anger, humiliation, and hurt that I'd been juggling for days caught up with me, as did my fatigue, my financial stress, and my anxiety about finding another job soon enough to keep myself going. I felt ready to collapse, and I could hardly form a coherent thought. I swayed a little, feeling a bit dizzy.

"Are you okay?" He reached out to steady me, then evidently remembered my reactions tonight to his attempts to touch me, and stopped himself. "Esther? You look a little . . . Are you all right?"

"Yeah. I'm just really tired." My voice sounded dull and distant to me. I *felt* dull and distant now.

Lopez rested his hands on his hips, looked at the floor, and let out his breath slowly. "All right, look. Maybe this isn't the time—"

"I'm still taking my pills." I'd been on that prescription for several years. It helped stabilize my erratic cycle and control my symptoms. "And I'm definitely not pregnant." Nature had made that quite clear in recent days.

He nodded. "Okay," he said quietly.

I knew I was really mad at him, but I just couldn't feel it now. Everything had shut down. I just wanted to lie down and go to sleep. Nothing else mattered.

"Are we done?" I asked wearily. "Can I go?"

"Yeah. But I want you to wait here a minute, okay? I'm going to get a squad car to take you home."

Since I couldn't afford to waste money on a cab, and the logistics of getting home by foot and subway at five o'clock on a frigid winter morning seemed overwhelming just now, I nodded my agreement.

A few minutes later, Lopez escorted me outside, where it was dark and bitterly cold, and put me in the backseat of a squad car. A uniformed policewoman was behind the wheel. Her male partner sat in the passenger seat. I nodded in response to their brief greeting.

Lopez said to me, "They'll wait in the street until they're sure you're inside your apartment. Turn on a light so they'll know, okay?"

I nodded again, too tired to speak.

He said to the cops in the front seat, "Miss Diamond lives on the second floor, and her living room faces the street. Don't leave until you see the light go on."

"Understood, detective."

And then, despite how apathetically exhausted I was now, Lopez managed to enrage me one last time.

"I'll call you," he promised me.

It was like being poked with a cattle prod. My temper ignited immediately, my energy suddenly renewed. "I can't *believe* you! The *nerve*. The gall! The—"

"I just said the wrong thing, didn't I?" he guessed.

"It's exactly what you said when you left my bed a week ago," I fumed. "And then you never called!"

"He slept with you and then didn't call?" said the policewoman at the wheel of the squad car. "For a *week?*"

"That's right!" I said.

"God," said Lopez, "I just hate my whole life right now."

"Men," said the policewoman.

"Oh, come on," said her partner. "That's not fair. We're not all like *him*."

"Take Miss Diamond home now," Lopez instructed them. "*Right* now."

"Men," I agreed, as Lopez slammed the car door shut and walked away.

I fumed in stony silence all the way home, huddled in the backseat of the police car while the two cops in the front seat bickered about . . . I don't know. Mars, Venus, men, women, Lopez, and me. Something like that.

After I let myself into my shabby but welcoming apartment in Manhattan's West Thirties, I turned on the light, then went to the window and waved at the bickering cops in the car on the street below, so they'd *go away*.

My daypack by now felt like it was stuffed with bricks. I slid it off my shoulder and dropped it on the floor. Then I headed toward my bedroom, unzipping and unbuttoning my coat. As soon as I slid it off my shoulders, I shivered. My apartment was freezing. I quickly stripped off my clothes, leaving them lying in a heap on the floor, and donned heavy flannel pajamas, followed by a thick, fuzzy bathrobe. After a quick trip down the hall to the bathroom, I crawled into bed, still wearing my bathrobe, and collapsed facedown on my pillow, so relieved to be there.

I was just drifting off to sleep, trying to banish the random thoughts and images that were floating through my head, when I realized who *hadn't* witnessed my embarrassingly public fight at Bella Stella with Lopez about extremely private things. Who hadn't been in the police van, either, along with me and the other prisoners.

Once again living up to his nickname, Alberto "Lucky Bastard" Battistuzzi had escaped OCCB's sweep of the Gambello crew.

When the cops barreled into the restaurant, shouting "NYPD!" and everyone else started screaming in response (in particular, I remembered Ronnie shouting, "It's a raid!"), Lucky had been in the men's room, trying to clean splattered lasagna off his clothes. Alerted to what was happening, he must have made his getaway.

I assumed the cops had all the exits covered, but it didn't surprise me that Lucky had managed to slip away undetected. He was wily, experienced, and quick-thinking, and he knew that building well. He was also, well, *lucky.*

I wondered where he was now. He presumably couldn't go home, and I doubted he'd gone to Victor Gambello's house—that would be too obvious to be safe. Besides, for all we knew, the cops were executing a search warrant there, too.

Well, wherever Lucky was tonight, I thought drowsily as I drifted off to sleep, I hoped he was all right.

4

老師

Laoshi

An elder teacher, sage, and role model who has devoted his life to knowledge and wisdom.

Job hunting was not going well. Employers were letting go of holiday staff in the early days of January, not hiring new people. I filled out applications online and in person. I applied at restaurants, retail stores, and temp agencies. I answered employment ads and looked for signs in windows. Some places with "Help Wanted" signs posted told me that those notices were left over from last month and should really be taken down.

"Gee, y'think?" I muttered.

Other places said they just weren't hiring. "It's the economy," they'd tell me with a resigned shrug.

Some places had already filled the positions I inquired about. With so many people looking for work these days, I supposed this wasn't surprising.

While overpaid politicians with self-righteous smirks and media pundits with patent-leather hair, all of whom had enjoyed paid holidays last week, daily shrieked insults into TV cameras about the lazy, no-good, leeching poor and unemployed of America, I skidded across icy pavements and waded through ankle deep slush each day, looking for work.

Every morning, I left my apartment around nine o'clock, after mixing my breakfast smoothie from a discount container of nonfat yogurt and a bag of fruit I'd found at the back of my now-empty freezer. For thirty minutes each afternoon, I'd "grab lunch" by pretending to be a shopper at the upscale food emporiums where they handed out free samples. At night, I'd get home around nine o'clock and heat up some beans and rice for dinner.

Naturally, during my darkest moment one evening, when I was morosely wondering if I'd ever work again at all, let alone as an actress, my mother called.

She has an uncanny ability to sense when I am at my lowest and immediately phone me. And then she manages to make me feel even worse. It's her gift.

"You should have known better than to work for a criminal organization," she said after I explained as briefly and vaguely as possible what had happened to my job.

In other words, it was *my* fault that I was out of work now.

I tried to change the subject by asking a few questions about things in my parents' lives back in Madison, Wisconsin, where I'd been raised. My father is a history professor at the university, and my mother is a youth employment counselor. They're active in the local community and bedrock members of their synagogue.

But my mother was not to be thwarted in her efforts to find out just *how* bad things were going here.

"So you haven't had an audition lately?" she asked. "Not any at all? *None?*"

"No, Mom, not for a month. Things have been slow."

She decided to send me money. I declined the offer with thanks—sincere thanks, in fact.

My parents didn't understand my lifestyle; but, to give them credit, they loved me anyhow, and they didn't fight me on my choices. My mother was critical and my father was bewildered, but they had recognized me as a mystery child many years ago, as someone who'd been born into their family via some cosmic joke, and they had decided to accept it. (Jews are good at enduring. Not *silent* about it, but good at it.)

My only sibling, Ruth, was four years older, and

she was much more the sort of person they had expected to raise. Married to a Jewish lawyer in Chicago, she was a professional woman with two small children and a good salary. (She was also invariably so stressed out that on the few occasions I saw her, I always had the jitters for days afterward.)

I appreciated that despite their not understanding me—and despite their phone calls not always being a source of undiluted joy for me—my parents accepted that I had chosen this path in life and was committed to it. They tried, in their way, to be supportive and show an interest in my work.

And I had always felt that my obligation in our silent pact, since life is a two-way street, was not to trouble them with the problems that inevitably arose from this lifestyle. I knew they wouldn't mind sending me money now and then; but I thought it just didn't seem right to ask or accept. It somehow felt a bit like asking to them help me cover the cost of converting to Christianity and getting baptized. (Well, without the hysterical threats of self-immolation that my mother would immediately start shrieking in such a situation.)

Accepting money from them might also open the door to their suggesting that I should think about quitting this life, and that wasn't a conversation I wanted to have with them. Partly because acting isn't just what I do; it's who I am. I'll never give it up. And partly because that's just too painful and irrational a conversation to have when you can't afford to eat, let alone pay your rent.

So when my mom pressed me, obviously worried about my circumstances, I lied and pretended I had enough money to get by for a while. Then I changed the subject again and asked how my father's recent speech had gone at a big conference. My mother told me about it, and I could hear my father in the background, interrupting repeatedly to correct her and provide additional details.

I smiled. My dad never really knew what to say to me, so he seldom got on the phone with me. Instead, he hovered annoyingly around my mother when she called me, so he could listen and keep interjecting the whole while. It was his way of visiting with me, and it suited us both.

After we finished discussing my father's news, my mother turned the conversation back to me by asking whether I was seeing someone special.

"No, there's no one," I said, not even flinching. I had expected the question. She always asked.

I ended the call a few minutes later, after turning down one more offer to send me money.

Then I did some mental calculations, working out exactly how bad things were. I still had a little cash left over from my interrupted New Year's Eve shift at Stella's, but it wouldn't last much longer, despite my careful hoarding.

However, on the bright side, at least I didn't have

to tell my mother I was involved with an Irish-Cuban cop who'd been raised Catholic. Lopez seemed open-minded about religion, but nonetheless faithful to his own; I knew he attended Mass every week. There was no way I could pretend to my mother he might convert.

So it was just as well he and I weren't dating. If we were, I'd have to listen to my mother fret about how we'd raise the children.

Besides, *his* mother hated me. I'd met Lopez's parents while I was working as an elf at Fenster & Co. And even when I thought about it long and hard, I couldn't imagine how that encounter could have gone any worse. Not without gunplay, anyhow.

So maybe he and I just weren't ever really meant to . . .

Oh, forget about him, would you? After all, you're starving because of him!

Every time I found myself thinking of Lopez, I tried to focus on how angry I was at him for shutting down Bella Stella. If he hadn't done that, I'd have a job right now. I'd be able to buy groceries, pay for utilities, and save toward next month's rent.

Being so angry at him about *that* kept things simple for me. And with our relationship in tatters, my career going nowhere, and financial collapse looming directly over my head, I *needed* things to be simple. Thinking about the way he had treated me . . . Well, that generated feelings too complicated and powerful for me to cope with while my life was in such dire shape. So I just tried not to think about it. Not now.

I regrouped after my mother's phone call by reviewing practical matters. Stella Butera had been released on bail, as expected. Based on her attorney's advice, she was lying low and not talking to anyone. Some of the Gambellos who were arrested that night were considered serious flight risks and were still in custody, including Tommy Two Toes and Ronnie Romano; others had been released after posting hefty bails and surrendering their passports.

I still didn't know where Lucky was. Which I assumed meant the cops didn't know, either. The bust at Bella Stella was high-profile, OCCB had made additional Gambello arrests since then, and Lucky was too well-known a figure for his arrest to go unreported; but when I checked the news each day, there was no mention of him.

I didn't kid myself about what kind of life Lucky had led, and I could only guess at how much trouble he was in, now that OCCB was really cracking down on the Gambello family. But that didn't change the fact that I was attached to him—and, indeed, had trusted him with my life, more than once, in very dangerous circumstances. I knew he was a survivor, so I wasn't exactly worried about him as the days passed without any word, but I was a little anxious. I also knew that even if he was still using the phone number I had for him, which seemed very unlikely,

I shouldn't call him. Lopez knew that Lucky and I were friends, which meant that OCCB knew. So it would probably be safer for Lucky if I didn't try to contact him.

Safer for me, too, I thought, recalling Napoli's ire when he'd ordered Lopez to arrest me. Detective Charm would really sink his hooks into me if he found evidence that I was phoning the old hit man whom OCCB was hunting.

And that's how things still stood the following afternoon, some five days after Lucky escaped arrest. I was coming out of yet another restaurant where I'd filed a job application when my cell phone rang. An icy wind whipped down the street as I fumbled in my pocket for it, my heart giving a little leap. Even as I peered at the LCD readout to see who was calling, I was mentally kicking myself for hoping it would be Lopez.

Stop thinking about him, would you?

"Ah!" My heart gave a little leap, anyhow, when I saw who my caller was. My agent was finally getting back to me. I put the phone to my ear and said, "Thack! How was Wisconsin?"

Thackeray Shackleton (not his real name) was from Oshkosh, a town in my native state; like me, he had moved to the Big Apple after college. We had met here three years ago, when I was seeking competent representation (which is not so easy to find in my profession). A Lithuanian-American, he came from a long line of hereditary vampires—reputedly descended from Gediminas himself, the medieval Lithuanian warrior-king who'd started that whole thing. But Thack was mostly a non-practicing vampire; a debonair gay man who wore tailored suits and was first in line to try every new fusion food fad, he was much more comfortable in his adopted lifestyle as a New York theatrical agent, bon vivant, and man-about-uptown. And he hated visiting his family in Wisconsin, so I expected him to be in a sour mood. But he surprised me.

"Not as bad as I expected," he said. "The family's pleased with me for stepping up to the plate—sort of—during that whole crazed-Lithuanian-vampire-serial-killer mess that you and Max got me mixed up in this fall."

"Oh, like it's *my* fault when your people turn bad," I said.

He ignored that. "Even so, there was, as usual, more ritual drinking of human blood in honor of Christmas than I care for. So *please* remind me not to visit my family for about five years." I had gathered that Thack's family was fairly casual about their Catholicism but pretty rigid about their vampire traditions. He continued, "And although we didn't fight, there was just enough familial tension that I wanted to kiss the ground when I landed at LaGuardia."

"Eeuw," I said. "You really *don't* want to kiss the ground there."

"Anyhow, I've checked my messages and caught up on your news. I'm sorry to hear about Bella Stella, though I suppose it was bound to happen sooner or later. And, really, I've been anxious about your working there ever since that Gambello *capo* got shot dead at his dinner table while you were serving him."

"But the tips were good there," I said morosely. "And I am *so* broke, Thack."

"I'm afraid there's not much going on right now," he said apologetically. "I was hoping things would pick up once the holidays were over, but it's still slow. It's the economy, I guess."

"I'm so tired of hearing that," I said crankily.

"But there are a few rumblings from *Crime and Punishment*," he added. "They'd still like to find the right spot for you."

The New York-based *C&P* empire of prestigious TV police dramas had a lot of money and a lot of weekly shows to cast—*Crime and Punishment* (the flagship program), *Criminal Motive, Street Unit,* and *The Dirty Thirty.* I had done a couple of very minor roles for *C&P*, and then this past summer, I had been cast in a juicy part on *The Dirty Thirty* (affectionately known to fans as *D30),* the production company's most controversial show. I'd played Jilly C-Note (not her real name), a homeless bisexual junkie prostitute suspected of killing her pimp. Although they had no solid evidence against Jilly for that murder, the morally bankrupt cops of the corrupt Thirtieth Precinct pressured her over that crime in order to pump her for information about other criminal activity. One of the detectives also used Jilly for sex.

Cops hated *D30*. Lopez could barely even choke out the show's name, he loathed it so much.

Nonetheless, that was a powerful episode in an overall strong show with great writing and talented actors. But my role had been unexpectedly reduced after Mike Nolan, the actor with whom I'd had most of my scenes, suffered two heart attacks before the episode was completed. My character got dropped out of the replacement scenes that were hastily written to cover his absence. When it became clear after the second heart attack that Nolan wouldn't be coming back for a few months, the rewrites included having his character suddenly shot twice, off-screen, and being hospitalized indefinitely. Since then, Nolan had only appeared a few times on *D30*, always in brief scenes where his character was lying in a hospital bed.

I had worked well with the cast and crew of *D30*, and the *C&P* people kept saying they felt bad about cutting down my part so much as a result of circumstances. They told Thack they'd find something for me on one of their shows, to make it up to me.

I appreciated this; but I'd read for two *C&P* roles in late November, hadn't been cast in either of them, and there had been nothing from them since then but vague "rumblings." So I wasn't enthused when Thack now said that they were rumbling once again.

"I need something more concrete than that, Thack," I said. "I need an audition. A reading. I need to be *cast*. I need income."

"I will goose them and see if I can't get something more than a rumble," he promised. "Meanwhile, I've got my ear to the ground, my hand on the phone, my nose to the wind. Hang in there."

"Hmph."

The gunmetal gray sky opened up and started sleeting soon after I ended our phone call. The wet, frigid, windy downpour soaked my coat, streaked my daypack with rivulets of melting ice, and made my teeth chatter. Although I really needed to keep looking for gainful employment, I was just too cold, tired, hungry, and discouraged to stick with it any longer today. It was only late afternoon now, but I decided to call it quits. Tomorrow was another day, after all.

Greenwich Village was my job-hunting territory today, so I decided to walk over to my friend Max's place and fling myself on his mercy. He would give me a cup of hot tea and seat me by his little gas fire so I could thaw out.

Zadok's Rare & Used Books was on a quiet side street in the West Village. A specialty store for occult books, it didn't get much foot traffic, but it had a devoted clientele. If its proprietor, Dr. Maximillian

Zadok, were a more engaged businessman, he'd get online, since his store was well stocked with rare and exotic volumes, and he'd probably do brisk business on the internet. But the store was sort of a modestly paying hobby for Max, or a cover story. His real work was confronting Evil in New York City, as the local representative of the Magnum Collegium, an old, revered, and extremely obscure worldwide organization.

Gifted with mystical mojo and supernatural talents (though he always insisted the word "supernatural" was inaccurate), Max had first befriended me when I was in danger of becoming the next victim in a series of magical vanishings aimed at (as we eventually discovered) securing a human sacrifice to use for summoning a people-eating, power-granting demon. Since then, Max and I had helped each other resolve additional sticky problems that arose when Evil intruded, demons were summoned, dark gods were bribed, and dimensions rubbed each other the wrong way.

People just got up to all *kinds* of dangerous shit in this city. Sometimes it was almost enough to make a starving actress think about moving to Los Angeles. (At the moment, though, I'd be hard-pressed to scrape together cab fare to Harlem, never mind a ticket to the West Coast.)

Anyhow, what with one thing and another, Max had become a cherished and trusted friend—and exactly the right person to cheer me up when I was feeling so low. I should have come to the bookstore before now, I realized, as I entered the old townhouse where the shop resided. Max and I hadn't seen each other since Christmas Day, which I had spent here.

"Hello?" I called. "Max?"

On a wet, cold, dreary day in early January, I wasn't surprised to find the shop apparently empty of customers.

"Esther? Is that you?" he replied from somewhere in the book stacks.

"Woof!" A dog the size of a small horse came trotting across the floor to greet me.

"Hello, Nelli." I patted her head and then pulled gently on her immense floppy ears. Excited to see me, she bounded around a little and batted me playfully with her paws, nearly knocking me over.

Nelli was Max's mystical familiar. She had emerged from another dimension in response to his summons for assistance in fighting Evil—after his apprentice from the Magnum Collegium hadn't worked out, what with plotting to mystically murder much of Manhattan and ruthlessly rule whoever was still left standing.

Whatever mysterious powers had helped Nelli assume canine form so she could pursue her noble mission in this dimension, they evidently hadn't realized how crowded New York is. She was an inconveniently *large* animal for such close quarters. Trying to transport Nelli from one area of the city to another had been a logistical nightmare until Max recently developed a relationship with a pet-transport service that had a vehicle big enough to hold her. And wherever we were, it usually felt as if Nelli was taking up most of the available space.

A healthy dog in the prime of life, she was well muscled beneath her short, smooth, tan fur. Her massive head was long and square-jawed, and her teeth were so big they might look terrifying if the immense size of her floppy ears wasn't such a distraction from them. Her paws—which, like her face, were darker in color than the rest of her—were each nearly the size and density of a baseball bat, and the skin of her feet was as rough as coarse sandpaper.

So I was glad I was wearing thick clothing as Nelli batted at me with her paws in playful greeting.

"Esther, what a nice surprise!" Max beamed at me as he appeared from behind a tall, overstuffed bookcase with a duster in his hand. "I was just about to do a little cleaning, and your arrival gives me the perfect excuse to postpone it."

He was a short, slightly chubby, older white man with gentle blue eyes, slightly long white hair, and a neatly trimmed white beard. His English was completely fluent, though his faint accent revealed his origins in Central Europe. He was dressed tidily today, as he usually was, and obviously in good spirits.

I smiled and kissed Max's cheek in greeting, then suddenly shivered.

"You're soaked!" he said in alarm. "Here, let me take your coat. Come sit by the gas fire. Shall I make some hot tea?"

"Yes to all of that," I said gratefully, feeling pleased that, for the first time in longer than I could remember, things were going according to plan.

I settled into a comfortable chair near the gas fire, which was glowing warmly. Nelli lay down beside me and panted happily for a while, then decided to take a little nap. Nelli spent *much* of her time resting up for any possible future confrontation with Evil.

Max bustled around, filling the electric kettle, setting it to boil, and brewing a pot of tea. Before pouring me a cup, he arranged an assortment of cookies on a plate; he maintained a small refreshments station here that was usually stocked with goodies. Nearby, there was a large, careworn walnut table with books, papers, an abacus, writing implements, and other paraphernalia on it.

The shop had old hardwood floors, a broad-beamed ceiling, dusky-rose walls, and rows and rows of tall bookcases overflowing with books about the occult, printed in various languages. Some of the volumes were modern paperbacks, many were old hardback volumes, and a few were rare leather-bound books of considerable value. Downstairs, where only trusted friends and colleagues were invited, was Max's private laboratory. It was the place where Nelli had first come into being in canine form.

My empty stomach rumbled in eager reaction as I bit into a cookie. I sighed with pleasure, glad to relax in comfortable, familiar surroundings while Max chatted amiably. I realized from his cheerful demeanor and easy small talk that he had no idea what had happened at Bella Stella. The police bust was in the news, of course, but Max seldom followed current events. So his not knowing about it mostly meant that Lucky hadn't been in contact with him. Which didn't surprise me. Although the two men were friends, due to having confronted Evil together on various occasions, I hadn't really thought Lucky would come to my companion for help in this matter. He wouldn't risk turning Max (who'd had his own problems with the NYPD) into an unwitting accomplice or accessory by going to earth here.

So I broke the news about Bella Stella to Max. My account omitted most of what had happened between me and Lopez; it was too painful and embarrassing to go into. Especially with someone like Max. He was a man of the world, but he was also a gentleman of the old school. *Very* old, in fact.

Although he didn't look a day over seventy, Max's true age was closer to three and a half centuries, due to having unwittingly consumed a mysterious alchemical potion in his younger days, way back in the seventeenth century. It hadn't made him immortal, but it had unnaturally slowed his aging process. The secret of that life-prolonging potion had died with the mage who'd administered it to Max as a cure for a feverish illness. I knew that Max, mostly due to the exhortations of the Magnum Collegium, had searched for the secret to his longevity for some time—before finally deciding not to waste any more of his long life in trying to figure out *why* it was so long.

Anyhow, although he recognized the nature of my interest in Lopez and, after centuries of living an eventful life (albeit a celibate one for quite some time), certainly wouldn't be shocked to learn we had slept together . . . I wouldn't be comfortable talking about it with him. And I certainly didn't feel like discussing the humiliations that had followed. So, in describing the events of New Year's, I left out all the . . . well, all the juicy bits.

Max was distressed to learn that Lucky was probably in hiding now, sympathetic about my loss of employment, horrified to learn I had been arrested (I mostly glossed over the reason for it), and relieved that the NYPD had released me without a stain on my character.

"And how is Detective Lopez?" Max asked with concern. "Considering his fondness for you, closing down your place of employment and imprisoning your employer, with whom I gather you have a very cordial relationship, must have been a severe trial of conscience for him."

"I'm not sure Lopez has as much conscience as we thought," I said sourly, finishing the cookie I was consuming and reaching for another.

"You know him better than I do, of course," said Max, "but he has consistently seemed to me a person of honor and integrity, as well as intelligence, perseverance, and courage. Though perhaps a little rigid and judgmental."

Since that was a pretty accurate description—or so I had always thought, anyhow—I wondered for the first time if Lopez had wound up favoring his duty over his libido. Maybe he decided he had to choose between me and his job, and his job won. Was that why he hadn't called—because deciding to shut down Bella Stella meant dumping me?

"He should have at least told me," I muttered. "Just *not calling?* There's no excuse for that!"

"Pardon?"

"Huh? Oh, nothing. Um, are there any more cookies?"

"Yes, of course." Max rose from his chair, paused to turn on some more lights now that it was dark outside, and investigated his refreshments cupboard.

My cheeks burned every time I thought of the night Lopez had spent in my bed—every time I thought of the passionate, mind-blowing, intimate sex we'd shared. I hadn't held back anything; I didn't think he had, either. Heat gushed through me whenever I remembered those hours, despite all the water under the bridge since then. Most painful of all was my memory of his sleepy, affectionate departure for work at dawn on Christmas Day. I had been so relaxed and open with him, just assuming everything between us would be fine from now on, despite the rocky path our relationship had always been on before.

Right, I thought now with heavy self-derision. *Because sex always makes everything else just fine between two people. Gosh, everyone knows* that, *Esther.*

What an idiot I was.

Max set a fresh plate of cookies in front of me as he said, "Since you had occasion to observe Detective Lopez during the events you have described, I feel compelled to ask if you noticed any . . . interesting phenomena?"

"You mean things exploding or catching fire?" I willed myself not to think about sex as I said those words. "No. Nothing like that. It was all very . . . mundane." Well, in Max's sense of the word, anyhow: non-mystical.

"Hmm. Did he seem to be under stress at any point during the proceedings?"

At various points in the "proceedings," I thought Lopez had seemed like his head might explode. So I said, "Yes, at times. Why?"

"Well, one possibility for the incidents that you and I have previously discussed is that they are coincidence. After all, mathematically, coincidences are more common and more probable than most people suppose. But the other possibility, of course, is that Detective Lopez possesses mystical power of which he is unaware," said Max. "In which case, I theorize that extreme stress triggers these interesting events. His emotions and his focus become powerful enough for him to affect matter and energy, though it's not conscious and he doesn't realize it's happening."

When we were all trapped in a pitch-dark church with a murderer who was prepared to turn me into the next victim, electric light had suddenly been generated by the sabotaged system at the exact moment that Lopez (very *loudly)* wished for it. When Lopez was in an underground tunnel with a killer who was (literally) about to rip off another cop's head, suddenly there was a huge, fiery explosion that Lopez and the other cops survived while the killer perished. When a villain had tried to escape from Lopez by holding a gun to my head, he'd been foiled by an exploding shower of fiery light inside Fenster & Co. And on one occasion, when Lopez and I were having a particularly volatile evening, my bed had burst into flames—while we were on it together.

In other words, strange things happened around him.

"Always involving fire and light," Max mused.

"Quite intriguing, when you consider that, during our search in Harlem for a Vodou sorcerer who was bargaining with dark powers, Detective Lopez was briefly possessed by the spirit of Ogoun."

"A warrior," I said, remembering what Max had told me as I fretted over Lopez's unconscious body in the aftermath of that incident. "A protector."

"And a spirit of fire."

Yes, during Lopez's involuntary possession trance in a Vodou ceremony, there had been quite a bit of playing with flames and red-hot coals.

"So this power that you suspect he possesses . . ." I said.

"May well be focused in or derived from fire," said Max. "I postulate some form of pyrokinesis. Innate, obviously, rather than learned."

"But Max," I said, shaking my head, "how could he possess that sort of power without knowing? I mean . . . wouldn't you *notice* if you had an innate ability to make things burn, explode, or light up?"

"Oh, no, not necessarily," Max said, shaking his head. "If it's an ability he's had since birth or his early years, then the unconscious processes that create these events would feel so normal to him as to be unnoticeable. And if these incidents occur only in moments of extreme stress, as so far seems to be the case, then they are probably too irregular for any mundane person in his life—including himself—to perceive a pattern, let alone to identify *him* as the source of that pattern. Moreover, Detective Lopez is quite prone to seek—indeed, to insist on—conventional explanations even for phenomena he finds puzzling and outside his experience."

"That much is true," I said, recalling my many arguments with Lopez, who thought I was a flake—and who thought Max was crazy and possibly dangerous.

"Such gifts are quite rare," said Max, "but failure to recognize them is not. Well, not in the contemporary Western culture that Detective Lopez inhabits, that is. Had he been born in a superstitious village a century ago—or, indeed, born almost anywhere in the world when I was a young man—then his fate might well be quite different. In those days, a person around whom *multiple* strange incidents occurred would soon have attracted the worst sort of superstitious fear and suspicion."

As he said this, I realized again how perilous so much of Max's existence must have been.

I thought over everything he'd said, then settled on what struck me as the most relevant questions. "Do you think this gift makes Lopez unintentionally dangerous? Or places him in danger?"

"Well . . ." I could tell from Max's expression that these questions had already occurred to him. Some time ago, probably. He said gently, "Danger of some sort is always among the possibilities of possessing such a gift, but never the only possibility. And much like a material gift, a mystical gift can be recognized or neglected, valued or wasted, and used with wisdom or with profligacy."

I didn't know what "profligacy" was, but I got the gist of his meaning. I picked up another cookie and munched as I thought it over. "If you're right about him, then I think this gift is going to remain unrecognized, Max. Things are pretty strained between us these days, but even if they weren't, I can easily imagine Lopez's response to my explaining he has mystical power and just doesn't know it." I'd get a more serious response if I told him I was the Pope in disguise.

"Indeed. And since I am theorizing rather than speaking with certainty," said Max, "there would be little point in pursuing the matter with him at this juncture."

"Well, that's a relief." Because I really couldn't picture that conversation going well.

"You seem quite hungry," Max said as he watched me reach for another cookie. "May I offer you dinner?"

"Dinner." I nodded enthusiastically, enthralled by that suggestion. The cookies were waking up my stomach and making me realize how ravenous my tight budget had made me.

The bells chimed, indicating that someone was entering the bookstore. Nelli woke up and lifted her head.

"Hello?" It was a man's voice. "Dr. Zadok? Are you here?"

"Back here," called Max, rising from his chair to greet the visitor. Then he said to me, "How about some Chinese food, Esther? We could avoid this nasty weather by having it delivered."

"Good idea," I said, picturing crunchy egg rolls, plump dumplings, chicken stir-fry, and rice pancakes stuffed with pork in a rich sauce. (I don't keep kosher, obviously.)

A tall, handsome Chinese-American man who looked like he was my age or a little younger came around the bookcase that blocked our view of the doorway. He was carrying a brown paper bag in his arms. There were some Chinese letters on it. Below that, in English, was printed the phrase: Kwong's Chinese Carry-Out.

I looked at Max in surprise. "That was fast."

"Indeed." Max looked down at himself with a puzzled frown, as if wondering whether he had managed to conjure the food delivery without realizing it.

"Dr. Zadok?" the man asked.

"Yes. But, er, I don't think we order—"

"Here's your delivery!" The man held his finger up to his lips, indicating we should be silent.

Max and I exchanged a perplexed glance as the guy set the food bag down on the walnut table, shoving aside a pile of books to make room for it. He had a lean, athletic build, slim without being skinny. Neatly combed black hair framed an attractive face. He was also unusually well dressed for someone delivering carry-out. He wore a black wool coat over a black suit and tie, with a crisp white shirt. I noticed that his polished black shoes were wet from the sleet outside.

Having shed the carry-out bag, he reached into his breast pocket and pulled out a folded piece of paper. After again indicating that we should be silent, he handed it to Max.

As he did so, he was saying, "Egg rolls, steamed dumplings, shrimp in garlic sauce, spicy duck, roast pork . . . Is that everything you ordered?"

"Oooh! Is that really what you brought?" I asked eagerly.

Both men turned to look at me.

"Um, never mind." I rose from my chair and approached them as Max unfolded the paper he'd been handed. The enticing aromas wafting from the carry-out bag distracted me, and I decided that no matter what this stranger's odd arrival was actually about, I was going to investigate that bag in a minute. But first, I peered over Max's shoulder as he started reading the note written on the creased sheet of paper:

I think there's been a murder. The kind you specialize in. If I'm right, you know how messy that can get. So we got to look into it and nip this thing in the butt.

"The butt?" I said. "Don't you think he means bud?"

The tall stranger put his finger to his lips again, reminding me not to speak. I gasped as I realized who must have written this note, and I promptly continued reading over Max's shoulder.

My seminary will bring you here so we can talk. Bring Nelli with you. We may need her. BURN THIS NOTE!

"Seminary?" Max said.

"Emissary," I guessed, looking at the well-dressed young man. Seeing how puzzled Max still looked, I silently mouthed, "Lucky."

Max's eyes widened. We both turned to look at the stranger, who nodded to confirm my guess. He pulled a lighter out of his pocket, took the note gently from Max, and set it on fire. After he dropped it into a tea saucer, where it turned to ashes, he made a gesture indicating that we should leave the bookstore with him.

We nodded in unison and started bustling around the shop, gathering our things and putting on our gear. While I slid my daypack over my shoulders, atop my heavy coat, Max donned his furry Russian cap. The hat complemented his long, tailored coat with its dramatically flaring hem. His brightly colored waterproof boots didn't match his otherwise elegant winter attire, but they were practical.

While Max wrestled Nelli into her thick winter vest ("I fear her short fur is not sufficient protection against New York's climate at this time of year"), I went back to the table and peered inside the bag of carry-out food. It smelled *wonderful*. My stomach growled. My mouth watered. I decided I would rather let Evil have its way with Manhattan than miss this meal, so I picked up the bag and carried it with me to the door.

The stranger held open the door for me as Max clipped Nelli's pink leather leash onto her collar. I exited the building and entered the night, with the rest of my party right behind me.

As I turned to ask where we were going, I slipped on some ice. The man caught my elbow and steadied me. Sleet hit my face, cold and stinging. I felt a drop of it trickle down my neck, a chilling sensation.

Max was tugging gently on Nelli's leash, trying to urge her to come outside. She hung back, looking dubiously at the freezing precipitation coming down on us and the filthy slush soaking into our footwear.

"I brought a car," said the stranger, much to my relief.

"Will our dog fit?" I asked him.

"Sure. That's why I brought it. Um, our mutual

friend suggested it. He said Dr. Zadok would be bringing a big dog."

"Actually, 'dog' is not quite accurate," Max explained, still trying to coax Nelli out the door. "She is a mystical familiar who has chosen to manifest in canine form."

"A very *large* canine form," our companion noted.

"Nelli, come *on,*" I said firmly, taking her leash from Max and giving it a sharp tug. She skittered toward me and tried to seek shelter under the hem of my coat (not a very practical strategy) while Max closed the shop door. I asked the well-dressed stranger, "Where's your car?"

"Right over here. I got lucky with parking," he said, leading the way. A few seconds later, he stopped at a big black hearse and opened the tailgate so Nelli could climb into the back.

"A hearse?" I blurted, clutching my warm bag of food.

"I thought it would be too conspicuous, but our mutual friend insisted I bring it. Now I know why," he added with a grin as he closed the door on Nelli, who was settling herself comfortably. "Anyhow, being *in*conspicuous was the idea with the carry-out. I was trying to seem like I had an ordinary reason for entering the shop to find Dr. Zadok."

"Delivering food in a hearse?"

"Not my smoothest plan ever," he admitted with

another smile. "Here, you don't have to keep holding the bag."

"Yes, I do." I took a step back when he reached out to take it from me.

As Max helped me into the back seat of the hearse, he said to our escort, "May I ask were we are going?"

"To a funeral," was the reply.

"Of course," I said as I dug into my bag of food.

White

The color of death and mourning, ancestral spirits and ghosts.

As we turned south on 7th Avenue, I extracted a container of egg rolls from the bag. "Does anyone else want something to eat?"

Nelli whined a little, and although I didn't want to encourage bad habits, I tossed an egg roll into the back for her, rather than feel her mournful brown gaze bore into me while I ate. Our escort was busy dealing with bad driving conditions and heavy traffic, and Max was too nervous to eat. (Not because we were on our way to confront Evil, but because cars terrify him. Born in the seventeenth century, he's still having a little trouble adjusting to motorized transportation.) So I ate alone, munching on the remaining egg roll with relish as I investigated the other contents of the bag.

After we crossed Houston and continued going south, Max unclenched his tense jaw enough to ask, "Where exactly is this funeral we're attending?"

"Chinatown," said our driver.

When traffic became so thick that the hearse came to a standstill, I asked, "Who are you, by the way? Or can't you tell us?"

"Oh, I'm sorry! I should have introduced myself," said the stranger, turning to look at us both. "I'm John Chen. How do you do?"

We exchanged greetings.

Then John said with a self-deprecating smile, "Uncle Lucky got me so focused on secrecy, in case your shop is bugged by the cops—"

"Uncle?" I said in surprise.

"Bugged?" Max blurted.

"—that I forgot to say something after we were outside."

"Bugged," I repeated to Max with a nod. As soon as I had realized the message was from Lucky, I'd understood why we were supposed to be silent. "I really doubt it, Max, since it's not as if you're a 'known associate,' and OCCB's resources probably aren't so endless they can spy on everyone who knows Lucky. But I guess that being so cautious is one of the reasons he's never gone to prison." Then I asked our chauffeur, "Is Lucky really your uncle?"

John returned his attention to traffic as things started moving again. "No, we just call him that. My brother and I. I've known Lucky all my life. His uncle—a real one—and my grandfather were business partners, and ever since they died, the business has belonged to Lucky and my dad. But he'll explain all that to you."

I wondered what sort of business we were talking about. Underworld stuff? I didn't think Lucky would get me and Max mixed up in Gambello business. Not in the current circumstances. And John seemed like a respectable guy, not a third-generation hoodlum. Then again, what did I know about Chinese criminals? I'd seen gangbangers stalking the streets of Chinatown occasionally, when I was there shopping and eating (prices are good in Chinatown, so I go there often), and they looked just like thugs of any other ethnicity. But for all I knew, maybe Chinatown associates at Lucky's level of business all came across like John—who gave the impression of being a courteous, well-spoken professional with nice manners. One who slowed down when the traffic light changed from green to yellow, I noted, rather than speeding through it.

"So, John, whose funeral are we going to?" I asked, opening a container of dumplings. "Is there sauce with this?"

"Huh? Oh, um, there should be," said John. "I'm taking you to Benny Yee's funeral. Well, his visitation."

"A Chinese funeral?" Max said with concern. "I don't think we're properly dressed for that."

"How should we be dressed?" I asked.

"In white," said Max. "It's the color of mourning."

"I'm not mourning the departed," I pointed out. "We never even met." I was wearing dark brown slacks, black boots with low heels, and a nice sweater in forest green, which I thought ought to be acceptable garb for a stranger paying her respects at a visitation on a miserable winter night like this.

"Don't worry, Dr. Zadok," said John. "People in Chinatown mostly dress just like you and Miss Diamond would for a funeral. A lot of the old ways don't survive long in the New World. Or in the twenty-first century."

"Oh. Yes, of course." Max murmured thoughtfully, "I should have realized. The last time I was at a Chinese funeral was in China, and it was a long time ago."

Knowing Max as I did, I realized that "long time" could easily mean a hundred years or so.

"And, actually, I'm not supposed to take you straight to Benny's send-off," said John. "Uncle Lucky wants to see you first. Which means meeting in private. I guess you already know, he can't be seen in public. And Benny Yee's wake is pretty public. Lots of people will be paying their respects."

"I gather Mr. Yee is an influential man?" said Max,

clinging to his seat as we skidded a little when turning onto Canal Street.

"*Was,* you mean," I said, deciding not to open the sauce I'd found, since the ride wasn't that smooth. I bit into a juicy dumpling and sighed.

"He was a Chinatown businessman," said John. "And a pretty prominent member of the Five Brothers tong."

"Ah-hah!" I said, perceiving the connection with Lucky. "A tong. That's like the Mafia, right? Only Chinese."

"Well, not really. I mean, yes, there's a certain aspect of—"

"Perhaps you should keep both hands on the wheel," Max said anxiously to John, who had lifted his right hand for a moment to waggle it ambiguously in response to my question.

"We'll be there soon, Dr. Zadok," John said soothingly, returning his full attention to the road.

So was John a tong member? Or was he simply, like me and Max, a normal person inadvertently connected to some underworld figures? (Well, "normal" in the sense of not being professional criminals.)

Traffic was heavy here, as it usually was, as well as perilous. On Canal Street, Chinatown's main east-west artery, a two-way thoroughfare that was crowded with impatient drivers and daredevil cabbies, pedestrians were crossing the street against the lights, wading through moving cars, and stepping off the curb without warning. But despite Max's obvious anxiety and occasional little gasps of alarm, John was handling this big vehicle well in the tight traffic, and he was alert in his reactions to the human obstacle course. So I thought we had a good chance of reaching our destination without mowing down a reckless pedestrian.

I heard panting in my ear and felt Nelli's breath on my neck as she peered over my shoulder, from her commodious spot in the back of the hearse, to examine the steamed dumplings. Rather than argue about it, I gave her one, being careful not to let her accidentally take a finger with it.

"But that's the only one you're getting," I said firmly.

As always, Chinatown was an explosion of light, color, bustle, life, and chaos. Even in this rotten weather, outdoor vendors lined Canal Street. The merchants, huddled deep in their coats and hooded parkas, were eagerly waving down pedestrians on the crowded sidewalks, urging them to stop, shop, and buy. We drove slowly past restaurants with duck carcasses hanging in the windows, their crispy skin burnished reddish-bronze by flavorful sauce and slow roasting. Chinese women carrying shopping bags bartered with fish vendors whose fresh-caught wares lay on piles of ice and glistened under the bright electric lights. A profusion of red, yellow, white, and green signs and billboards displayed Chinese calligraphy. The Chinese characters on all the stores and shops were followed, almost as an afterthought, by brief English translations: Happy Family Chinese Bakery; Shanghai Gourmet Restaurant; Glamorous Clothes; Kosher Dim Sum (food being a bond between Chinese and Jews); Herbal Remedies; Tea Imports.

When we stopped at another traffic light, John pointed to a nearby building with golden pagoda-like flourishes around the doorway. "Speaking of tongs, as we were . . . Have a look at the Chinese characters above the window there, Miss Diamond."

"Call me, Esther."

"Esther," he repeated with a nod. "See the third character there? The one that looks sort of like a stick-figure man wearing a big straw hat?"

I peered at it. "Yes."

"Ah," said Max with a nod. "The symbol for *tong.*"

"You read Chinese?" I asked Max, not that surprised. I had heard him speak it once, and I knew he read English, Latin, Greek, Hebrew, French, and German.

"Oh, no," he said, shaking his head briskly to disclaim any such accomplishment. "I only know a few dozen common Chinese characters. You'd have to be familiar with several thousand to read the language competently."

I'm no linguist, but I knew that in contrast to the phonetic way that Western writing had developed over the millennia, with each alphabetical symbol representing a sound, Chinese writing had arisen from ideograms and pictographs. I nodded in response to what Max had said, adding, "Because every word in the language has its own unique symbol, right?" I'd learned my ABCs when I was a small child, which is where literacy starts in our language. Kids in China don't have it nearly so easy. If you memorized twenty-six symbols in Chinese, you'd only know twenty-six words, rather than knowing all the symbols used to write your whole language.

"And a lot of the characters are easy to confuse with each other, too." John added ruefully, "I'm a good student, but my father finally gave up hoping I'd ever learn to read Chinese."

"But you can read that symbol?" I asked. "The character for tong?"

"Well, there are a hundred or so symbols that are so common—especially in daily life in Chinatown—that most people around here know them," John replied. "Even people like me who were hopeless at our Chinese lessons. Or immigrants from the bottom rungs of society who never really learned to read and write."

"That's why I recognize it," said Max. "I know even fewer characters than our able young escort, but tong is a common one. And easy to remember."

I found Chinese writing beautiful and exotic, but it all just looked like abstract art to me, without identifiable patterns, so I had never noticed this symbol—or any other—in particular, though I came often to this part of town.

"A stick-figure man with a straw hat," I said to John with a smile. "I'll remember that."

"It's one that you'll see all over Chinatown," he said.

"That seems very bold," I commented. "Sort of an in-your-face challenge to law enforcement, isn't it?"

I really couldn't picture the Gambellos—or the other Mafia families with whom they competed—writing *La Cosa Nostra* on their buildings.

As traffic started moving again, John said, "No, not at all. The literal meaning of *tong* is 'gathering place' or 'meeting hall.' It applies to any space in which people congregate, for whatever reason."

"Oh, I see," I said, understanding now. "It's similar to the way 'family' is a common word with a harmless meaning—unless we're specifically talking about something like the Gambello family." In which case, *family* meant a criminal organization, most of whose members weren't actually related to each other.

"Um . . . yeah," said John, keeping his eyes on the road.

I wondered if it had been tactless of me to bring that up, given that Lucky was evidently relying on the Chen family while he was hiding from the cops. Still, in for a penny, in for a pound. I was curious and a little puzzled now, so I asked more questions as we proceeded through the center of Chinatown, passing Mulberry, Mott, and Elizabeth. Fortunately, John didn't seem to mind answering.

"But I'm sure 'tong' has some kind of criminal connotation," I said. "I sometimes read in the news about tong leaders being investigated or arrested for running extortion, prostitution, and gambling rackets. And whenever there's a sweep of street gangs in Chinatown, the media usually describe the gangs as the enforcers for the tong bosses."

"Yes, that's certainly an aspect of Chinatown's tongs," said John as the hearse approached the Bowery. "A well-known one. They're secret societies, in a sense, like Uncle Lucky's work family—which my brother and I were never allowed to ask him about. Being kids we asked anyhow, of course, but my parents chewed us out if they found out about it, and Lucky mostly just told us not to ask."

Ah. So apparently the Chens had not raised John and his brother to go into a similar line of work. Which would explain why he came across as respectable—he evidently *was*.

John continued, "But the tongs are also fraternal organizations. Community benevolent associations, you might say. There's criminal activity—really bad stuff, in fact. But the tongs are also involved in helping immigrants, assisting families, supporting community activities and local businesses, and working on civic problems. It's all based on the way Chinatown evolved, separate from the rest of the city. Self-contained and self-reliant. A lot of those old ways and established customs have far-reaching effects. Especially in a community where there are always a lot of new immigrants who don't really speak English, don't trust government authorities, and aren't always here legally."

When we slowed down for the traffic light at the Bowery, the windy north-south boulevard that bisects Chinatown, I wondered how far east we were going. Historically, Chinatown was a very small, densely packed neighborhood. Still densely packed today, it had expanded geographically in recent decades to take over much of Little Italy, which is north of Canal, and most of the Lower East Side, which was historically a Jewish neighborhood—way back when the Diamonds came to America from Eastern Europe in the early years of the twentieth century.

"Tongs are complicated," John concluded as he turned south on the Bowery. "Well, *most* things in Chinatown are complicated."

That much I had always gathered. In keeping with the long tradition of New York City as a gateway to America, there's a constant churn of population in Chinatown, with new immigrants (legal and illegal) arriving here and working hard to scrape out a fresh start in a new land, and previous arrivals moving on after a few years—or after a generation—as they seek to turn their initial foothold in the New World into middle class prosperity. Much the way that my own forebears came to these shores more than a century ago, survived in overcrowded tenements on the Lower East Side, and labored long hours for low wages as garment workers, before ultimately saving enough money to move on to better jobs and decent apartments elsewhere. Their children, in turn, grew up as Americans, started successful businesses, and owned suburban houses. It's the perpetual cycle of realizing the American dream, generation after generation.

The Chinese got a late start on this path, despite migrating to America as early as the mid-nineteenth century to build the railroads that eventually crossed the continent. The racist Chinese Exclusion Act severely limited Chinese immigration to the US for some sixty years, including decades during which there were no immigration quotas or restrictions for other nationalities. The act prevented Chinese men from becoming US citizens, and prevented their wives and families from joining them here.

Even Jews were treated better than that. Not a thing one often has a chance to say about my people, historically speaking.

During the decades that the Exclusion Act was in effect, the Chinese in America became a small, isolated bachelor society, largely self-governing and separate from the general population. Hence the establishment of historic Chinatowns in various major cities, which are still destinations for new Chinese immigrants every year.

The Chinese Exclusion Act remained in effect until World War Two, and the motivation for eliminating it was political, not moral. In the Pacific war against the Japanese, the US became allied with China. This made the typical American characterization of the Chinese as the Yellow Peril a tad inconvenient for the US government, which finally lifted the virtual ban on Chinese immigration that had been in effect since the Victorian era.

But, you know—world at war, tens of millions perishing, the Japanese occupation of China . . . There wasn't exactly a huge rush to get in the door the moment the Exclusion Act was abolished. It wasn't until the 1960s that the Chinese population in the States really started booming. So the Chinese have made major inroads in American society in a relatively short time. And in the process, much of lower Manhattan has now turned into Chinatown.

Hey, you learn a lot about a people when you spend your whole life eating their food twice a week and every Christmas. Especially if your father is a history professor.

Still making cautiously slow progress, the hearse turned once more, cruising down to the south side of

Chinatown's historic area and doubling back toward Mulberry and Mott, where they each came to a dead end in this tangle of old streets. I realized that the claustrophobic one-way traffic system of this neighborhood had forced John to bypass our destination and circle back around to it. He pulled into a parking garage and swiped a plastic key card through a machine at the entrance. A moment later, we were granted access to the garage, and John parked the hearse in a large ground floor space that was, I noticed, reserved for Chen's Funeral Home.

The penny dropped, as Ronnie Romano might say.

"So this family business that Lucky is in with your father . . . It's a funeral home?" As we all got out of the vehicle, I realized with consternation that John's mode of transport had been a pretty big clue.

"Yes." He went around to the back of the hearse so he could let Nelli out. "I'm sorry, I guess I didn't make that clear."

"No need to apologize," said Max. "The hearse was self-explanatory."

Indeed.

It was starting to dawn on me how Lucky, while hiding from the cops, had uncovered disturbing information about the recent death of a Chinatown businessman. John's family was obviously handling the funeral, in the business which they co-owned with their Uncle Lucky.

"Okay, I think I'm caught up now," I muttered.

Having consumed most of the carry-out appetizers, I was still hugging the bag in my arms. I hoped we were headed some place comfortable enough for me to sit down and finish my dinner.

Nelli leaped out of the hearse in a burst of energy and then gave herself a bracing little shake. She wagged her tail gaily as Max took her leash from John and we all headed toward the exit.

"Are you a mortician?" I asked John curiously. I didn't think I'd ever met one socially before.

"No. I mean, I help out, of course. It's the family business, after all. But I'm in grad school. Biochemistry. My older brother is the mortician. He'll take over running the funeral home, when the time comes."

"In that case, your father must be pleased with both his sons." One would be a scientist and the other would follow in the father's footsteps. My own parents, who must often wonder if I was a changeling left for them by fairies with a malicious sense of humor, would be hard-pressed to hide their envy of the elder Mr. Chen.

John grinned as he shook his head. "Chinese parents are never pleased with their kids, Esther."

"Well, then, that's another bond between Jews and Chinese," I replied, and he laughed.

"Or if they're pleased," he added, "they don't show it. That would never do, you know."

The sleet was turning to snow as we left the garage, so I pulled my hood over my head. As the wind whipped down the street, blowing damp flakes into my face, Max paused to settle his fur cap more firmly on his head. Nelli huddled close to him, clearly skeptical about the wisdom of venturing forth on foot in this weather.

Following John's lead, we started walking in the direction of Mulberry Street. I estimated that our destination, which must be close now, was roughly halfway between the Fifth Precinct house, which was the Chinatown police station, and One Police Plaza, which was just a few blocks from where we'd left the hearse. So Lucky must really trust the Chens. There were a lot of cops nearby, if the family happened to decide they didn't really want a Gambello hitter hiding out here. Or if any of the Chens happened to be a little too loud or indiscreet, unable to resist gossiping about the notorious mobster hiding out with them.

Thanks to my recent memories of being arrested and incarcerated, I also wasn't thrilled to see how close we were to the immense, ugly façade of Manhattan Central Booking, where a lot of people were probably having a grim night. I always thought that building's architect must have been a huge fan of Stalin and Mao; the place had that sort of look. Feeling a little spooked as I glimpsed that stark edifice looming ominously over Columbus Park by night, I reminded myself that I was a free woman—and would remain so, thanks to Lopez making a mess of the procedure after arresting me.

Thinking of him made me start wondering where he was now, and whether he . . .

No, stop there. Stop right *there.*

"We're almost there," said John, startling me.

"Huh?"

"It's just ahead." He was squinting against the snowflakes flying into his eyes. They clumped on his dark lashes.

Max and I looked in the direction he was pointing. It was a turn-of-the-century building, crowded between others, with an elaborate Italian façade: thick marble pillars framed the doorway, above which there was an elaborate relief sculpture of trumpeting cherubim being blessed by a plump angel, surrounded by flowers, vines, and leaves. On a less profusely decorated portion of the building, swooping gold letters identified the place as Antonelli's Funeral Home.

"That's a Chinese funeral home?" Max asked doubtfully.

"It's the Italian side of the business," John said. "This used to be Little Italy."

"Ah." I nodded. "Of course."

The magnificently restored Eldridge Street Synagogue is now in Chinatown, on a street that was in the heart of the Jewish Lower East Side back when the synagogue was built in the 1880s. (I like their annual Egg Rolls and Egg Creams festival.) The oldest Jewish cemetery in the city, Shearith Israel, which dated back to Max's childhood, was just a short distance on foot from this spot. And the Church of the Transfiguration, smack in the center of Chinatown's historic district, had originally been Irish, then later Italian. Now Chinese Christians worshipped there, with services in English, Mandarin, and Cantonese.

So finding a funeral home in Chinatown that looked like it belonged in Naples wasn't that surprising. Layer upon layer of living history survived in these streets.

John made what looked like a time-out gesture with his gloved hands. I realized a moment later he was giving us an illustration, when he said, "It's an L-shaped building. You just can't tell from here, because the other buildings are all crowding around it. You'll see after we're inside. The Chinese half of the business—Chen's Funeral Home—opens on another street. All the bodies get processed in the middle."

Which went a little way toward explaining how Lucky Battistuzzi wound up in business with a Chinese funeral parlor.

"Actually, these days, we do more Chinese funerals than Italian ones on this side of the building, too," said John as we approached the door. "Things are slow tonight—Benny Yee is our only customer. But when it's busy, we use both sides of the building for Chinese. We keep it looking Italian, though, or otherwise we'd lose all our white customers."

He opened the door, and we scuttled inside, grateful to escape from the weather. We entered a grand old foyer with marble floors, paneled walls, traditional art, several elaborate chairs, and two enormous vases positioned on either side of a large gold-framed mirror. Our footsteps echoed in the silent hall as we passed several closed doors. Max, Nelli, and I were following John, who led the way to the back of the building and through a door which he unlocked for us. The décor on the other side of that door was contemporary and utilitarian, dramatically different from the Italianate hall we had just passed through. These were obviously the offices and working rooms of the business.

"Uncle Lucky?" John called softly.

"In here!" responded a familiar voice.

John gestured for us to precede him. We entered a room that had a couple of desks and computer monitors, a lot of standard office equipment, paperwork, and file folders—and an old mobster who was rising from one of the chairs to greet us.

"Lucky!" Relieved to see him, I gave him a big hug.

"Hey, you're all wet," he said to me. "Is it stinkin' rotten out there tonight?"

"Yep."

He shook hands heartily with Max, then greeted

Nelli. Lucky was a favorite of hers, so she was delighted by this unexpected surprise and barreled violently into him, panting, whining, and hopping up and down in her excitement. Her long, thick, bony tail wagged back and forth furiously, its whiplash motion threatening the safety of everyone (and everything) in the room. John cried out in pain and staggered away from her after this menacing appendage struck him in the leg.

"All right, calm down," Lucky said to the dog. "You're hurting people."

"I'll go get a couple more chairs." John limped out of the room.

I set my brown bag down on one of the desks. "Lucky, you're really part-owner of a funeral business? I mean, you've actually *got* a perfectly legitimate business interest?" I had never expected this.

"I inherited it from my mother's brother," he said. "He was never involved in any Gambello business. Running a funeral home, though, he turned a good profit from some of our work."

"No doubt," I said.

"And straight away after this place come down to me," he continued, "I put it in my daughter's name. Her *married* name."

"So you don't think the cops or the FBI know about your connection with it?" I asked as Max helped me off with my coat.

"I don't think so . . ."

He didn't sound very sure, but instead of questioning him about that, I asked curiously, "How did your family get into business with the Chens?"

"My uncle brought old Mr. Chen into the funeral business after that guy saved his life by pulling him out of a burning car one night right after an accident on Canal Street."

"Good heavens!" Max looked at me. "Speed kills, Esther."

"That kinda thing creates a bond."

"I'll bet," I said.

"Those two guys was in business together for forty years. Italian funerals on one side, Chinese on the other, and their partnership was always as smooth as glass." Lucky continued, "My uncle didn't have any kids, so I was kinda like a son to him. Which is why he left me the business. Anyhow, I don't advertise my association with the Chens, since I got complications in my life that my uncle never liked and the Chens don't need, but we've always been able to count on each other."

As Lucky finished his story, John returned to the room, carrying a couple of folding chairs. While he set them up, he said, "That's for sure. When my mom died suddenly fifteen years ago and my dad was devastated, Uncle Lucky took care of everything. Looked after me and my brother . . . Looked after my dad, really. He was the rock in our lives when we needed it."

"Oh, my dear fellow," Max said, obviously moved.

"Whatever," Lucky said gruffly. He noticed the carry-out bag and asked me, "Hey, did you bring dinner?"

"Yes!" I was ready to get this party started. "Have you got plates and forks?"

"You really want to eat in a funeral home, kid?" Lucky asked me doubtfully. "There's a dead guy lying in his coffin just across—"

"*You've* been eating here, haven't you?" I said dismissively as I began unpacking what was left of the food. I assumed he had been stuck inside this building ever since escaping the bust at Bella Stella.

"Sensitive, but not squeamish," the old gangster said with a grin. "I've always liked that about you."

"My dad's got stuff here for when things are so busy he has to eat at his desk." John opened a cupboard and pulled out some paper plates and napkins, plastic forks, and a few bottles of water.

As we all sat down at the desks to eat, Lucky said to me, "So, kid, did you really clobber a couple of cops during the arrest at Stella's? Including your boyfriend?"

"Lopez is not my boyfriend," I said, shoveling rice onto my paper plate. "I did hit him, though."

"Hmm." Max frowned. "Actually, Esther, I'm still puzzled about *why* you struck Detective Lopez. Perhaps I've missed some key aspect of the stor—"

"How do you know what happened during the

bust?" I asked Lucky quickly. "I assumed you got yourself out of there as soon as you realized that the NYPD had just stampeded through the door."

"You bet I did," said Lucky as he accepted a container of roast pork and vegetables from John. "But I've got my sources. I can't stand going five days without any news at all. I been trying to find out how bad the damage to the family is and how much worse it's gonna get."

"I've been reading the papers," I said, "in case your name appeared." I passed the spicy duck along to Max.

"OCCB executed a search warrant on the boss' home in the middle of the night," said Lucky, "but they didn't find nothing. He's a careful man, after all. And he still ain't been arrested, so maybe they just can't get him."

"At least, not until someone who *has* been arrested decides to cut a deal and turn state's evidence," I said.

"Hmph. We don't need *that* kinda talk at dinner." Lucky spoke sternly and dug into his meal with a scowl.

Nelli was watching us with riveted attention, but Max—who otherwise tended to spoil her—had established a strict rule against begging at the table. So she was lying by the door, occasionally cocking her head alertly, as if hearing something interesting. I supposed her enormous ears could detect a few sounds from Benny Yee's wake. Which reminded me . . .

"So Lucky, what was the meaning of your note?" It had sounded serious. And talking about it would take his mind off the Gambello family's problems.

"Ah, yes! I am most intrigued," said Max. "I deduce that you believe Mr. Benny Yee has been murdered by mystical means?"

Lucky set down his plastic fork and nodded. "You bet. I think Benny Yee was killed by a fortune cookie!"

6

堂

Tong

"Let me get this straight," I said to Lucky. "You think Yee was murdered by a cookie?"

"No." Lucky gave me an impatient look. "A *fortune* cookie."

"Oh. Well that makes all the difference," I said. "I stand corrected."

"A fortune," Lucky said. "The piece of paper inside the cookie. That's what killed him!"

"Hmm. What leads you to believe this?" asked Max.

"It had a death curse on it," said Lucky.

"Interesting," said Max.

"A death curse? In a fortune cookie?" I frowned. "Seriously?"

Lucky nudged John, who was eating shrimp with garlic sauce. "Tell them."

John nodded. "It was a death curse. That part is true."

"What do you mean *that* part?" Lucky snapped.

"Wait." Max held up an admonishing finger. "Someone please begin at the beginning."

John started to speak, but Lucky scowled at him and said, "*I'll* tell it."

John nodded and went back to eating.

"Benny Yee, who's a *capo* in the Five Brothers tong—"

"They don't call them *capos*, do they?" I interrupted.

"No," said John, without looking up from his plate.

"Esther, please, let's not interrupt unless we must," said Max.

"Sorry."

"Three days ago," Lucky continued, "Benny Yee receives this elaborate fortune cookie at his office. One of them gourmet things. It's kinda big, drizzled with dark chocolate, wrapped in see-through silver cellophane. Very fancy. It was left on his secretary's desk while she was down the hall for a couple of minutes. She thinks there was a card with Benny's name on it, but no one could find it later."

I spooned some roast pork onto my rice and then kept eating. It was amazing how much better lots of good food was making me feel about my prospects in life.

"So Benny takes the cookie into his office, where he's planning to spend the rest of the day working, and closes the door. And I guess he got a little hungry, because he broke open the cookie. To eat it, we figure."

Since Lucky seemed to be awaiting a response, I said, "Uh-huh."

"Later that day, his wife shows up by surprise. Some excuse about showing him her new hairdo. But word on the street is that she thinks Benny's having an affair with someone and plans to catch him at it."

"*Was* he having an affair?" I asked.

"Oh, yeah," said John with an emphatic nod. "With his secretary, in fact. And he wasn't discreet. His wife is probably the only person in Chinatown who *hasn't* seen him pawing her."

"But on this occasion, when the wife arrives, Benny's alone in his office, and the secretary's getting ready to leave for an appointment with Benny's lawyer, who's helping her fix a prostitution rap," Lucky added. "She was on the game before Benny gave her a job in his office. Benny's been getting that all straightened out for her."

"In other words, she's got no motive to kill Benny, and several reasons to keep him alive." Presumably Mrs. Yee wasn't going to keep paying the secretary's legal fees now that Benny was dead, even if she didn't know about the affair.

Lucky nodded and continued, "But Benny doesn't answer when his secretary buzzes him to say his wife's here. So his wife knocks on the closed door. Still no answer from Benny. So the two women go in—and Benny's lying there, dead on the floor, with the broken fortune cookie sitting on his desk. His head's split open and there's blood everywhere."

John set down his fork. "I didn't know we were going to go into this much detail."

I wondered if a touch of squeamishness was why he wasn't going into the family business.

"The doc needs to know everything," Lucky said to him. "Any detail might be the key to the whole thing."

"Uncle Lucky, there isn't any 'whole thing,' " said John. "All that happened—"

"*I'm* tellin' it."

John let out his breath, nodded, and fell silent again.

"A bloody head wound," I said, digging into some spicy duck. "Was he attacked?"

"Nope. The medical examiner figures Benny got up from his desk without taking a bite of the cookie after he cracked it open. Maybe heading for the door. Anyhow, almost as soon as he got up, he tripped and fell. On the way down, he hit his head so hard on the corner of his desk that it killed him."

"His secretary didn't hear this?" I asked.

"Oh, she probably did," Lucky replied. "She remembers a *thud* coming from inside his office a couple of hours before she and the missus found him. But it wasn't that loud, and he didn't call for her. She thought he just dropped something. Or threw something—I guess Benny had a temper on him."

"He did," said John.

"Oh, that poor young woman," said Max. "It must torment her to imagine Mr. Yee lying there dying, while she sat on the other side of the door, unaware that anything was wrong."

John shook his head as he said, "Benny died so fast, it wouldn't have made a difference if she'd known and called for help."

"Lucky, I'm not really seeing the connection," I said. "Benny opens the fortune cookie. He sets it down. He gets up, he trips, he dies." I shook my head. "The homicidal nature of the cookie isn't apparent to me."

John laughed at that. Lucky glared at him, then said impatiently to me, "The fortune cookie contained a death curse. Don't you *get* it?"

"Hmm," said Max.

I looked at John. "Do you think Benny was cursed with death?"

"No," he said. "I think Uncle Lucky has been cooped up in here for too long, with too little to do besides worry."

"That does sound plausible," I said to Lucky.

He glared at me, then said grumpily to John, "So tell them *your* theory, Mr. PhD Candidate."

"Okay." John looked at me and Max. "Benny was the kind of guy you asked about when we were talking in the car, Esther. He was a bigshot in the Five Brothers tong and involved in plenty of stuff on the wrong side of the law. He had enemies."

"And one of them," Lucky said, "cursed him with death!"

"Hmm," said Max.

"It's John's turn to tell the story," I pointed out.

"Like a lot of older Chinese," John continued, "Benny was superstitious. He was known for it, in fact. For example, he wouldn't visit the fourth floor of any building, no matter how important a person or an appointment it might be."

"Um, why?" I asked.

"Four is a bad-luck number," John explained. "The Chinese word for it sounds like the word for 'death.' Sure, plenty of people think it's inauspicious. But Benny had a real phobia about it. And that's just one example."

Realizing where John was going with this, I said, "So this very superstitious man who has a lot of enemies receives a mysterious gift, and when he cracks open the cookie, he reads a fortune there that curses him with death. And he panics?"

"Exactly. He drops the cookie and jumps out of

his chair. Maybe he was just moved by agitation. Maybe he was headed for the door to tell his secretary they had to find out where the fortune cookie came from. Either way, he trips, falls, hits his head, and dies." John shook his head. "I think it was a malicious prank, a practical joke that was intended to wind him up. To make Benny jumpy and skittish. But it had much worse consequences than the sender ever expected."

"Hmm," said Max.

"It might even have been sent by a friend or colleague," said John.

"Not a very nice one," I noted.

"I don't think Benny hung out with nice people," John replied. "Anyhow, there's no trace of where the fortune cookie came from. And now that it has led to his death, no one will ever—"

"So it was really a *mis*fortune cookie," I said, thinking of Benny's superstitions.

"You got it, kid. And ain't nobody ever gonna admit to giving that misfortune cookie to Benny," said Lucky. "That's one thing John and I agree on, at least."

"How did you guys find out about this?" I asked. "Did Mrs. Yee just blurt out the whole story when she was making funeral arrangements?"

"No, I heard it from Benny's nephew," said John. "He heard it from the widow."

"And I eavesdropped." Lucky shrugged. "I was

bored. I really *don't* have anything to do besides worry."

"Why did the nephew tell you all this?" I asked John.

"I know the family," he replied. "Ted and I grew up together, and Susan and I were in some undergrad classes together in college."

"Who is Susan?"

"Ted's sister," he said. "And, of course, I'm helping with Ted's film, so we see each other a lot these days."

"Ted's film?" I repeated.

John replied, "Benny's nephew, Ted, is shooting an indie film here in Chinatown. I'm doing the hair and makeup for it. I've had a lot of practice at that kind of thing." Looking at me as if concerned about how I'd react, he added, "I do most of the hair and makeup on the customers here."

I realized he meant corpses, but something much more important had caught my attention.

"Ted's shooting this film now?" I asked.

"Yes."

Max said to John, "In order to review this matter thoroughly, I need to know what has become of the—"

"Have all the parts been cast already?" I asked.

"Well, when I say *now,*" John said, "I guess I'm wrong. Between Benny's death and Mary breaking her leg, we haven't filmed for the past few—"

"Does anyone know," Max asked, "what became of the—"

"Who's Mary?" I asked.

"Mary Fox," said John. "She's one of the two female leads. Well, she was. Now that she's laid up with a broken—"

"Is she Chinese?" I asked urgently. I'm versatile, but there was no way I'd be cast as a Chinese character.

"No, Mary's white. The lead character in the movie is an ABC who's trying to choose between two women. One of them is—"

"ABC?" I repeated.

He smiled. "American Born Chinese. Like me."

Max said, "About the fortune that was in this cookie . . ."

"So Mary Fox was playing the white girl?" I said. "And now that she's broken her leg, the role will have to be recast?"

"Um, I don't know. I would think so," said John. "But that's Ted's call. And he's got a lot on his mind right now, since—"

"Yeah, Benny's death," I said. "Whatever. Look, John, I'm an actress."

"A professional," Lucky added helpfully. "Esther's been on TV."

"Oh?" said John with interest. Then: *"Oh."*

"Can you introduce me to Ted?" I asked.

"Of course," said John. "I'm sure he's here tonight. The deceased is his uncle, after all."

"Oh. Right." That sank in now. "Sorry. I should have . . . I mean, this might not be the best time for me to ask to read for his movie."

"Oh, it's probably all right," said John. "To be honest, Ted won't miss Benny—just his money."

"Pardon?"

"Benny was backing Ted's film."

"Ted's lost his backer?" I asked in dismay.

"Well, there's still cash left from Benny's initial investment," said John. "And Ted is optimistic about getting more investment."

"Okay. Good. I'd like to meet him. Right away." I stood up.

So did John. "All right."

"Does anyone know," Max asked loudly, "what happened to the fortune that may have cursed Benny Yee with death?"

"Oh, sure," said Lucky, looking surprised by Max's volume. "I got John to ask Mrs. Yee for it today."

John said wearily, "He really did get me to do that."

"I figured you'd want to see it," Lucky said to Max. "And since handling it after Benny's death didn't kill the missus, I didn't think it would kill us, either."

"She kept it?" I asked curiously.

"When she saw it, she wasn't sure what to make of it," said John. "She thought it must be something to do with the Five Brothers. So she took it home with her."

"In case it turned out to be evidence?"

"Maybe. Or maybe just to keep it out of strangers' hands. I'm not sure."

While John was speaking, Lucky was retrieving a sealed plastic bag from a drawer in one of the desks. Inside the transparent bag was a slip of black paper, barely an inch wide, maybe three inches long. Lucky didn't open the bag when he showed it to us. The black paper had a single Chinese character on it, painted in delicate white calligraphy.

"White," murmured Max. "The color of death."

The symbol looked like expressionist art to me, like a few random brush strokes arranged in a pleasing shape. It was hard for me to see why it would have inspired fear in Benny Yee.

"What exactly does this character mean?" I asked John.

"It depends on context," he said. "Which we don't have here. But the meaning can be die, dead, death, condemned to die. Any of those."

"I'm going with 'condemned to die,'" said Lucky. "It's a curse!"

"May I take this back to my laboratory to study it?" Max asked.

"Yes. In fact, I'd prefer that," said John. "I don't

consider myself superstitious, but I wish Uncle Lucky hadn't insisted on having this thing here, and I'll be glad to get rid of it. It was written with malice, and it led to someone's death."

That much seemed certain. The question I knew Max was pondering, as he studied the item in the bag, was whether it had *inflicted* Benny's death. If so, then we needed to figure out how and when the next victim would be chosen. Because if this *was* mystical murder, then there would certainly be another victim sooner or later—probably sooner. Max always said that Evil was voracious, and events had repeatedly proved he was right about that. So although I thought John's interpretation of Benny's death was reasonable, I knew that Max had to investigate, in case Lucky was right.

"Before you take that home with you, though," said Lucky, "you gotta check out the suspects."

"Pardon?"

"Benny's wake." Lucky jerked his chin in the direction of the Chinese funeral parlor. "If you mingle, maybe you can spot the killer there. I'd bet fifty grand that he's here tonight."

"Why?" I asked. "Attending your victim's wake seems unnecessarily melodramatic."

"Not to mention being in questionable taste," added Max.

"People do it all the time," Lucky insisted. Which made me realize *he* might have done it.

John met Lucky's eyes. "Uncle Lucky might be right. Whoever sent Benny that cookie must have known him. And everyone who knows Benny is bound to turn up for his send-off."

"Well, then." Max slipped the death curse into his pocket. "Let's go meet the visitors. Come, Nelli. The game is afoot!"

"Um, Dr. Zadok," said John. "I don't think you can bring a dog to the visitation."

"Oh, I really think I should," said Max. "It would be advantageous for Nelli to examine the corpse for remnants of mystical influence, in the unlikely event that any such residue lingers now that the deceased has been prepared for burial."

"Huh?"

"And if there are demonic or mystical beings present, she may well be able to detect them."

"O . . . kay." John looked to me and Lucky for help.

"It's best to go along with this," said Lucky.

I nodded my agreement, though I felt sorry for John, who'd have to explain to his father, his brother, and probably the Yee family why he had allowed an enormous dog (and not a particularly well-behaved one) to prowl around the wake.

"You two go ahead," said Lucky. "There's something I need to discuss with Esther in private. She'll catch up."

John nodded. "Dr. Zadok and I are the only two

people at this wake who you know, Esther, so we should be pretty easy to spot when you come through the door."

I nodded and watched them exit the room, with Nelli stepping lively as she accompanied them out the door. Then I turned to Lucky. "What's up?"

"I got a little additional problem that I need your help with. I don't like to drag you into this, but it's important," he said. "And most of my resources ain't available for the time being."

"I'll help you in any way I can, Lucky." As long as he didn't ask me to break the law, that was. "What is it?"

He blew out his breath with his lower lip. "Well, your boyfr . . . I mean, Detective Lopez is poking around Chinatown."

"What?" I blurted in surprise. "Do you think he suspects you're hiding here?"

"I don't know. I haven't been able to find out enough to be sure. It don't seem like he's looking in the right places, but I can't think of why else he'd be in Chinatown right now."

"Oh, no." I realized what this favor was. "You want me to find out why Lopez is here?"

"And you need to do it without him knowing that's what you're asking. Because he's the type who'll figure out real quick *why* you're asking, once he realizes *what* you're asking." Lucky asked, "Do you think you can do it?"

"Oh, man," I said grumpily. "This means I'll have to *talk* to him, Lucky."

He frowned. "I know you had a big fight with him at Bella Stella, and he wound up arresting you. But maybe . . ." Lucky sighed and shook his head. "Wait a minute. Forget it. What was I even thinking? I'm sorry, kid. If I wasn't climbing the walls here, I wouldn't even have asked. I know better. I shouldn't be sending you to talk to that guy after—"

"No, no, it's important," I said quickly. "And I want to help you. And the Chens, too, who I'm sure you don't want to put in danger."

"No *way* do I want them to get in trouble because of me."

"So I'll just have to talk to Lopez," I said firmly. "For your sake. And theirs."

"Are you sure?" he asked with concern.

I lifted my chin. "I can do this. Don't worry about me, Lucky."

God, you're pathetic, Esther. And despicable.

I had no idea how I was going to approach Lopez, let alone how I'd manage to sound casual while quizzing him about his activities in Chinatown and/or the hunt for Lucky Battistuzzi. But at least I'd get to talk to him. Once I could think of a suitable pretense for it, that was.

You swore you'd stop thinking about him. You swore you'd move on!

Especially after the god-awful events of New

Year's. When I tried to imagine how that night could have been any more humiliating, I came up blank.

Yet here I was, volunteering—more or less—to get in touch with Lopez.

I didn't even know *why* I wanted to see him.

To demand an apology from him? To get an explanation for his behavior? To say all the cutting things to him that I only thought of *after* the squad car had pulled away from the curb that night?

Or maybe I'd tear off his clothes, indulge in hours of steamy sex with him, and then just *not call* him—not even after *promising* to call.

Okay, stop right there. There will be no *removing of clothes and* no *indulging in sex. Are we agreed? If not, then you can't get in touch with him. I absolutely forbid it.*

Well . . .

Agreed or not?

Oh, fine, then. *Fine.* No sex. Clothes stay on. Agreed!

"Maybe I should just bring him a misfortune cookie," I muttered.

"Don't even joke about that," said Lucky. "I'm telling you, I got a real serious feeling about this. Benny Yee was cursed with death. And you know what that means."

I nodded. "I know."

"The killer ain't gonna stop with Benny." After a moment, he added, "You better go join them at the wake. Oh, and I forgot to tell Max—keep Nelli away from the food."

"They've got food?" I asked. "At a *wake?*"

"Offerings to nourish the spirit of the departed. It's a Chinese thing." Lucky added, "We can't have our favorite familiar stealing food from a corpse. It won't make a good impression."

7

孝

Filial piety

Respect and veneration for one's parents and ancestors.

Benny Yee's wake was so crowded that I thought the odds were good that John and Lucky were right about the killer being here—simply because half of Chinatown seemed to be here.

Well, "killer" if the misfortune cookie had inflicted Benny's death; "malicious prankster" if his reaction to reading that menacing fortune had led to a fatal but mundane accident in a moment of distracted anxiety.

The latter possibility was making me think about how uncertain life was. Anyone's candle could be snuffed at any moment. Just by tripping and cracking open your head, for example. As I searched for John and Max in the crowded funeral hall, phrases like *carpe diem* and "live each day as if it were your last" kept running through my head.

Since Chen's Funeral Home was in a downtown Manhattan neighborhood, rather than in a sprawling modern suburb, it was too small for such a big send-off. But people here were accustomed to that, so everyone just crowded in without reserve, shoulder to shoulder, cheek by jowl. A lot of people had shown up this evening to pay their respects to Benny Yee. Traditional music was playing on the sound system, but with so many people here, I could hardly hear it, though most of the mingling visitors kept their voices respectfully muted as they chatted. As I squeezed my way through the throng, I felt glad I'd left my coat and belongings in the office with Lucky, since the collective body heat was making this hall rather warm.

The Chinese side of the L-shaped funeral complex was decorated in elegantly somber shades of gold and red. Several large, beautiful tapestries hung on the walls, as did some banners that displayed graceful Chinese calligraphy. I assumed the latter were blessings or prayers for the departed. There was an alcove in which several tables, all draped in white linen, were covered with offerings. Lucky was right about the food; there were plates and baskets of prettily wrapped candies, little Chinese egg tarts (my favorite), mooncakes, dried mushrooms, bright orange clementines, and dark purple plums. Several people had left bottles of liquor for the deceased.

Fortunately, Nelli didn't seem to have been here. Everything appeared to be tidy and intact, and there was no sign of drool.

I wondered whether the person who'd left a basket of fortune cookies here knew how Benny Yee had died. In any case, these were the small, plain sort of cookies that you could find in any Chinese restaurant, not the elaborate, chocolate-drizzled, gourmet variety that someone had sent to Benny.

Still searching for John and Max, I continued making my way through the gathered mourners. As John had predicted, they were all dressed pretty much the way I'd have dressed if I had known I'd be attending a wake this evening. Most of the men were in suits, most of the women wore skirts or nice slacks, and the dominant colors were black and navy blue. In my brown slacks and dark green sweater, I looked a little casual compared to most of the people here, but not out of place—well, except for the fact that Benny didn't seem to have known many Caucasians. Max and I were apparently the only white people in attendance. However, we were in contemporary New York City, not imperial Peking, so no one noticed me, let alone did a double take, as I made my way through the crowded hall.

Or so I thought.

Just as I stumbled on the guest of honor, so to speak, lying in his open casket, I heard someone near me say in an oily voice, "Hey, pretty lady, are you here all by yourself?"

I kept my gaze fixed intently on the deceased, fervently hoping that the voice was not addressing *me.*

Benny Yee had been a man of modest stature, probably in his early sixties, with a receding hairline, snub nose, and thin lips. He wore a gray suit, a gold wedding ring, and an expensive wristwatch. A large framed photo of Benny was displayed near his corpse; I noticed that he hadn't really looked that much more animated in life.

"You look lonesome," said the same oily voice, closer now.

The coffin was lined in white silk and elegant white drapes hung behind it, with additional heavy white swags framing the area around the casket and the profusion of funeral wreaths and floral tributes surrounding it. A small altar near the coffin held a statue of the Buddha, chubby and laughing—a portrayal I always found very comforting, compared to Yahweh's dour attitude throughout the Old Testament or the suffering Jesus nailed to a crucifix in Catholic churches. There were also small incense burners from which aromatic smoke was wafting, as well as special offerings, skillfully fabricated from brightly colored paper, of the things Benny had evidently enjoyed in life and wouldn't want to be deprived of in death: cars, money, a house, gold ingots, airplanes, more money.

"I think you need some company, cutie." The guy with the oily voice wasn't going away, despite being ignored.

There were more baskets of food on the altar, too, filled with fresh fruit, fortune cookies, and Chinese pastries. I was glad I had eaten before paying my respects, or this wake would be torture for me.

Visitors who approached the coffin to pay their respects crossed themselves as they gazed down at Benny, or they pressed their palms together and bowed three times; some people did both things. Many of them also paused at the altar beside his casket. Then they moved on to the group of people seated nearby, in two rows, most of whom were wearing black armbands. They must be Benny's family. An older woman with well-styled hair and a drab black dress seemed to be the focal point of this group, and her face bore an expression of stoic grief, so I figured she was Benny's widow.

I wondered if one of those mourners was Benny's nephew, Ted the filmmaker. I needed to find John and get an introduction.

"How well did you know Benny, doll face?" the oily voice asked.

Doll face? Oh, please.

With a sinking feeling, I looked at the speaker. Sure enough, he was staring right at me.

"I came here with friends," I said coldly, knowing full well that a little coldness was never enough to get rid of guys like this.

His rather stupid face contorted into a predatory smirk. "So where are these 'friends?' "

"Mingling."

"I'll take care of you while they do that." He winked at me.

He spoke with a slight Chinese accent, and he appeared to be about my age. His long hair was slicked back and tied in a pony tail, he sported a little mustache and goatee that didn't suit him, and he was dressed so inappropriately for a funeral that I didn't want anyone here to think I knew him. He wore blue jeans, boots decorated with silver studs and chains, a garish shirt, and a black leather jacket.

"No need," I replied. "I'm going to rejoin them now."

As I turned to go in search of Max and John again, this guy stepped into my path, blocking my way. "I'm Danny Teng."

"I don't care who you are," I said.

He made a little hissing sound and grinned. "I *like* a girl with spirit."

I repressed a sigh. Some women met nice men while jogging in the park or attending a friend's wedding. I, on the other hand, came to a wake and, while standing within ten feet of the corpse, got hit on by a guy who'd look right at home in a police lineup.

Police . . . No, stop. Don't think about him.

Actually, I was going to have to think about Lopez. I had just promised Lucky I would talk to him.

Oh, great, *Esther. Just great.*

"What was I thinking? God, I'm an idiot," I said with weary exasperation. Then to Danny Teng: "Now get out of my way."

"Fiery temper. Mmmm. *Lots* of potential. You know what I mean?" He winked again.

I was about to speak sharply to him when someone near us burst into noisy sobs. Distracted, I looked over my shoulder. A pretty young woman in a tight black dress (one that was better suited to a cocktail party than a wake) was weeping uncontrollably as she gazed at Benny in his coffin. Her elaborate hairdo (better suited to opening night at the opera) gleamed under the lights as she shook her head in anguished denial while staring at the departed. Her dangling earrings sparkled, and long, fake eyelashes fluttered as tears streamed down her face.

"I guess Benny will be missed," I murmured.

"Yeah," said Danny Teng. "Benny was good to her."

"Oh." I realized who the girl must be. "She was his secretary?"

"That's one word for it," he said with a snort.

Realizing this guy had known Benny, I reluctantly decided to see what I could learn from him. While the secretary continued sobbing over the corpse, I said to Danny Teng, as cheerfully as if he weren't intentionally blocking my escape route, "So this is quite a wake, huh? A big turnout."

"Sure. Benny had some juice."

"I'll bet," I said with a nod. "All those floral wreaths. Some of them are really elaborate, too. All these offerings. So many visitors."

"It's important to show face when a guy like Benny dies," said Danny. "A big funeral, no expense spared, a lot of mourners. It's a sign of respect. The way it should be when your number comes up—if you were anybody that mattered, I mean."

"How well did you know Benny?"

Danny shrugged. "I guess I knew him a long time."

"How did—"

"So why don't you and me get outta here, babe?"

"For someone who knew him a long time, you don't seem that broken up about his sudden passing," I noted.

"I know a lot of dead people," Danny said, and I believed him.

"How did you know *this* dead person?"

"You could say we were business associates." He leaned closer to me, his breath hot on my face. "How about we go somewhere for a drink?"

"Business associates?" My gaze flickered over Danny's attire. "What sort of business are *you* . . . Oh. Wait." John had said that Benny Yee was the sort of tong boss I read about in the news, involved in crime and violence. And Danny looked like the epitome of a Chinatown street thug.

"You're in a gang," I guessed.

"Is that a turn-on?" he asked in what he evidently thought was a seductive voice. "A lotta girls like that."

"You worked for Benny?" I asked. "For the Five Brothers?"

"I work for *me,*" he snapped. "No one gives Danny Teng orders."

"But your gang is associated with his tong?" I persisted.

His expression changed. "Oh, shit, you're not a reporter, are you?"

Since that possibility obviously repelled him, I didn't deny it. "Who are the Five Brothers?"

"Like you just said, it's a tong."

"No, I mean, who are the five brothers the tong is named after?"

"Oh, who cares? They're long gone. That was, like, a hundred years ago."

"The tong is that old?" Well, most of them were, I recalled. There had been tong wars in Chinatown since the nineteenth century.

"We could skip the drink," he said. "Just go straight to my place."

"Was someone after Benny?" I asked. "Do you think he might have been murdered?"

"Jesus, you *are* a reporter," Danny said with disgust, turning away.

"I know he had enemies. Do you think one of them . . . ? Never mind," I said to his retreating back.

Above the sobs of Benny Yee's secretary, I suddenly heard a woman shouting in Chinese. I looked in that direction and saw that the widowed Mrs. Yee had shed her expression of stoic grief in favor of an animated look of outrage. She was on her feet, pointing a finger at Benny's weeping secretary and shouting a torrent of words at her which, based on the appalled expressions of the relatives surrounding her, I was glad I didn't understand. Several men in the family were trying to appeal to Mrs. Yee to calm down, but she shook them off and continued hollering angrily at the secretary, whose sobs turned into a high-pitched screeching wail that made me wince.

A beautiful middle-aged woman dressed in a black knee-length cheongsam, that elegant, body-hugging style of Chinese dress, joined the men of the family in trying to persuade Mrs. Yee to calm down. She didn't have any effect, either. When she put her hand on Mrs. Yee's shoulder, the other woman impatiently shook her off.

Having been rebuffed, the woman in the cheongsam cast a frowning glance at a young man who was still seated in his chair. He was looking the other way and evidently trying to pretend that this noisy family scene wasn't occurring. She spoke to him sharply in Chinese, but he seemed not to hear her. Her tone grew exasperated as she switched to English. "I'm speaking to you, Ted!"

"Huh?" he said vaguely, looking in her direction now.

"Ted, please do something!"

Ted, I thought with interest. *The filmmaker.*

He looked pretty unprepossessing. But then, directors often do. (And writers usually look like they should be in a padded cell.) He was younger than I expected—early twenties, probably. Very skinny, he wore his long hair in a messy shag that kept getting in his eyes, his white shirt was half-untucked and wrinkled, his tie was loose, and he was the only male family member who wasn't wearing a suit.

He shrugged and said something to the woman whom I now took for his mother, but I couldn't hear him above all the shouting.

Whatever he'd said, it caused his mother to turn away from him with an expression of resigned disappointment that I had a feeling Ted saw often on her face.

Then a pretty woman in her twenties started saying in American-accented English, loudly enough for everyone to hear, "Aunt Grace is right. That woman has some nerve showing up here!"

The beautiful woman in the cheongsam said firmly, "Susan, please."

But Susan—Ted's sister, whom I remembered John mentioning earlier—ignored this. She said directly to Benny's secretary, "Get out of here! Can't you see you're upsetting my aunt? Show some respect!"

The secretary's grief turned to anger, and she started shrieking at Mrs. Yee and Susan.

Apart from Susan, who continued using English, everyone was still speaking Chinese, so I didn't understand what was being said; but it didn't take much imagination to guess what Benny's wife and mistress were shouting at each other over his dead body while his offspring and relatives watched with horrified embarrassment. I looked around and noticed that virtually all the visitors I could see were also focused on this scandalous scene, watching the players with riveted interest—and very glad, I suspected, that they had braved tonight's rotten weather to pay their respects at what was turning out to be quite a memorable wake.

I returned my attention to the shouting match—which was when I realized what should have occurred to me before: If Benny had been murdered, then Mrs. Yee was an obvious suspect. I had watched enough episodes of *Crime and Punishment* to know that the spouse often turned out to be the killer.

John had said that Benny Yee had a lot of enemies;

but closer to home, he had a wife he was cheating on—and based on the determined way she was advancing on Benny's mistress right now, she didn't seem like a woman you could expect to cross with impunity. Mrs. Yee roughly shook off the restraining hands of her anxious young male relatives (her sons, I assumed), stopped at the altar near Benny's coffin to pick up a bronze incense burner, and then leaped vengefully at Benny's screeching secretary.

"Hey!" Without conscious thought, just acting on reflex, I jumped into the fray and threw myself bodily against the secretary, slamming her sideways so that Mrs. Yee's deadly swipe at her skull with that heavy object missed its target.

Inevitably, the girl and I flew straight into the coffin and landed facedown on top of Benny's corpse. We were both winded for a moment. Then she realized where we were and started screaming and flailing. I had landed on Benny's embalmed legs, in their well-tailored trousers. The body didn't feel particularly eerie—mostly, it felt like landing on a very solid mannequin—but falling on top of a *dead* guy was still pretty disturbing. So I gasped in startled revulsion and vaulted backward—straight into a broad chest and a pair of strong arms.

"Did you *intend* to fling yourself on the corpse?" John asked.

Dangling from his arms for a moment, I said breathlessly, "No! I was trying to . . . Trying to . . ."

"I know. I saw."

He set me on my feet, waited to make sure I wouldn't sway, then let go. Then he went to assist the woman who was flailing and floundering atop the open coffin, still screaming her head off.

Mrs. Yee had apparently struck herself in the leg when she missed her nemesis' skull. The bronze incense burner lay on the floor while she limped back to her chair, moaning in pain and supported by two sons.

"Esther! Are you all right?" Max asked, appearing at my side. Nelli was with him, panting anxiously.

"I've been looking for you," I said, getting my breath back. "Where were you?"

"Due to the demands of Nelli's corporeal form, we had to step outside for a few minutes." I assumed he meant she had needed a little walk. Max looked at the injured woman who was limping toward a chair, then he looked at the hysterically shrieking woman who was still flailing atop the corpse while John tried to disentangle her. "What manner of cataclysm occurred in our absence?"

"Benny's mistress showed up. His wife attacked her."

"Ah, and you rescued the young woman? I see."

"I don't think *she* sees," I said, looking in her direction.

Benny's mistress, now back on her own two feet, was pointing at me and shouting angrily. John, who was speaking to her in English, with a few Chinese phrases thrown in, was not having any success with trying to calm her down. When she saw me gazing her with a bemused frown, that was evidently the last straw. She took off one of her high-heeled shoes and, holding it overhead like a weapon, lunged for me.

Max stepped into her path and, with a quick gesture and a word in Latin, caused the shoe to fly out of her hand. Due to the woman's uncoordinated movements and her hysteria, it almost looked natural, despite her startled reaction. I wasn't sure anyone else saw it happen, anyhow, since Nelli had started barking ferociously the moment the woman's attack began, and a dog that size is pretty distracting when she behaves that way.

John grabbed the woman, restraining her, while Max soothed Nelli.

A nice-looking, neatly dressed man who appeared to be in his thirties rushed to the coffin and started tidying up Benny's appearance. He looked over his shoulder and said, "Get her out of here, John!"

I realized that must be John's older brother.

"Right." Speaking calmly to her, John retained a firm grip on the woman as he started dragging her away. "Let's go find a taxi for you."

As they started making their way through the crowd, the woman now sobbing again, I said to Max, "I've never been to a Chinese funeral before, but you have. Are they usually this eventful?"

Rather than answering, he said, "We were able to examine the corpse earlier. Nelli exhibited no peculiar reaction to it."

Watching John's brother fuss over Benny's body, I asked, "How did you get Nelli close enough to the coffin to—"

"John has told his family and the Yees that Nelli is a therapy dog and that I brought her here to comfort those who have trouble expressing their grief. Since we are in America, this explanation was received without the incredulity it would produce in most societies."

I looked at Nelli. She drooled a little.

"I gather she hasn't noticed any demonic entities at this festive gathering?"

"No," said Max. "Have you noticed anyone suspicious in your perusal of the visitors?"

"Well, there's a gang member here. He knew Benny a long time, so he must have known how superstitious he was. But I think street gangs usually go in for something more direct than murder by cookie."

"Hmm."

John's brother finished repairing the damage to Benny, then went to check on the Yee family.

Realizing I was a little mussed after my tumble across the room, I patted my hair and straightened my clothing. Then I turned to Max to continue our conversation. I was about to suggest Mrs. Yee as a likely murder suspect when a woman said in an American accent, "Oh, my God, that was the best *ever!* I have to thank you."

I turned to find Susan Yee greeting me. A pretty woman with a short, chic haircut, she wore black slacks and a simple black silk blouse. She exchanged introductions with us, pointed out that Nelli was an impractical size for a therapy dog in Manhattan, and then said to me, "Jumping in the way you did, you saved my aunt from an aggravated assault charge."

"By happy coincidence, I also saved the other woman from a crushed skull."

"Oh, she deserved it. But I wouldn't want to see my aunt go to prison over trash like that. And watching that disgusting woman go flying into the coffin that way, and then getting dragged out of here by John!" She laughed, then covered her mouth and looked around, apparently remembering she was at a wake. She leaned forward and said in a low but enthusiastic voice, "It was priceless!"

"She seemed to be, um, close to your uncle," I said.

"Close? That's one word for it, I suppose," Susan said with a sneer. "But no one expected Aunt Grace to blow her top like that. We thought she didn't know."

"Didn't know that her husband was, er, personally involved with that young woman?" Max asked.

"Well, Aunt Grace certainly had her suspicions

that there was someone. Especially since it's happened before—Uncle Benny keeping a woman, I mean." Susan seemed to be as indiscreet as she was harsh. Maybe she noticed the surprise in our expressions, since she said, "Yeah, I know, I know. Don't speak ill of the dead, and all that. *Especially* not if you're Chinese."

"Ah." Max nodded. "Reverence for ancestors."

"And for elders," she added with a courteous nod to him. "But in all honesty, my uncle was kind of a pr . . ." She hesitated, looking at Max, then said to me, "Uh, not a very nice man."

"That must have been hard on your aunt," I said.

"Well, *I* sure couldn't be married to a guy like that," she replied. "But you know the older generation. Benny was a good provider, gave Grace three sons, and didn't ever come home drunk or violent. So she thought he was a good husband."

"Despite his infidelities?" I asked. If Susan was willing to gossip about her relatives, then I was certainly willing to encourage her.

"That upset Aunt Grace, of course. She got really furious with him a few times—well, you've seen her temper. But she's also got an old-fashioned 'men will be men' attitude, and she never threatened to divorce him for playing around."

I wondered how to ask tactfully, only a few feet away from Benny's coffin, whether his wife had ever threatened to kill him for it.

Susan said with a puzzled frown, "Anyhow, I know she suspected lately that Uncle Benny was having another affair, but I was sure she didn't know who it was. In fact, just this morning, she was saying to my mother that maybe the family should try to help Benny's secretary find another job. Man, did I have trouble keeping a straight face when I heard her say *that*."

"It didn't occur to her that your uncle's secretary might be his girlfriend?" I asked.

"It sure didn't seem like it. But then, Uncle Benny had a lot of practice at this sort of thing, so I guess he covered his tracks well. I can remember Grace telling my mother about how stupid and vulgar Benny said his secretary was, the ignorance and mistakes he put up with, all so he could earn merit by keeping this uneducated immigrant girl from turning to prostitution because she'd never find another decent job. Stuff like that."

I figured that if Mrs. Yee had really accepted that story from a serial adulterer, then she wasn't the first woman who chose to believe whatever improbable fiction would help maintain stability in her marriage.

Or, as an alternate explanation, maybe she just wasn't the brightest bulb in the chandelier.

"So this morning, your aunt wanted to help the young woman?" Max mused. "Yet this evening, she attacked her when she showed up here."

I said, "I guess all that weeping over the casket gave the game away, and Aunt Grace realized the woman was more than just a grateful employee."

"Maybe," Susan said with a shrug. "Or maybe someone blabbed. Half of Chinatown knew what Uncle Benny was up to. He kept Aunt Grace in the dark, but he wasn't discreet."

"Telling her about the affair now would so unkind, though," I said. "She's a new widow, after all."

"Even so," said Susan, "people gossip."

"How true," Max said gravely.

"Anyhow, Esther, you flinging that awful woman into the coffin like that—it was the best thing I've seen all year," Susan said with a grin.

"Well, the year's only a few days old," I said modestly.

"Your year," she said. "But ours is nearly over."

"Oh, right," I said. "That's coming up soon, isn't it?"

She nodded. "Two weeks."

The traditional Chinese calendar is lunar, like the Jewish calendar, and none of the annual milestones coincide with the Gregorian solar calendar that's used throughout the West. Rosh Hashanah, the Jewish New Year, usually occurs in September, but occasionally it falls in October. The Chinese New Year is sometimes celebrated in January, sometimes in February.

So as Susan had just noted, in the Chinese calendar, the old year was in its final days now.

The Lunar New Year is always a big event in Chinatown. It kicks off with the firecracker festival, in which impressively costumed lion dancers roam the streets, accompanied by musicians. They go from shop to shop throughout the neighborhood, dancing outside the doorways (and sometimes going inside) to demand "lucky money" in red envelopes for the New Year. They're also fed big heads of cabbage, which they "chew" up and "spit" out at the gathered crowd, to share the good luck and abundance that the green vegetables represent. If you don't mind getting cabbage and firecracker confetti in your hair, it's a fun day out. The famous Dragon Parade, which is usually on television, wends its way through Chinatown a week later.

Given what a bust the recent New Year had been for me, starting off jobless and in jail, maybe I'd aim for the Chinese New Year as my chance to start over, shed bad habits, and get a certain man out of my system.

"So how did you two know Uncle Benny?" Susan asked us. "If you're two of his dearest friends, then, *boy,* am I embarrassed. But, no, I guess I'd have seen you around before now, if you were close to him. Did you do business with him or something? I know he did business with a *lot* of people," she added, looking around at the dense crowd.

Max and I exchanged a glance, realizing at the same moment that we hadn't prepared an explanation for our presence at this wake. Susan had just handed us a good reason for being here, but I wondered what sort of business we should say we had done with Benny.

Then inspiration struck me. "I'm an actress. Benny told me he was backing a film and there might be a part in it for me."

"Seriously?" Susan rolled her eyes. "Oh, *no.*"

People in New York often react that way to meeting actors, so I ignored it. "He said there's a female Caucasian character, about my age, in the story. I guess the actress who originally had the role recently broke her leg?" I hoped I was right in thinking that had happened before Benny died, rather than after.

"Believe me, Esther, you don't want any part of my brother's piece-of-crap film."

"All the same," I said, "I'd like to talk to him and see—"

"Forget it. If you're serious about having an acting career—"

"I *have* an acting career," I said defensively.

"—then working on this film would be a complete waste of your time."

Some distance behind her, I could see John now. He had returned from evicting Benny's mistress and was mingling with the Yees. He checked on Mrs. Yee, who grimaced a little as they spoke but didn't seem to need emergency medical care. Then he zeroed in on Ted, who was still sitting apart from the others and looking like he wished he was somewhere else.

Susan continued, "Anyhow, now that Uncle Benny's dead, there won't be a film. Benny was Ted's only backer. And my cousins didn't approve of the investment, so my aunt won't continue throwing good money after bad."

"Because her kids will tell her not to?"

"That's right."

I tried to picture what it would be like to have a mother who did what I told her, but my imagination just wouldn't stretch that far.

"Esther," said Max, "I think John is trying to get our attention."

"You know John Chen?" Susan asked in surprise, looking over her shoulder at him.

"We have a friend in common with him," I said.

"Is that how you met Uncle Benny?" she asked. "Through John?"

"In a manner of speaking," I said. "You're right, Max. John's waving at us. Let's go see what he wants. Please excuse us, Susan."

"And please accept our heartfelt condolences on your bereavement, Miss Yee," Max added. "Come, Nelli."

Face

Social credit; crucial to reputation and status, for oneself and one's family.

When Max and I reached John's side, I smiled gratefully at him, since he obviously intended to introduce us to Ted. I was even more pleased to discover that John had already broken the ice for me.

"So John says you're, like, an actress?" said Ted. "And you're interested in reading for my film?"

"That's right." I nodded eagerly.

"So, like, have you done any acting?"

I gave him a verbal rundown of my résumé, which included some TV roles—the best of which had been on *The Dirty Thirty*—as well as a long list of stage credits, including playing one of the two female leads in the Off-Broadway production of *The Vampyre* in autumn.

"Whoa, that's awesome," said Ted. "You're, like, a real actress."

"That's exactly what I'm like." Fudging a little, I added, "And I gather you need to cast someone quickly so you can continue production."

"Well, um . . ."

First I'd get him to offer me the part. Then I'd get Thack to make sure I got paid as much as this production could afford. It was obviously non-union, so this would be a matter of finesse and negotiation.

"I'm free tomorrow," I said to Ted. "When can we meet?"

"We're burying my uncle tomorrow."

Feeling gauche, I said, "Oh, of course. I'm sorry. Maybe a day or two after th—"

"No, no, tomorrow's cool," he said absently. "I'm just wondering how long this funeral thing will take."

John was right; Ted would apparently miss Benny's money more than he'd miss Benny.

"Mom?" Ted called. "Hey, Mom!"

"Ted, this is a wake," his mother admonished as she approached us. "We should keep our voices down."

"Oh, come *on,* Mom. Aunt Grace and that hooker from Benny's office just went at it right in front of the coffin like—"

"Ted, please," said his mother with a long-suffering expression. "Your aunt or your cousins will hear you."

"By the way, Esther," said Ted, "the way you jumped in there, walloped Aunt Grace, and threw that girl on the coffin—it was totally awesome!"

"I *didn't* wallop your aunt, I—"

"How do you do? I am Lily Yee, Ted's mother," the older woman interrupted with a pleasant smile. She spoke English precisely, with a delicate Chinese accent. "I'm pleased to meet you."

I introduced myself, then said, "And this is my friend, Dr. Maximillian Zadok."

"How do you do, sir?"

Rather than respond, Max stared mutely at Lily Yee, looking dumbstruck. His blue eyes were wide, his mouth hung open slightly, and he seemed unaware that I had just introduced the two of them.

"Max?" I prodded.

"Hmm? Oh!" He blinked. "Pardon me, madam. I am very pleased to make your acquaintance. I, uh . . . I . . ."

He went back to staring at her. And I looked at both of them, wondering at Max's reaction.

Yes, Lily was a beautiful woman, elegantly dressed, with a gracious manner. I assumed she was at least in her mid-forties, since her daughter looked mid-twenties; and Lily might well be in her fifties, for all I knew. Good bone structure, good skin, and good grooming made her age hard to guess. She wore her black hair in a heavy bun at the nape of her neck, which complimented her traditional dress. Her style was very different from that of her modern American son and daughter, and it suited her well.

Yet there was nothing about her to explain Max's thunderstruck reaction to meeting her. His great age certainly didn't prevent him from noticing—and sometimes reacting to—pretty women. But I'd never before seen a beautiful face rob him of the power of speech.

So I looked at both of them, seeking some clue to Max's odd behavior; but I just couldn't see anything. Lily seemed a little perplexed by his manner, but not disconcerted, and her smiling courtesy remained unruffled.

"So, Mom," said Ted, oblivious to the way Max was staring at his mother, "what time will we be done with the funeral tomorrow? I want to meet Esther afterward."

"Oh, really? How nice!" Lily seemed to think he meant we were going on a date. Given her daughter's reaction to my being an actress, I decided not to correct her. "You can certainly meet in the evening. Or late afternoon."

Max stirred himself enough to say, "Er, what is . . ."

We all looked at him.

Apparently unaware that he was interrupting, or

even that there was anyone else in the room other than Lily Yee, he said to her, "May one ask your given name?"

"You wish to know my Chinese name?" She smiled. "Of course. It is Xiaoling."

"Xiaoling," Max repeated. "How lovely."

"My late husband called me that," she added, gracefully imparting the information that she was a widow. "But to almost everyone else, ever since I came to America when I was young, I am Lily."

"Also a lovely name," Max said. "Very fitting."

She smiled again.

"So listen, Esther," said Ted. "Like, here's the thing . . ."

"Yes?" I turned to give him my full attention while Max and Lily continued chatting quietly.

"I think it's cool that you want to read for my film, but you're a different type than Mary."

"I'm versatile," I assured him.

"You heard her résumé," John said to Ted. "That's some range. She'd be great in Mary's part."

I smiled at him.

"Yeah, but Mary is, you know, a Betty," said Ted, with a doubtful glance at me. "The actress in this role needs to be really hot."

"Esther's really hot." John added to me, "No disrespect intended."

"No problem." I appreciated John's support, but I hadn't taken offense at Ted's comment. This was business, not personal, and actors need to know what people see when they look at us. My looks are all right, but I'm no Hollywood bombshell. On the other hand, I also knew that what Ted was seeing right now was an incomplete picture. I didn't have any of my headshots with me, and I certainly wasn't dressed for an audition—let alone to try out for the role of a "really hot" love interest.

So I said to Ted, "Look, I came here through sleet and snow, at the end of a long day of pounding the pavement, and then I wound up in the middle of your aunt's violent brawl with a hooker and a corpse. So you're not seeing me at my most attractive. Put me in good makeup and hair, with the right clothes, and I can play a Betty." And when I did my reading for him, I would convince him by showing up dressed for the role.

"I think you look nice," said John.

"Well, I suppose I really do need to recast that part," Ted said unhappily. "Mary says there's no way she can come back to work. Her broken leg was just one thing too many."

"I'm not surprised," John said. "She's a trooper, but she's really had a rough time lately."

"So I guess I should hear you read, Esther," Ted concluded with unflattering reluctance.

I smiled warmly at him. I wanted work more than I wanted flattery, after all. "Great!"

We agreed to meet late the following afternoon on

the set where Ted hoped to resume filming soon. It was a loft on Hester Street, which served as the main character's apartment in the film.

Then John, who was scanning the crowd, drew in a quick breath. "Look who just arrived."

Ted followed his gaze, then said with pleasure, "Oh, good, he's here."

Other people in the hall were also murmuring about the new arrival, as were members of the Yee family.

Lily paused in her conversation with Max to look in the same direction as everyone else. I noticed that her warm, animated expression suddenly grew cold.

Ted whispered to John, just loud enough for me to hear, "I really need to talk to him."

Quite curious by now, I watched as the crowd parted to let a short, homely, plump older man in a cheap suit approach the coffin to pay his respects. He bowed three times before Benny with his palms pressed together, then paused at the altar before coming over to greet Grace Yee and her family.

My business with Ted was concluded, so I was reluctant to continue intruding on the family. I tugged on John's arm to pull him some distance away from them. Max remained with Lily, whose gaze was fixed coolly on the new arrival. It was clear from everyone's behavior that he was an important man. Grace Yee seemed particularly pleased to see him. Despite her sore leg, she rose from her chair to speak with him.

"Who is he?" I murmured.

"Uncle Six." John's answer made me think of Fleming's Double-Oh-Seven or *Star Trek's* Seven-of-Nine.

"Who?"

He smiled. "It's what people call him. Real name, Joe Ning. He's head of the Five Brothers tong."

"Ah."

" 'Uncle' is respectful, a way of saying he's everyone's benefactor. And six is a good number. It represents wealth, prosperity, and success in business."

"He doesn't look wealthy and successful," I noted.

"He's one of the most powerful men in Chinatown," said John. "But he's traditional. He's ruthless about maintaining his power, but he doesn't flaunt his wealth."

I noticed that Uncle Six was soft-spoken and his manner was humbly courteous. He took time to speak to each member of the Yee family. Due to Max's proximity to Lily, Uncle Six even made a point of patting Nelli on the head. She accepted this cheerfully, then went back to looking around the room with interest.

When Uncle Six greeted Lily, I was surprised by how friendly she seemed; it was a contrast to the negative way she'd reacted to his arrival. I supposed she didn't want to slight such an important man, especially not when the rest of the family seemed so pleased by his arrival.

Now that he was closer to us, I could see his features more clearly. His face was chubby and a bit froglike, but there was nothing cute about it. His eyes were too shrewd and intense for that—and also cold, even when he smiled, as he was doing now. Watching him as he spoke with more members of the family, I found it easy to believe that Uncle Six was a ruthless man.

"He's showing a lot of respect, spending this much time with them," said John. "It's a little surprising, since he didn't like Benny. But it's good for the family. They're regaining some of the face they lost when Benny's girlfriend showed up and Mrs. Yee jumped her. Plus there was this whole thing with a white girl flying through the air and landing on the corpse."

"You'd have had another body to embalm if I hadn't done that."

"True. And killing someone at a wake is *such* bad manners, the Yees would never be able to regain face if you hadn't walloped Grace and tackled the girl."

"I *didn't* wallop . . ." I realized he was kidding and rolled my eyes at him. "Anyhow, surely going to *prison* would have mattered more than losing face?"

Having recently been jailed, I had strong feelings on the matter.

"Not around here. Almost nothing matters more than losing face," John said seriously. "If anything, it's a custom that's even stronger in Chinatown today than it was back in the old country. You can survive a prison sentence, or the death of a family member, or anything else as long as you still have face. But without face, life is very tough in Chinatown. And the Yee family is well established, so they have a lot of status to protect. It's a lot more visible to everyone in the community if they lose face than if a penniless, unknown sweatshop worker with no connections does."

"Hmm. So maybe Mrs. Yee thought she'd lose more face by letting Benny's overdressed girlfriend weep over his body in front of all these people than by clobbering the girl in the middle of her husband's wake," I suggested.

John smiled and shrugged. "Maybe. Or maybe for a few minutes there, Mrs. Yee just wasn't thinking at all. She's got a hot temper, after all."

"So I gathered." I changed the subject. "By the way, thank you for introducing me to Ted."

"You're welcome. I think it would be fun to have you on the film."

I asked a little more about the Yees and learned that Lily's late husband, Benny's younger brother, had died of cancer several years ago, after a long battle with the illness. He had been a successful merchant who'd left Lily a thriving Chinatown souvenir shop that was bequeathed to him by his father—who had cut Benny out of his will for being involved in the criminal world.

It seemed like a complicated family. But as John had said, *most* things in Chinatown were complicated.

Uncle Six finished paying his respects to the Yee family, then started to mingle with the crowd. He was obviously very well-known around here. I saw Danny Teng approach him and, from then on, stick to him like a burr, which the old man accepted as if accustomed to it. But I also saw perfectly respectable-looking people warmly greet and chat with Uncle Six, and I recalled what John had said about the complex nature of Chinatown's tongs.

Ted joined me and John then, and the three of us talked a little about his movie. It was called *ABC* and was the story of Brian, a young man trying to find his own path as a first-generation American in a Chinese immigrant family. His conflict was represented by his attraction to two very different women: Mei, a FOB (Fresh Off the Boat) immigrant living and working in Chinatown, who represented the Old World that Brian found restrictive; and Alicia, a modern American woman who represented the New World and freedom.

I made sure that "freedom" did not mean I'd be expected to take off my clothes.

Ted assured me it wasn't that kind of movie.

"It's about ideas and culture, identity and meaning, old values and new temptations." After a moment, he added, "There are a couple of love scenes, though. That's okay, right?"

I started to say that it was absolutely fine, as long as certain private parts of my body remained private; but I closed my mouth when I saw Lily approaching us. Max accompanied her, with Nelli at his side.

Lily asked Ted to go find his sister. "It is time to go home."

Ted said, "Actually, I want to stay a little longer and see if I can talk some more to—"

"We are leaving now, Ted," Lily said firmly. "Please tell Susan, and then get our coats."

Ted sighed, said he'd see me tomorrow, and then went off to do as he was told.

Max said to me, "Perhaps we should also depart, Esther."

I nodded, and John offered to give us a lift home, which we accepted; the hearse was a very convenient way to transport Nelli.

Max turned to Lily and took her hand in a courtly gesture. "It has been a great pleasure to meet you, Lily, and I hope we meet again soon."

"I hope so, too," she said with a smile. "You have been very kind."

We said our goodnights, then made our way to the private back rooms again, where Lucky was waiting to confer with us. After we recounted the evening's events to him—he'd heard some of the shouting and wondered what was going on—we discussed possible murder suspects.

"You met Danny Teng?" John said to me with a grimace. "I feel like I should apologize to you for that, since it happened in my family's place of business."

"Yes, normally a girl has to go into an alley after dark to meet someone like him," I replied.

"Who is this guy?" Lucky asked with a frown.

"*Dai lo* of the Red Daggers," said John.

"*Dai lo?*" I repeated.

"Gang leader." John added, "Literally it means 'big brother.'"

"The Red Daggers." Lucky nodded. "I heard of them. Bunch of street punks with matching tattoos. Always in a lotta messy trouble. They're enforcers for the Five Brothers. So, comin' to Benny's wake, that guy's probably just paying his respects, like a good soldier."

"Probably," John agreed. "There were other Red Daggers there, too, but they stayed out in the lobby. My father, who's a braver man than I am, asked them not to come into the visitation room. I think he said their attire might insult the family, or something like that. He's an elder, so he got away with it, and they stayed out there. But, obviously, he couldn't ask their *dai lo* not to come inside and pay his respects directly to the deceased. Danny would lose face, and that wouldn't be forgiven."

"This 'face' thing really complicates life," I said.

"You bet," said John.

"Yes, but having social credit—in other words, maintaining face—is crucial, because social relationships have been the central structure of Chinese society for thousands of years," Max said, speaking up for the first time since we'd taken our seats in here. He had been unusually quiet and obviously distracted, which I attributed to Lily Yee's mysterious influence. "The family, the clan, and the community in Chinese society are much more important than the individual. And people in China survived centuries of warring states, civil wars, volatile warlords, foreign invasions, unjust rulers, and colonial domination by relying on their social and personal relationships—rather than on laws or government—for protection, justice, and mutual aid."

John nodded. "Traditionally, that's how Chinatown has always functioned, too."

I was pleased to see Max behaving more like his usual self, so I didn't interrupt as he continued lecturing—which he was prone to do.

"Therefore, if one person loses face or is dishonored, it doesn't reflect only on him, but on the whole social fabric in which he is merely one thread. His family, his clan, his guild or brotherhood—any or all of these will endure shame because of *his* shame. Thus their influence will be reduced and their position damaged in all their social relationships, making them vulnerable and weak, diminishing and even endangering them." Max said pensively, "It's a strong enough system to have worked effectively for many centuries, but it is not an easy way of life."

"And tonight Esther helped the Yee family save face," John said with a smile, lightening the mood, "when she prevented Grace Yee from committing murder at her own husband's wake."

"Good work, kid," Lucky said to me. "I been to two funerals where someone got whacked before the stiff was even in the ground. I just hate it when that happens. People oughta show more respect for the dead."

9

壞

An evildoer

Since John had just raised the subject of Grace Yee, I said to my companions in the offices of Chen's Funeral Home, "Speaking of the merry widow . . ."

"What about her?" asked Lucky.

I posed my *Crime and Punishment* theory about Grace (i.e. the spouse is always whodunit). But I was skeptical now, after what Susan had said—which information I summarized for Lucky's benefit.

"So if the wife didn't know about Benny and his secretary . . ." The old mobster shook his head. "Then what's her motive? Would she kill him just because she thought he *might* be playing around with *someone?*"

"I suppose she could be an extremely clever

woman who was just *pretending* not to know, in order to divert suspicion away from herself when she killed him." However, I was skeptical about this theory, too, and I added, "But that level of self-control and planning really doesn't match the woman who flew into a rage and tried to pulverize the girlfriend's skull tonight in front of many witnesses."

"And the niece—Susan?—said Benny had played around before, right?" said Lucky.

"He had," John confirmed. "I don't really follow gossip about that kind of thing, and even I knew."

"Why would the missus kill him this time, when she didn't kill him any of those other times?" Lucky asked. "I don't see it."

John added, "Plus, she gave me the death curse from the cookie as soon as I asked her for it. If she was behind it, wouldn't she be cagey about it? But she seemed relieved to get it out of their apartment. Pretty much the way I'm relieved that Dr. Zadok is taking it out of here tonight."

Lucky looked at Max. "What do you think, Doc?"

"Hmm? Oh." Max looked distracted again as he patted the pocket where he had put that menacing slip of paper earlier tonight. "I need to take it back to my laboratory to study its properties."

"No, I mean, what do you think about Mrs. Yee?" Lucky clarified.

"A lovely woman," said Max. "Very, um . . . That is, she reminds me . . ."

"He means Grace Yee, Max," I said quickly. "Benny's widow."

He blinked. "Oh. Er, yes, of course. I only exchanged a few formal words with her, so I didn't form much of an impression. Well, not beyond noting that she seems to be a woman of volatile temper."

"And cursing someone with death in a fortune cookie," Lucky said, "is a *plan.* Cold and calculating. Not something you do in a fit of temper."

"*If* a curse is what we're talking about here." I looked at Max.

"Well, you all know what *I* think," John said, shaking his head.

"Yeah, yeah, we heard from you, Mr. Mundane," said Lucky. "Now the ball is in the doc's court. Right?"

"Indeed," said Max, rising to his feet. "I shall take this fortune to my laboratory now and try to determine forthwith if it has mystical properties . . . or was merely a vicious mundane prank."

"Let's go," I said, eager to find out whether Evil was going to intrude on my film role—because tomorrow, I was going to convince Benny's nephew to cast me in *ABC* even if I had to get Nelli to sit on his chest and show him her fangs in order to persuade him that I was right for the part.

We said goodnight to Lucky as we donned our coats, gloves, and hats. Then John, Max, Nelli, and I made our way through the silent Italian portion of the funeral home and back out into the wintry night. A thin blanket of fresh snow coated the sidewalks now. It had stopped coming down, but the temperature had dropped and the wind had picked up.

Shivering a little even inside my warm coat, I took Max's arm and huddled close to him and Nelli, following John as he led the way back to the parking garage.

"Lily Yee made quite an impression on you," I said quietly to Max.

"Hmm?" He'd obviously been lost in thought again. "Oh. Yes . . ." He was silent for a long moment, then said, "She reminds me of someone."

"Someone special, I gather?"

"Yes. Someone who was quite special." It was too dark to see his expression, but his voice sounded sad.

"Is Lily a lot like her?"

"In appearance, very much so. In circumstances, not at all, I suppose." He thought it over. "In other ways . . . I don't know her well enough to say."

"Who was she, Max?" I asked, curious about someone who was obviously a powerful memory for him.

"Li Xiuying," he said on a sigh. "Beautiful Flower."

"What happened to her?"

"Oh . . . she died."

"How?"

He shook his head. "It was a long time ago, Esther."

I was even more curious now, since Max wasn't usually reticent about his past. On the contrary, he could be loquacious to a fault. But I could tell that if I pursued this subject, I would be intruding on something he didn't really want to talk about. Max was not a moody man by nature, so I realized there must be heartbreak behind the name Li Xiuying. I supposed he would tell me about it when he was ready—or perhaps not at all.

I was a little concerned about him, but not hurt that he didn't choose to confide in me. After all, I kept a number of things private about my relationship with Lopez. We all have things we'd rather not discuss, not even with someone we trust.

After we reached the parking garage, Nelli hopped readily into the back of the hearse and settled down. The streets were less crowded now, and the shift in the weather had improved visibility, so the drive back to the West Village was uneventful. John, Max, and I talked a little more on the way home about our impressions of the wake and the visitors, but the conversation was desultory.

When we got to the bookstore, John offered to drive me to my apartment, but I declined. I knew Max would go down into his laboratory now, rather than upstairs to bed (he lived above the shop), and I was as eager as he was to find out whether the death curse had mystical properties.

So I entered the bookstore with Max and Nelli, shed my coat, and warmed up with a quick cup of hot tea. Nelli lay down by the gas fireplace, though Max didn't ignite it for her, and promptly fell asleep.

Max pulled the death curse out of his pocket, still in its little plastic bag, and turned it over in his hands, studying the black piece of paper and its sinisterly graceful white symbol.

"I don't suppose it gives off a vibe or something?" I asked.

"Alas, nothing so self-explanatory," he said.

"So how do you plan to determine whether that thing is mystical?"

"I've been thinking about that all the way home."

"Oh! I thought you were thinking about . . ." I paused, not wanting to bring up Lily Yee's name again. I concluded awkwardly, "Exactly that."

He didn't seem to notice, absorbed as he was in examining the dark fortune. "I have an idea . . . I once dealt with a matter which had features not dissimilar to our suspicions about the misfortune cookie."

"In China?" I asked as I followed Max to the back of the bookstore.

"No, in Sicily. That strange episode was . . . oh, well over two hundred years ago, certainly. Goodness! Where do the years go? Nonetheless, I remember it well."

I recalled that Max once told me he had been questioned by the Spanish Inquisition in Sicily, which had remained active there until the late eighteenth century. But I decided not to ask him any more questions tonight about memories he might not be keen to revisit.

We entered a little cul-de-sac at the back of the shop where there was a utility closet, a powder room, and a door marked PRIVATE. The door opened onto a narrow, creaky stairway that led down to the cellar.

At the top of the stairs, there was a burning torch stuck in a sconce on the wall. It emitted no smoke or heat, only light; it had been burning steadily ever since I had met Max, fueled by mystical power.

I descended the steep, narrow steps behind him as he said, "The situation in Sicily involved miniature replicas of body parts rather than a written fortune—"

"Ugh! That sounds gruesome."

"Well, not necessarily. As with fortune cookies—which did not originate in China, by the way, though they have become a part of Chinese cuisine throughout America, whether the meal is humble or grand . . . But I digress."

Now that he was focused on work, he was obviously feeling much more like his usual self. Whatever memories of Li Xiuying haunted him, they had retreated, and he was chatting with engaged enthusiasm as he reached the final step and entered his laboratory.

"Miniature replicas of body parts are normally part of a positive ritual in Sicily. And *un*like fortune cookies, whose origin was probably in twentieth-century California, the custom is very ancient."

"What custom?" I asked.

"Sicilians leave these miniature replicas at the shrines of their favorite saints to entreat their blessings for health and their help with healing."

"Ah-hah!" I said triumphantly, recognizing the nature of this custom. "Sympathetic magic."

"Precisely." Max sat down at his workbench and gestured for me to take a seat on a nearby stool. "But during a dark episode in the eighteenth century, an evil adversary started using such effigies to curse his enemies with ill health and injury."

"It figures," I said. "Someone always has to spoil a good thing."

Like fortune cookies, for example. What evildoer, I wondered, whether mystical or mundane, had taken something so innocent, tasty, and fun, and decided to turn it into a menacing messenger of death?

Max continued, "And since these effigies of human body parts were so common in Sicily, it was essential to devise a means to determine whether any given replica was harmless or cursed."

I looked around the laboratory and guessed, "So you're going to use that method to analyze Benny's fortune?"

"That is what I propose," he said. "I have my notes from those days, and they contain the formula I used. I know it's here somewhere . . ."

He rummaged around for a few minutes in the bookcase near his workbench, muttering to himself. After he found what he was looking for, he began gathering ingredients for his recipe from 200-plus years ago.

Max's laboratory was cavernous, windowless, and shadowy. The thick stone walls were haphazardly covered with charts, plans, drawings, maps, lists, and notes, some of which were very old, and some of which had been added since my last visit down here. Bottles of powders, vials of potions, and bundles of dried plants jostled for space on cluttered shelves. Jars of herbs, spices, minerals, amulets, and neatly sorted varieties of claws and teeth sat on densely packed shelves and in dusty cabinets. There were antique weapons, some urns and boxes and vases, a scattering of old bones, and a Tibetan prayer bowl. And the enormous bookcase near where Max was sitting was packed to overflowing with many leather-bound volumes, as well as unbound manuscripts, scrolls, and modern notebooks.

I was always afraid to touch anything in here, so I sat with my hands folded, just watching Max work.

I had forgotten that fortune cookies were not actually Chinese in origin, but I now recalled my father telling us something of the sort many years ago, over one of our regular family meals of Chinese food. There seemed to be several stories about who had invented this combination of cookie and after-dinner entertainment; but regardless of which version was correct, few people disputed that fortune cookies had originated in America, as Max had asserted. According to my father's account, fortune cookies were virtually unknown in China, despite their long association with Chinese food in the US.

This led me to a fresh thought. "Max, since fortune cookies aren't originally Chinese, do you think Benny's cookie might have been created by someone who's not Chinese?"

He was peering into a small black cauldron that was full of newly measured and mixed ingredients, which he was simmering over a Bunsen burner on his workbench.

"It's possible," he said absently, and I realized this theory had already occurred to him. "I am not inclined to think so, since the fortune cookie has been closely associated with the Chinese in America since before Mr. Yee's birth. But one should nonetheless keep an open mind about—Ah! It's boiling."

He reached for a jar with some golden-yellow powder in it, carefully measured a small scoop of the stuff, then tossed it into the boiling brew. A few moments later, the mixture emitted a deep vocal moan, so human-sounding that I hopped off my stool and gaped in alarm, ready to bolt.

"I'm sorry, Esther. I should have warned you," Max said, noticing my anxiety. "Don't worry. This is perfectly normal."

"I wouldn't say *that,*" I muttered, climbing back onto my stool. As a cloud of yellow smoke wafted through the room, I gagged. "Blegh! What is that *stench?*"

"It's the sign that the potion is ready." Max turned off the flame beneath the cauldron. Then he pulled Benny's fortune out of his pocket and unsealed the plastic bag. Using a pair of tweezers, he extracted the black piece of paper and then held it over the smoking, stinking cauldron. "This is the part of the experiment I'm a little concerned about."

"Oh?"

"The replicas I tested in Sicily were always made of solid materials, not paper."

"Oh! You're afraid that . . ."

"If this process doesn't work, I may damage the fortune so much by immersing it in liquid that I will be unable to perform further experiments on it."

"Hmm. I see your point, but I'm afraid I don't have any alternative suggestions, Max."

"Nor do I. So here we go." He took a steadying breath, then dropped the fortune into the small cauldron.

There was a long moment of silence. Max's face fell, and I feared the experiment had been a failure.

"Now what?" I asked. "Can we—*Whoa!*"

The pot suddenly shuddered with life and shrieked with such ear-splitting horror that I fell off my stool in surprise.

I could tell from Max's pleased reaction that this was the result he'd been looking for. As the cauldron continued screaming and shaking, he said to me, shouting to be heard above the din, "We have our answer! It was a mystical curse!"

"Yeah, I think I got that!" I shouted back, standing well away from the workbench and not inclined to come any closer.

A moment later, the pot went still and the room went silent.

"Oh, thank God that's stopped." I put a shaking a hand over my pounding heart.

"What a satisfyingly clear result!" Max said. "Sometimes I'm not always so sure."

"Yes, I'd say that was unmistakably . . ." I took another step back as a throaty growling emerged from the cauldron. "What's happening now?"

"I'm not sure." Max leaned over the pot to peer into it—then flinched and fell off his stool, too, when its contents exploded in a fiery burst of pure white flames.

White, the color of death.

High-pitched maniacal laughter emerged from the little cauldron now, rising with the flames.

At the top of the stairs, I heard Nelli start barking hysterically. I didn't know if she was summoning us for help, trying to warn us about what was down here with us, or just panicking.

As the sinister laughter got louder and the white flames grew fatter and higher, I was backing away from this frightening phenomenon, stumbling clumsily in the direction of the stairs.

"Max, let's get out of here!" When he didn't respond, just kept staring intently at the flames, I said, *"Max!"*

"Yes," he said, taking a few steps in my direction as the high-pitched laughter turned to a deep-throated, gravelly roar. "Yes, perhaps we should . . ." He paused again. "Wait, there's something . . ."

"Max!" I shouted insistently. "Come *on!*"

Nelli's barking got more ferocious, and then I heard her thudding footsteps as she thundered down the stairs toward us, evidently having decided to give her life to protect us from whatever this *thing* was that we had summoned.

As she reached the bottom steps, Max shouted, "Nelli, no! Esther, stop her!"

Obeying him blindly, I grabbed Nelli's collar as she rushed past me, intent on attacking . . . the cauldron, I supposed. I threw my whole body weight in the reverse direction, trying to halt her. But Nelli outweighed me, as well as being more muscular than I, so this only had the effect of making her stumble sideways—which, in turn, offset my balance. I fell down on the concrete floor, banging my knees and elbows painfully, while Nelli lunged at the table, barking aggressively, her fangs bared.

"Stay back, Nelli!" Max commanded. "Look!"

Dazed, terrified, and in pain, I lay sprawled on the cellar floor as I looked up to see . . . a black piece of paper float up out of the cauldron, rising to the top of the wildly undulating white flames. As the walls of the laboratory reverberated with the throaty, menacing laughter coming from the pot, which was by now at deafening volume, the piece of paper—which I recognized as Benny's death curse—exploded into flames and went up in smoke.

A second later, the ear-splitting, growling laughter ceased and the white flames vanished, disappearing into the cauldron, which now sat still and silent on the table, just an ordinary little black pot again.

Nelli stopped barking and, for a merciful moment, the room was quiet, except for everyone's frantic breathing. Then our favorite familiar started whining loudly. I didn't blame her.

I sat up slowly, my chest heaving, my heart thudding. Still whining, Nelli skittered over to me and tried to crawl into my lap. I clung to her, scarcely noticing the discomfort of having a dog the size of a small car sitting on top of me and panting anxiously into my face. As I watched, Max tentatively approached his workbench, gingerly poked the inert cauldron, then leaned over to peer into its contents.

Apparently satisfied that the danger was over, he breathed a little sigh of relief. Then he met my eyes and said with certainty, *"Mystical."*

I nodded. *"Evil."*

10

剥

Bo

When things fall apart or deteriorate; when incompetent people gain power and make a situation worse.

It took a few days, but I finally found a good excuse to call Lopez. So good, in fact, that I'd probably have phoned him even if I hadn't promised Lucky I'd try to find out why Lopez was investigating in Chinatown.

Shivering inside my heavy coat as the wind whipped down the street on a bleak January day, I pulled my phone out of my pocket and speed-dialed Lopez's cell. (None of my vows to get over him had led me to delete his number.)

He answered on the third ring. "Esther?"

"Yeah, it's me," I said as another gust of icy wind

blew down Doyers, the little L-shaped street in Chinatown that runs between Pell Street and the Bowery.

"Are you all right?" he asked. "You sound funny."

"I'm just cold." I tried to keep my teeth from chattering. Under my heavy coat, I wasn't dressed for this weather.

"Where are you?"

"Chinatown."

"Oh?" He sounded surprised. "Me, too. I'm working on a case here."

"Really?" I said, as if also surprised by our proximity. "Oh, good!"

In fact, I had assumed Lucky would be right about that. He hadn't survived all these years in his line of work by relying on bad information.

"Good?" Lopez repeated. "Does that mean you're speaking to me?"

"Do you have to start right off with trick questions?" I said crankily.

"Sorry. I mean, no. I mean, uh . . ." He cleared his throat. "I'm glad you called."

"Oh, really?" I hadn't intended to be snippy with him, but I couldn't seem to help myself.

I was standing outside of a well-known little eatery. Ted Yee was inside with the cast and crew of *ABC*. I looked through the restaurant's big storefront window and waved to Officer Novak, the uniformed cop who was with them. Then I pointed to my phone and nodded, to let him know I had succeeded in contacting the detective I had told him I was going to call.

"Yes, really." Lopez took a breath. "Look, can we talk? And I don't mean that as a trick question."

I turned my back to the restaurant so that Novak and my colleagues, if they were watching, wouldn't see me scowling.

"If you wanted to talk," I said, feeling incensed with Lopez all over again, "you could have called me."

I was already way off script here, and I was kicking myself for it. But, well, he had that effect on me.

"I know, but when I put you in the squad car that night . . . morning . . . whatever . . . Well, when I said I'd call, you got so mad, I wasn't sure I *should* call after that."

"I got *mad* because—"

"And," he continued, raising his voice, "it's not as if talking was going all that *well* between us that night . . ." After listening to my stony silence for a long moment, he added, "Or right now."

I sighed. "All right, look, I don't want to talk about any of that right now."

"Okay," he said quickly.

His prompt agreement to drop the subject of his transgressions made me mad again. "What do you mean, *okay?*"

"Huh? You just *said*—"

"Oh, never mind," I interrupted, in no mood to

hear a reasonable rebuttal. I took a deep breath, refocused, and plunged in. "I'm calling you because I need your help. And you always . . . Well, you . . ." He had told me on several occasions, including the time he *broke up* with me, that he wanted me to call him if I ever needed his help. But although I had intended to remind him of that, I now found that the words stuck in my throat. Or formed a lump there. Or something. I gave myself a shake, gritted my teeth against the bone-numbing cold that was whipping down the street, and concluded lamely, "Look, I just need your help. So can you come here?"

"Yes. Do you need me there right now?"

In the background, I heard a man say irritably to him, "*Now?* We're kind of in the middle of something here."

So I said, "No, I guess not." I didn't want Lopez to drop everything, rush over here, and then be annoyed with me when he discovered that my problem wasn't exactly a life-or-death situation. I wanted him to help me, after all. "Will what you're doing right now take very long?"

"Hang on a second, Esther." I could hear him conferring with someone, though I didn't catch what the two of them were saying. Then he said to me, "I can be there within an hour. Is that all right?"

"That should be fine." I hoped I was right.

"Where exactly are you?" he asked briskly.

"Doyers Street." I gave him the name of the popular eatery where I'd be waiting.

"Sure, I know that place," he said. "I'll be there as soon as I can."

"Okay. Good." After a moment, I added, "Thanks."

After we ended the call, I put my phone back in my pocket and stomped my chilled feet as I looked down Doyers, one of the oldest streets in the neighborhood, wondering which direction Lopez would come from. In traditional Chinese folklore, ghosts and spirits could only travel in straight lines, so local merchants had built this street to be crooked in order to keep out evil spirits. Or, at least, that was the story that Brian, the protagonist of *ABC*, was supposed to tell my character, Alicia, as we strolled down Doyers Street together today.

Being a cop rather than a filmmaker, Lopez would probably be more familiar with the street's criminal associations. The little L-shaped street was sometimes known as the Bloody Angle because of all the gang wars and murders that had taken place here over the years. But that wasn't in Ted's script, which took a decidedly romantic view of Chinatown.

Even with the heavy lacquer of industrial-strength hairspray holding my 'do in place and my hood pulled up to protect it, the wind out here was messing up my hair. I also felt my nose running and my eyes starting to water from the cold. John wasn't around to fix my hair and makeup, so I decided I'd better go inside before I got any more disheveled—even though we obviously wouldn't be doing any more filming for a few hours.

I opened the door of the restaurant and went inside, giving a sigh of relief as I entered the warm building. It was only eleven o'clock in the morning, but the place was already so crowded that the noise level meant I'd had to step outside to phone Lopez. And considering the way our conversation had gone, I'd certainly been right not to sit in here, shouting over the phone to him while surrounded by my curious *ABC* colleagues.

"Is your friend coming?" asked Bill Wu as I sat down again at our table. He played Brian, my boyfriend in the film.

I nodded. Then I added to the cop hovering near us, "Detective Lopez will be here within an hour."

"An *hour?*" Officer Novak repeated in dismay.

"I'm sorry." Fudging a little, I said, "He's in the middle of a big Chinatown investigation. It's the soonest he can get here."

"If it's so big, then why haven't I heard about it? This is my precinct, after all."

Novak looked so young and fresh-faced, I thought he was probably brand new to the force, and it seemed likely that *lots* of things went on in the Fifth Precinct that no one told him about.

Hoping to placate him, I leaned toward him and said in a confidential tone, "He's OCCB."

"Oh. *Those* guys." He nodded, sighed, and tipped his cap back, apparently settling in for the wait. "I get it."

I glanced around and saw that my *ABC* colleagues looked puzzled but impressed.

"You don't really want to stand there for an hour, do you?" I pulled out the free chair next to me. "Please have a seat, Officer Novak."

Everyone seated at this table chimed in, urging him to sit down.

Novak hesitated for a moment, then smiled and accepted the invitation—as well as the hot cup of tea I insisted on pouring for him.

An apple-cheeked blond guy, Novak had shut down today's production when he discovered us filming in Doyers Street and blocking traffic without any permits. His intervention was how *I* learned that we were there without the proper permits. But he had been very nice about not charging Ted for violating various local laws and ordinances—after I said that if he would be patient and not call this in, then an NYPD detective would come vouch for us and help clear up this misunderstanding.

So it was just as well, really, that I hadn't followed through on my intention to kill Lopez after he'd arrested me.

"So your police friend is going to straighten this out for us, Esther?" said Ted. "Excellent! Why don't we go ahead and have lunch while we wait?"

Everyone agreed with this suggestion, including Officer Novak. Enticing aromas were wafting through the crowded little eatery, so it would have been hard to resist.

And, fortunately, I could actually *afford* to eat today. In addition to being cast in Ted's film a few days ago, I had recently been surprised and delighted to find my final paycheck from Fenster & Co. in my mailbox. Due to the way I had accidentally destroyed whole portions of the department store's fourth floor while Max and I were confronting Evil there, I had assumed they would withhold my pay. But the impersonal wheels of corporate bureaucracy had turned out to be a wonderful thing in this instance, and the retail empire's accounting system had simply spat out my paycheck along with all the others. I quickly deposited it before the company could change its mind, then I paid a utility bill, set some money aside toward next month's rent, and bought groceries.

Heigh ho, the glamorous life of a working actress.

Now, sitting in a cozy, no-frills Chinatown restaurant with Officer Novak and members of the *ABC* cast and crew, I ordered some soup dumplings, a delectable feat of culinary engineering in which hot broth is contained inside Chinese dumpling wrappers. It's one of my favorite things to eat on a cold day. Then I sipped my tea while everyone else at the table placed their lunch orders.

Ted Yee, who was sitting on my left, had plenty of flaws, as I was quickly learning, but he was a good-natured guy and, more to the point, unabashed in his enthusiasm for my work. He had declared himself "blown away" by my audition for him the day after his uncle's wake, and he'd hired me on the spot. Thack had called me the following day, after negotiating with him, to inform me of a pay rate that would barely cover my basic living expenses, but which was nonetheless at least double what Ted was paying anyone else. And I had been mentally prepared for the modest pay scale, since I knew the film's only backer had just died.

Although Aunt Grace had indeed declined to invest any more money in the film, she didn't try to demand that Ted repay any of the funds that Benny had already invested. Ted said there was enough cash left to cover another couple of weeks of filming; so I had a job for at least that long. He also said he was lining up another backer, and he was very optimistic about securing sufficient funds from this new mystery investor to finish the movie.

However, I had no idea how reliable that vague information was. Only a few days into this job, I had already realized that optimism and enthusiasm were among Ted's greatest strengths, while things like realism, practicality, and organizational ability were *nowhere* among his strengths. He had, for example, completely forgotten to secure permits for filming on location today. And upon realizing it this morning, rather than reschedule, he had blithely gone ahead with the location shoot as if that were a minor detail. Whereas, in fact, it was a major oversight that got our production shut down within an hour.

Luckily for Ted, though, the young cop who'd insisted that, no, we really *couldn't* take over a public street without the city's permission, had agreed to wait around for a more experienced officer to show up and decide what to do with us.

And since Lopez had cost me my previous job by arresting my employer, I thought grumpily, the least he could do was make sure *this* employer didn't go to jail, too. It wasn't as if Ted was laundering money for the mob, after all. He was just careless. Much like the sort of man who lets a whole week pass without calling a woman after sex, for example.

Stop, I told myself. *You can't bring that up today. Just follow the script.*

I would get Lopez to help us, and I would find out if he was in Chinatown to run Lucky to earth. Those were the two things I needed to stay focused on when he got here. No deviating into intimate matters. And definitely no shouting at each other in front of a whole restaurant crowd again. Been there, done that, determined not to repeat the performance.

The warmth of the restaurant and the hot tea I was drinking had succeeded in taking the chill off my bones, so I unbuttoned my coat. Underneath, I was wearing Alicia's costume, which was Ted's notion of what a "really hot" uptown white girl would wear while strolling around Chinatown on a windy January day with her date. I was dressed in a tight, low-cut knit top, a little black leather jacket, a miniskirt, sheer stockings, and boots that were designed to be sexy rather than warm. When not on camera, I wore a heavy coat over this ensemble so that I wouldn't promptly succumb to hypothermia.

John had done a great job with my hair; I wished *I* could get it to look this good. It appeared shiny and soft (though, in fact, it took the full-force gale in Doyers Street to make it move at all), falling around my shoulders in lush, rounded waves. Ted wanted a much more heavily painted look for Alicia's face than I did, and John was good at creating a look that satisfied Ted without making me cringe.

Maybe more hair-and-makeup artists in show business should train in mortuaries, I thought.

The cast had to be self-sufficient about doing our own touch-ups, though, since John was a very busy guy. In addition to working on his PhD in biochemistry at NYU (which was where he was right now) and helping out at his family's funeral home, he was also rehearsing to be one of the lion dancers roaming the streets during the upcoming firecracker festival.

It took two men to wear a lion costume and perform the dance. Bill Wu, who had the lead role in this film, was John's partner this year. He was telling Officer Novak about it as we waited for our food.

"It's sort of like a giant puppet that you wear," Bill explained. "One man is the lion's head, and the other is the body. The lion's head is very animated—the eyelashes flutter, the mouth opens and closes, the head swivels and bobs up and down. And the whole dance is very athletic. The training for it arises out of Chinese martial arts, so there's lots of jumping and kicking, crouching and leaping. And when two lions meet in the street, which happens often during the festival, they have to 'fight' or compete for the 'lucky money' and cabbage they've come to collect from the shopkeepers there." Bill added, "The fighting is just symbolic, of course. We try to outdance each other. John and I love doing this because we're really into the beauty and skill of martial arts, but we're not that interested in hitting anyone."

Ted said, "I thought John always did the lion dance with his brother, though."

"His brother didn't have time for training anymore. Not since his wife had their second baby a few months ago. So he decided to drop out," said Bill. "Which was when John asked me to partner with him this year."

Given John's other commitments, I was amazed that he had time or energy to train for the lion dance. And Bill was almost as busy. He was a pharmacology student who had reduced his course load to part-time this term so he could star in Ted's movie. He was hoping that success in *ABC* would convince his parents to agree to let him drop out of grad school and pursue acting as a full-time career, which was what he really wanted to do. His parents, however, expected him to get this youthful acting bug out of his system by doing Ted's film, then return to school full-time next term and become a pharmacologist—a future that Bill viewed without much enthusiasm.

Like John, Bill was twenty-five—just two years younger than me. And I couldn't imagine letting my parents play that big a role in my decisions about my adult life; not even if my parents happened to be people whom I listened to. But I was learning that things were often different for a first-generation Chinese-American than they were for me. Especially in Chinatown, where traditional influences remained strong.

"Those lion costumes are so beautiful and elaborate," I said to Bill. "Is it a lot of work to take care of them?"

"Oh, you bet," he said with a nod. "And they're expensive, too."

"I should write something for *ABC* that takes place during the firecracker festival," Ted mused. "We could film a scene where the characters are surrounded by lion dancers. Wouldn't that be cool?"

"As long as you remember to get a permit," said Officer Novak.

"Huh?" said Ted.

I repressed the impulse to roll my eyes.

"Well, the whole event sounds great," Officer Novak said to Bill. "I'm looking forward to it."

"You've never been to Chinatown during the New Year before?" I asked him.

"Nope. This will be my first time." He added, "But I'll be working that day. Crowd control."

"I'm sure you'll enjoy it, even while working," Bill said. "It's a great celebration."

I and everyone else at the table agreed with this. Besides Ted and Bill, we were seated with several crew members and two other featured actors in the film.

Cynthia Kwan, the only other woman in our group today, was playing Mei, the FOB girl who was Alicia's competition for Brian's affections. Cynthia and I got along well, whereas our two characters fought like alley cats every time they met in the story—such as when Mei bumped into Brian and Alicia kissing on Doyers Street, which scene we were supposed to film today. The only cast member besides me who had an agent, Cynthia had graduated last year from NYU's Tisch School of Performing Arts. I thought she was good as Mei, though—like me—she was somewhat hampered by the clumsy dialogue and one-dimensional stereotyping that dominated Ted's script.

The other cast member seated with us was Archie

Sung, who played Jianyu, an imaginary medieval warrior-poet who appeared to Bill's character, Brian, in daydreams and reveries, to give him advice, teach him cultural pride, and impart traditional values to him. There was no explanation or internal story logic for Jianyu's visitations; he just kept popping up in Ted's heavy-handed script, quoting Confucius and Lao Tzu, until Brian gradually realized that the hardworking and honorable Mei epitomized the traditional values he was coming to appreciate, while the selfish and materialistic Alicia would never even be able to understand them.

Archie was a martial arts pro, rather than an actor. He had won a number of competitions, and he ran a martial arts school uptown. He saw *ABC* as an opportunity to get his skills on film, which exposure he hoped would attract sponsors and students. So Jianyu delivered all his speeches while performing elaborate kung fu forms. Although this meant there was usually a disorienting lack of continuity between what Jianyu was saying and what he was doing, the gracefully athletic routines Archie performed while delivering his dialogue were certainly a welcome distraction from the tedious monologues that Ted had written for him.

I was warm enough to remove my heavy coat by the time our food arrived. Since I didn't want to risk getting food on my costume, I asked for extra napkins, which I tucked carefully over my chest and lap.

Cynthia and Archie did the same; but Bill, who mostly wore his own clothes when playing Brian, said he'd just go home and change shirts if he spilled something on himself. Like John, who lived with his father (John's brother had moved out upon getting married), and Ted, who lived with his mother and sister, Bill lived with his parents; and the family apartment was only a few blocks from here.

Archie (about whose personal life I knew nothing) had to be particularly careful with his costume, since Jianyu was dressed entirely in white: pants, slippers, tunic, sash, and robe. Even his sword belt was white. The sword itself currently lay sheathed on the floor under our table. While Mei stood exchanging insults on the sidewalk with Alicia, after finding her in Brian's arms, Brian would have a vision in which Jianyu performed an elaborate sword-form in the middle of Doyers Street while reciting a monologue about honor, wisdom, and virtue.

Well, that had been the plan, anyhow. Before it turned out that Ted had forgotten to apply for the necessary permits for a location shoot.

All things considered, I wondered if this film would really get made.

Although the soup dumplings which the waiter had set before me looked mouthwatering, I knew from experience not to bite into one immediately. They usually came to the table molten hot, so I was letting them sit for a bit.

So, since my mouth wasn't full, I made conversation. "Has anyone heard from Mary Fox? How's her leg?"

Although we weren't exactly filming a cult classic here, I was nonetheless very pleased to have this job—and keenly aware that it was available to me because the original actress had broken her leg. I knew how I'd feel if our positions were reversed, so although I didn't know Mary (and although I was *very* glad to have her role), I felt bad for her.

Ted, who was a surprisingly big eater for such a skinny guy, paused in his consumption of the enormous lunch he'd ordered. "Oh, yeah, that reminds me! I talked to her last night. She says we can still use her apartment."

I frowned in puzzlement. "For . . . ?"

"For the scene that takes place in Alicia's apartment," he said. "We need a designer-chic uptown sort of place for that, and when I asked you about where you live, it didn't sound like your place would fit the bill."

"Definitely not," I said. Alicia was well-to-do (though the source of her money was never explained in Ted's script), as well as materialistic; she wouldn't be caught dead in my apartment. "Mary's acting career must be going well if she can afford the kind of apartment Alicia would live in."

Ted shook his head. "Not really. Mary comes from old money. Trust fund and stuff."

"Ah." If I'd felt any guilt about taking her role, it was evaporating. Mary could still eat without this job; I couldn't.

Cynthia added with a smile, "But she's nice, even so."

"Mary *is* nice," Bill agreed. "She deserves better."

"Breaking her leg and having to drop out of the film must have been so disappointing for her," I said.

Bill nodded. "And she was already on quite a losing streak by the time that happened."

"Yeah, I really felt bad for her," said Cynthia. "It seemed like it was just one thing after another."

"I know how that goes," I muttered, poking my dumplings gently to let some steam out.

"But like I told Mary last night, it's almost the New Year," Ted reminded everyone. "A time to change your luck and turn your fortunes around."

"In the nick of time," I murmured.

I was hungry by now, so I hoped I had let the dumplings cool for long enough. I bit tentatively into one—and it was delicious. Still a little too hot, but not enough to burn my mouth. So I kept on eating.

I was nearly finished with my meal when I heard a cell phone ringing near me, but it didn't sound like mine. I looked at Ted, but he ignored the sound. So I glanced inquisitively at Officer Novak, who was on my other side. He heard the phone, too, and shook his head, indicating that it wasn't his.

Then I remembered. "Oh!"

I reached down into my purse, which was sitting between my feet on the floor, and extracted the unfamiliar ringing phone from it. It was a prepaid cell that John had given to me yesterday after he'd purchased it from a local vendor; Lucky wanted to be able to call me without using my regular number. Since I knew, therefore, who my caller must be, I realized I'd better go back outside. Apart from how noisy it still was in here, I should probably seek some privacy for this call.

So I shed my napkins, then I grabbed my coat and struggled into it as I headed for the door. "Hello?"

"No names," Lucky said immediately. "We're on the *phone.*"

"I understand," I assured him. The wind hit me like a block of ice as soon as I stepped outside. Since my coat took forever to button and zip, I just wrapped it tightly around me and held it in place with one arm while I talked. "What's up?"

"Any information about your boyfriend yet?"

"He's not my—"

"Any information yet?"

"I'm seeing him today, so I should have news very soon."

"Good. Why don't you come here later and tell me in person? Our mutual friend is also coming over later. To discuss certain matters."

"Our mutual friend?" I repeated, wondering if he meant John.

"He's bringing his dog," Lucky added.

"Oh, *that* friend. Okay, I'll be there later. After work." I'd be hungry again by then, so I said, "Ask him to bring dinner."

"Will do."

"Any news at your end?" Even though he was still hiding out in the back rooms of a funeral home, I knew he was in contact with some of his sources.

"Actually, yeah. I been finding out what I could about local matters ever since you and our mutual friend informed me that the sudden demise of a certain individual was definitely not as accidental as it looked."

After the unnerving experiment in Max's laboratory had confirmed that Benny was cursed with death by mystical means, we had returned to Chen's Funeral Home the next day to update Lucky. Since then, Max had concentrated on researching how to disable or defuse a misfortune cookie and how to reverse its effects once the curse was inflicted. And Lucky had been trying to find out who had wanted Benny Yee dead.

He said to me, "But I don't want to talk on the *phone* about what I've found out. It can wait until you get here."

"Okay."

Whether Benny was the first victim or just the first one whom we had so far detected, the success of that curse was bound to make mystical murder an irresistibly seductive solution to whatever other problems, enemies, or obstacles the killer faced hereafter. After all, as far as we knew, no one else even suspected Benny had been murdered. So doing it again—and *getting away* with it again—would simply be too tempting a prospect for the killer. Max always said that Evil was voracious and fed on its own appetite, and I had found that events kept proving him right about that. So I agreed that there was bound to be another misfortune cookie. We needed to be prepared for it.

"You're watchin' your back, right, kid?" Lucky asked.

"Yes," I said. "Of course."

"You gotta be careful."

"I am."

"Our mutual friend is holed up with his research. And I'm holed up with people who are practically family to me. But you . . ." He made a worried sound. "You're out there on the streets, a vulnerable target, if our anniversary gets suspicious."

"I think you mean adversary."

"So don't get careless."

"I won't," I assured him.

If I thought about it, I did feel a little anxious about working in Chinatown while the cookie killer was still roaming free and probably preparing to bake again. So I tried *not* to think about it. It just made me jumpy, and that wouldn't help the situ—

"Esther?" said a voice behind me.

"*Aaagh!*" My cell phone flew up in the air as I flinched in surprise and whirled around.

Lopez had good reflexes; though startled by my reaction to his greeting, he caught the phone before it fell to the pavement.

"Esther! *Esther!*" Lucky was shouting. "ESTHER!"

"Are you okay?" Lopez asked me.

"Fine." I seized the cell, not wanting Lopez to recognize my caller's voice. My heart was pounding as I put the phone to my ear and said loudly to Lucky, "I'm fine! Just *fine.* Someone startled me, that's all. Everything's okay. No worries. I have to go now. I'll see you later."

11

狗

Dog

The zodiac sign of the Dog represents loyalty, integrity, and bravery. Physical vigor and inner power make the Dog, who is always ready for action, a valuable ally to have.

I ended the call and fumbled to put the phone in my pocket. But my hands were stiff with cold, and my nerves were jangled by Lucky's warnings—and by Lopez coming so close to discovering that I was talking to Lucky. So I dropped the cell. Lopez missed his catch this time, and it hit the pavement.

Another man picked it up, examined it briefly, and handed it to me. "Here. I think it's okay."

I recognized him as the redheaded cop from the night I'd been arrested.

Lopez said to me, "Are you all right? You seem kind of jumpy."

"Stress," I said breathlessly. "I'm a little stressed, that's all."

"You should try working with *this* guy," said the redhead. "Then you'd know about *stress*."

Lopez gave him a quelling look, then introduced us. "Esther Diamond, Detective Andrew Quinn."

"We've met before. You may remember?" Quinn grinned at me. "It's a pleasure to see you again, Miss Diamond."

"Uh-huh," I said without enthusiasm.

"So what's this problem you need help with?" Quinn asked.

We both looked at him.

"Ah." He nodded. "You two probably want a moment alone."

"Yes," I said.

"Okay. I'll go inside where it's warm."

"Good idea," said Lopez.

Quinn turned toward the restaurant—then did a double take. "Whoa! There's a guy in there with a *sword*."

I peered through the window. Inside, I could see that Archie was on his feet now, demonstrating a few moves for Ted, probably for the scene we'd intended to shoot today. But to the uninitiated, I realized, Archie's pose as he held his elaborate sword poised directly above Officer Novak's head, while the patrolman watched him with riveted interest—well, it probably looked pretty menacing.

Quinn barreled into the restaurant shouting, "NYPD! Put *down* your weapon! Police!"

But Lopez, who was more accustomed to the kind of company I kept, looked at me for an explanation.

"Costume," I said. "Fake sword."

He peered into the restaurant and said judiciously, "It looks pretty convincing from this distance."

"It's pretty convincing up close, too," I said. "Quality workmanship. But it's made of rubber. You know, safety on the film set, and all that."

He looked at me. "Hey, does this mean you've got work?"

I nodded. "I've been cast in an indie film that's set in Chinatown."

"That's great." He smiled at me. "Congratulations!"

"Thanks." I looked through the window again. "See the skinny guy in the rumpled clothes who's standing up to talk to Detective Quinn? That's Ted Yee, the writer-director-producer."

"Looks like Andy's calming down now," Lopez commented as we watched the scene unfold. "And who's that guy?"

"Officer Novak."

"You mean he's a real cop? Not an actor?"

"Uh-huh. Local patrolman."

Novak had risen to introduce himself to Quinn.

Then Archie offered his sword to the detective, who took it and waved it around a bit, more relaxed now that he understood how harmless it was. After a moment, he smiled at Archie, and they started chatting.

"Crisis averted." Lopez turned back to me and looked at my costume, which was revealed by the open flaps of my winter coat. "Are you playing a hooker?"

"You'd think so, wouldn't you?" I said, looking down at my outfit. Then I started zipping and buttoning my coat so I could talk to him without freezing to death. "But, no, I'm playing an uptown girl who never feels the cold."

"Well, I'm really glad you found something," he said. "A job, I mean. An acting job."

"And that's where you come in. You see, Ted forgot—" I stopped speaking when his phone rang.

"Shit." He sighed. "I'm sorry, Esther. If I don't take this call, I'll never hear the end of it." I gathered from his long-suffering expression that the ringtone had warned him who his caller was. Lopez pulled his phone out of his pocket and answered the call without bothering to check the LCD screen. He said tersely, "This isn't a good time, Mom."

Ah.

A second later, he winced and held the phone a little way away from his ear. I could hear his mother's voice from here. She was obviously mad about something—which didn't surprise me at all, now that I'd met her. She was a beautiful woman with a temper that would have frightened the Mongol hordes into retreating.

He let her rant for a while, listening patiently until she wound down a little. Then, without bringing the phone closer to his ear, he said, "Yeah, well, since you kept calling just to tell me you're still not speaking to me, I didn't really see the point in answering."

Her reaction caused him to move the phone a little further away from his head. While Lopez waited for his mother to wind down again, another harsh gust of wind whipped down Doyers, ruffling his black hair and creeping under my tiny skirt.

"You're right," he said at last into the phone. "I'm a bad son. You know what would be a good punishment? Don't call me for a while. Now I've got to go, Mom. I'm in the middle of something here."

His expression was dark as he put the phone back in his pocket. "Sorry. There comes a point where her voicemails get so long, it's quicker just to take the call."

I was surprised by his obvious tension. For all that his mother was a volatile woman, I knew she was close to her youngest son (Lopez had two older brothers). He and she argued a lot, and they could be sharp with each other; but they talked regularly, and the flare-ups between them were usually brief—often lasting only a few minutes. This sounded more serious. Like they'd had a big fight and still weren't over it.

I also noticed that Lopez still looked stressed and tired, as he had on New Year's Eve. His skin was flushed from the cold wind right now and his dark hair was shining healthily in today's shifting light, but there were hollows under his blue eyes and signs of sustained tension in his face. He usually looked better than this. Even so, though, he looked so good to me after too long an absence. I wanted to drown in him.

I stared at him, trying to remember why I had asked him to come here today . . . and, at the moment, only able to remember what it was like to kiss him. When his gaze dropped to my mouth, I had a feeling he was thinking of the same thing . . . And my mind was flooded with memories of the way his lush, full lips had felt against my mouth, my neck, my—

Andy Quinn stuck his head out of the restaurant door to ask, "Are we going to be here a while?"

We both jumped.

"Huh?" said Lopez, blinking.

"I could eat." Quinn looked at me. "Whatever you want him to do, is it going to take long enough for me to have lunch?"

"Oh! Um . . ." I blinked, too, starting to remember why I'd asked Lopez to come here. "I guess so."

"Great," said Quinn. "Archie says the dumplings here are first-rate."

"Who's Archie?" Lopez asked.

But Quinn had already gone back inside.

So I said, "He's the guy with the sword."

"That guy? He doesn't really look like an Archie."

"Well, certainly not in his warrior-poet costume," I agreed.

Our gazes held as we fell silent, and I felt myself flushing. So I quickly rushed into a muddled explanation about Ted, our lack of location permits, Officer Novak, and my fervent desire to keep working.

"That's all?" Lopez looked through the window, to where Officer Novak was now playing with Archie's sword. "Sure, I'll talk to the rookie for you, Esther. It doesn't exactly look like it'll be a tough conversation."

"I guess the situation seemed more dire before Novak was full of dumplings and chitchat," I admitted.

Lopez smiled, then said, "This guy Ted sounds like a flake, though."

"He is," I said morosely.

"Like maybe you'll have this problem again."

"I have a feeling we will."

"I might be able to help with that, too."

"How?" I asked in surprise.

"The guy who was my first partner on the force is with the NYPD Movie/TV Unit these days. I could ask him to expedite Ted's location application for Doyers Street. A little grease ought to get your filming schedule back on track sooner rather than later."

"Really? Oh, that would be great."

Lopez added tentatively, "But you won't be able to continue filming here *today*. I'm afraid I've got to go along with Officer Novak on that, Esther. So if you were hoping I could arrange it for you . . ."

"No, no, I understand," I assured him. It hadn't even occurred to me that Lopez could help expedite Ted's application, and I certainly hadn't entertained any hope that we could resume filming on Doyers today. "I just didn't want our director-producer to get arrested. Or for the city to impose heavy fines on Ted for filming here without a permit this morning. Or for this problem to go any further than a stern talking-to, really. We're on a tight budget here, and Ted's lost his backer and is trying to get another one before the money runs out. So it wouldn't take much for this production to go belly-up. And I really want to keep working."

"In that case, are there other city locations Ted wants to use that he hasn't applied for?" Lopez's nose was getting red. It made him look a little boyish. "I could make sure we get this all sorted out at the same time, so that a problem like today's doesn't happen again."

"You'll do that for him?" I asked appreciatively.

"Of course not." Lopez stomped his feet against the cold. "I don't even know the guy. I'm doing it for *you*."

"Oh." I had asked him here to do me a favor, but

this caught me by surprise, even so. It wasn't exactly as if the two of us were on the most amicable terms lately.

He noticed my bemusement. "Of *course* I'm doing it for you, Esther. It's not as if I've forgotten how you lost your last job. And it's certainly not as if I don't know who you blame for that."

"Well . . ."

"Look, I'm glad you've got this job. Really glad. I know you need to keep earning. And this is a much better job for you, anyhow. You *should* be acting, not waiting on wiseguys." Lopez shivered a little inside his dark blue overcoat. "So if you need my help to keep this production rolling forward, then I want to help."

"Oh. Okay." I stared at him, feeling grateful, relieved, and pleased—and thinking *this* was the guy I had always thought he was. Not the guy who slept with me and then didn't call. And although I was still upset about that (also still angry, hurt, and humiliated), for the first time since late on Christmas Day, when I had started to suspect that he wasn't going to call me . . . I didn't want to talk about it. It was such a relief, for the first time in nearly three weeks, not to be *furious* with him, I just wanted to stay in this peaceful neutral territory for a little while.

Besides, I *did* need his help, and I had vowed to stay focused today, rather than revisit my grievances against him.

So I said, "Thanks. I appreciate it. And I'm sure we need your help. Ted's about as organized as a tropical storm."

"Don't say the word *tropical* right now. You'll make me cry," Lopez said as another wall of icy air hit us. "On days like this, I keep wishing I'd been born in Havana, despite everything my dad has ever said about Castro."

His father, I knew, had emigrated here from Cuba many years ago. In his sixties now, with three grown sons, he and his Irish-American wife still lived in the family home in Nyack, across the Hudson River from the city, and they craved grandchildren with zealous fervor.

"How is your father?" I asked politely, stomping my feet as they started to turn into blocks of ice.

"Not speaking to me," Lopez said. "Pretty much like my mother. Only her way of not speaking to me is much noisier."

So there *had* been a big family fight. I wondered if it had somehow involved Lopez's relationship with me, but I was reluctant to ask. That question could wind up being one of the worms in the can that I didn't want to reopen today.

So I just said, rather lamely, "Oh. Sorry to hear that."

He shrugged. "It'll pass." After a moment, he added, darkly, "Eventually."

I was sure he was right about that. His family was

volatile (I still felt like I needed to lie down every time I recalled meeting his parents), but they were devoted to each other. It seemed very much in keeping with their family dynamics that his mother kept calling him to *tell* him she wasn't talking to him. She wouldn't want to be out of touch just because they weren't on speaking terms.

"So how's your family?" Lopez asked politely.

"Oh, same as always."

"I'm sorry." He caught himself. "Um, I mean . . ."

"No, that's all right," I assured him with a wry smile. I loved them in my way, but I wouldn't want to live any closer to them than the eight hundred miles that currently separated us.

He smiled, too. Our gazes locked again. And for a moment, I forgot all the heartache and misery he'd caused me and only recalled how much I liked his company. How much I *missed* his company . . .

I shivered again and cleared my throat, forcing myself back to the subject at hand. "We *will* need your help. I'll bet there are other permits Ted hasn't applied for besides Doyers. And during lunch, it sounded like he's thinking now about adding a scene that'll be set during the firecracker festival."

"During the . . . ?" He rubbed his red nose with the back of a gloved hand. "Oh, you mean when all the lion dancers are running around Chinatown?"

I nodded, my teeth starting to chatter.

"That's coming up soon, isn't it?"

"In a little over a week," I said. "Chinese New Year's is early this year." And people in the neighborhood were already hanging out the festive red banners and traditional good luck symbols that marked the event.

"Then this is *really* late to apply if Ted wants to film on location that day," said Lopez. "It's not like asking to film in an empty side street on a cold weekday morning when nothing much is going on. That's a huge event, tens of thousands of people, dense crowds, streets closed off, extra cops brought in for crowd control, dealing with firecrackers going off, opening ceremonies, live performances, martial arts guys leaping all over the streets in their lion costumes . . ."

"Well, since it's not even in the script yet," I said, "I'm not as worried about getting a permit for that scene. Anyhow, maybe Ted was just blowing smoke."

"If he's serious, though, we need to make sure he understands he can't do it *without* a permit, that's for sure." Lopez started rubbing his gloved hands together, trying to get his blood circulating. "Okay, I need to meet this guy and figure out exactly what needs to be done. More than that, I need to get inside before my body parts start freezing and falling off."

"Me, too." I turned to enter the restaurant.

"You must be so cold in that outfit," he said as he opened the door for me. "I like your hair like that, though."

"John does a good job."

"John?"

"He does hair and makeup for the film," I said, still shivering. "Pretty skilled. Nice guy, too."

And since he habitually called a certain Gambello hit man *Uncle* Lucky, I was glad John wasn't here. He was very discreet, of course, but having him in proximity to two OCCB cops would nonetheless make me anxious about a possible slip of the tongue or revealing reaction.

Detective Quinn, who was sitting at the lunch counter enjoying his dumplings, nodded briefly to us as we entered the restaurant. The door closed behind us and we both sighed with relief as warmth enveloped us.

Thinking of Lucky reminded me of the additional reason I had called Lopez today. So as we stood there warming up for a moment, I tried a direct approach to that problem. "So what brings you to Chinatown, anyhow?"

Lopez grimaced. "An old case. From when I was in the Sixth Precinct."

"But Chinatown's in the Fifth."

"Criminals are so inconsiderate about that," he said. "We ask them to play nicely and stay within precinct boundaries, but they just won't cooperate."

I smiled but stayed on point. "An old case, you said?" I prodded, thinking with relief that this didn't sound like a search for a semi-retired *capo* who was hiding out in a Chinese funeral home.

"Yeah. It's coming up for appeal, and the defendant has got a hotshot lawyer working on it. Well, Ning's *brother* has got him the lawyer."

"Ning?" I repeated. "That name sounds familiar."

"You might have read about the case," Lopez said. "Paul Ning is a scumbag who murdered a man one night over a gambling dispute. He pursued the victim into the Sixth Precinct to kill him, which is how I wound up investigating it. My partner and I made a solid case, and the prosecutor did a good job. So if Paul were just *any* scumbag, I'd be nice and warm at my desk right now instead of pounding the pavement all over Chinatown helping make sure a three-year-old case will hold up and the conviction won't get overturned. But Paul is actually Joe Ning's youngest brother—"

"Okay, *that's* the name I've heard before," I said. "Also known as Uncle Six, right?"

He nodded. "I thought that might be why Paul Ning's name sounded familiar to you. His brother gets into the news a lot. Which is why Paul's trial was news—and why his appeal will be news, too. Especially since Uncle Six has deep pockets, so the lawyer he's hired is the kind of sleazebag who's always doing TV interviews." Lopez added with disgust, "He's also the kind of lawyer who gets killers off the hook, so we've got to be thorough, or Paul might walk."

I gestured toward Quinn, who was obviously

enjoying his lunch. "Was he the other investigating officer, then?"

"No, that guy left the force. Now he's making six figures a year in private security. And he's probably warm and dry today," Lopez said bitterly. "Andy's my new partner at OCCB. So, for his sins, he's out here stomping through ankle-deep slush with me."

"But at least he's enjoying his lunch." Thinking about how relieved Lucky would be, I added, "Well, good luck. It certainly sounds like Paul Ning is someone who ought to stay behind bars."

"He sure is," Lopez confirmed.

Warm enough now, I started unbuttoning my coat. "Come on, I'll introduce you to Officer Novak and to Ted." I led the way over to my colleagues' table.

Novak was by now really getting into playing with Archie's weapon, practicing the first few moves in a sword-form that the kung fu master was teaching him.

"Yes, you've got it now. That's right," Archie said approvingly to the patrolman. "You should start coming to my school. We could really develop your natural abilities."

"You think?" Novak said, looking interested.

I interrupted to introduce the patrolman to Lopez.

Novak blinked. "Who?"

"Detective Lopez," I repeated. "The person we've been waiting for."

"Oh!" Novak looked surprised—then embarrassed. "Oh, *right*." He handed the sword back to Archie. "Glad you're here, detective! Um, I guess I should have . . . I mean, I *know* I should have called this in, but Miss Diamond said—"

"Miss Diamond was right, and I want to thank you for waiting around for me," Lopez said, at his most cordial as he extended a hand to Novak in greeting. "I know you're probably eager to get back to your beat, so I'll only take a minute or two of your time."

Novak nodded, his mouth hanging open a little. He apparently hadn't expected the charm offensive.

"And this is Ted," I added, as our writer-director-producer rose to his feet.

For all his failings, Ted was a nice guy who'd been taught basic manners, so he thanked Lopez for coming here to help us out today. Lopez briefly explained that he was going to help with some other things, too, after he was done talking with Novak. He suggested that Ted organize his thoughts about what might be needed to keep production rolling and asked him to grab a copy of the script so they could go through it together.

Then Lopez said to me, "It smells so good in here, I can't stand it. Would you ask Andy to order something for me?"

"Sure." While Lopez took Officer Novak aside for a quick word, I joined Detective Quinn at the lunch counter and conveyed this request.

"Okay." Quinn signaled to the waiter, then said to me, "He likes pork, doesn't he?"

I realized I had no idea, so I shrugged.

"Is he the one who's allergic to shellfish? Or am I thinking of someone else?" Quinn added, "I'm the new guy at OCCB. Still figuring out who's who. And who eats what."

"I don't know if he has any allergies."

"I thought you were the girlfriend?" Quinn said. "Or recently ex-girlfriend? Or possibly the maiden to be wooed and won back?"

"I only know that he like chili dogs," I said stonily.

"Yeah, I did know about that one," Quinn said with a grin. "It's kind of an addiction with him. All right. Let's just get a few different things, and I'll eat whatever he doesn't want. The food here is great!"

Quinn placed the order while I gave a friendly farewell wave to Officer Novak, who was on his way out the door, looking satisfied with the way things had worked out.

"I'll see you soon, Archie," he called, so I supposed Archie had gained a new student today.

Lopez went back to the *ABC* table and sat down with Ted, who handed him a copy of the script.

Quinn looked at the two of them with a puzzled frown. "What's he doing now? Auditioning?"

"No." I explained the favor Lopez was doing for me.

"Man, as busy as we are, he's taking time out to

do that for you? He really *is* into you, isn't he?" Quinn looked me over and added, "Not that it's hard to understand the attraction."

"Seems the least he could do," I said. "After all, I lost my job because of him."

"No, you lost your job because you were working in a mob joint that got busted. And everyone who worked at Bella Stella lost their jobs that night, Miss Diamond," he pointed out. "But *you're* the only one Lopez is doing handsprings for, to try to make sure her new job works out."

"Not handsprings," I said, feeling a little uncomfortable. "It's a simple favor."

"Right," Quinn said. "Because a guy who's putting in overtime on a major OCCB case *and* trying to keep some scumbag killer from getting set free by the TV lawyer who his tong-boss brother has hired . . . That cop has *boatloads* of time left over to meet with your dipshit director and walk the kid's applications through NYPD's movie unit. Uh-huh."

"I thanked him nicely," I said defensively.

"How about you do something nice for *me*," Quinn said, "and cut Lopez some slack? Or work things out with him."

"What makes this any of *your* business?" I demanded, offended now.

"Because I'm his partner. I have to put up with him every damn day. You haven't been around. I have." Quinn gave a weary sigh. "I've only known him a few weeks. They tell me he's usually a pretty even-tempered guy. He's just going through a bad patch, they say. He'll pull himself together and get over it . . . But, I swear, there are days he's so hard to live with, I'm not sure it's a good idea for me to be carrying a loaded gun."

"Now you're scaring me."

"I'm just saying, when a guy acts like this . . . it's usually because of a woman." Quinn's attitude softened a little as he said, "Look, I know what he did to you. Well, okay, *everyone* who was at Stella's knows what he did."

"Yes," I said with resignation. "They do."

"And he should pay for it. If you ask me—"

"No one did."

"—he *is* paying for it. But the problem, Miss Diamond, is that I'm paying for it, too." Quinn looked imploringly at me. "So for my sake, couldn't you give him another chance?"

I thought about it for a moment. "Was he abducted by space aliens?"

"Huh?"

"That would be an acceptable excuse for not calling me," I explained.

"Oh." Quinn thought it over. "I'm pretty sure the answer's no. Would there be *any* other acceptable excuse that's a little closer to home?"

"I haven't thought of one yet."

"Hmm. You know, sometimes—"

"Ted!"

We both flinched. The whole restaurant flinched.

Susan Yee was standing in the doorway of the restaurant, her cheeks flushed, her eyes blazing as she stared at her brother. "Ted!"

Ted waved to her casually. "Oh, hey, Susan." Then he returned to conferring with Lopez, who (like everyone else) stared at Susan as she stomped angrily through the restaurant, making a beeline for Ted.

"Are you getting *arrested?*" Susan demanded.

"Nah, it's cool," said Ted.

"I heard that a police officer stopped your filming today," Susan continued, loud and furious. Everyone was watching with interest, including me and Quinn. "I heard that you were filming in the street without a location permit! Breaking the law!"

Lopez rose to his feet and introduced himself, then said, "You must be Ted's wife."

Oops.

I recalled that he tended to have cynical views about marriage. Not due to his parents, who seemed to be very happy together after nearly forty years of wedlock, but rather due to crime statistics and his experiences as a cop in dealing with domestic violence.

"I'm his *sister,*" Susan hissed.

"Oh. Sorry. My mistake."

"I should say so!"

"Susan, chill, okay? Detective Lopez fixed the whole thing for me."

"What?" Susan shrieked at Ted. "Did you *bribe* him?"

"On the other hand," Quinn said to me, obviously enjoying this, "working with Lopez is never dull. I gotta give him that."

"It was just a little misunderstanding and an honest mistake, Miss Yee," Lopez said. "We've talked about it, and Ted knows not to do it again."

"How do *you* know about this, anyhow?" Ted asked her in puzzlement.

"I know," Susan said tersely, "because the whole damn restaurant knows, Ted. Even *you* must have noticed people coming and going while you've been here? And by tomorrow, I assume half of Chinatown will know that my little brother was arrested in the *street* today—"

"I wasn't arrested," Ted protested mildly.

"—because of his stupid movie!"

Rushing in where fools would know better than to tread, Lopez said, "He wasn't arrested, Miss Yee. Ted's a good citizen who agreed to stop filming as soon as Officer Novak informed him that—"

"That he had no business being there?" Susan said shrilly. "That he was breaking the law? And making a spectacle of himself?"

"Man, we should turn her loose on Ning's new lawyer," Quinn murmured to me. "I'd sell tickets."

"And," said Lopez, raising his voice, "we're going

over the script right now to make sure it won't happen again. So it's all under control now."

"That's right," said Ted. "Detective Lopez is going to help me with everything, Susan. He's got a friend who handles the location permits for the city, so he's going to walk my applications in there personally and make sure everything is shipshape from now on. Right, detective?"

"Right," Lopez said wearily.

Quinn looked at me. "Can't you see how desperate our boy is to get laid again?"

"Oh, just eat your dumplings," I said.

"Detective Lopez is on top of this, Susan. So lay off, huh? Things are going to go smoother now that I've got him helping me."

Susan said to Lopez, "My brother needs to be taught a lesson. Can't you just arrest him?"

"I, uh . . ." Lopez looked in our direction and said vaguely, "I think my lunch is ready. Excuse me, Miss Yee."

"Here, take a copy of the script with you, detective," said Ted. "And we'll talk later, right?"

"Right." After he joined us at the counter, script in hand, Lopez muttered, "Does either one of you have something for a headache?"

Quinn shook his head, then reached for his cell phone when it started ringing.

"In my purse," I said to Lopez. "I'll be right back."

When Susan saw me, the woman whom she had warned away from her brother's film, she cast a glance over my outfit and sneered, then ignored me. She was still berating Ted, making a scene that all of Chinatown would surely know about before long, when I returned to the lunch counter and handed Lopez some painkillers.

"God, what a start this year has gotten off to," he said morosely.

Quinn finished his call and said to him, "We've got to go."

"Now?" Lopez looked sadly at the delectable dishes that had just been set before him for his lunch.

"*Right* now," Quinn said with a nod.

Lopez sighed and asked the waiter. "Can you put this in a carry-out bag?"

12

運

Fortune, luck

"And that's all Lopez said about being in Chinatown. So it looks like you got lucky again," I said to the notorious Alberto Battistuzzi as I spooned a modest portion of steamed crab in spicy sauce onto my plate that evening in the Chens' back office.

"I'm trapped in a funeral home," he said grumpily. "How lucky is *that?*"

"You're *safely hidden* in a funeral home," I corrected, "which should be treated as good news, given that you were worried about being rumbled."

The old *capo* sighed and nodded in acknowledgement of this. "I'm a little cranky, I guess. I got word before you got here that OCCB has arrested a couple more of our guys. This is a grim time for the family."

"Has Don Victor been taken into custody?" Max asked, helping himself to some food.

"No, that's the good news," said Lucky. "They still can't touch the boss. Not so far."

"Your loyalty to the head of your *famiglia* does you honor," said Max, which I thought was a tactful way of commenting on the situation.

"It's how I was raised." Lucky looked at me again. "So your boyfr—uh, Detective Lopez really don't seem to have any idea that I'm holed in up Chinatown?"

"No." I shook my head. "No hint of it at all. He seems to be in the neighborhood strictly to work on the Ning case."

"Then that's one problem we are spared," said Max, who had been apprised of Lucky's concerns about Lopez before my arrival this evening. "Beef with preserved ginger, Esther?"

"No, thanks, Max. I've got a costume fitting later, and I had a pretty hearty lunch today. So I'd better eat lightly."

Max had brought such a delectable dinner, though, that I was tempted to stuff myself despite how it would make me look in the tiny outfits that Ted insisted on for Alicia.

"I thought you were done working for the day?" Lucky said as I handed him the container of crab.

There was currently no one else (well, no *living* person) in the mortuary. John was still at the NYU lab, his father was playing mahjong this evening, and his brother had gone home for the night after letting me into the building and thanking me for preventing Benny Yee's widow from committing a murder here during her husband's wake.

Nelli lay by the door, contentedly chewing on a bone that Max had brought to keep her occupied. He believed this activity helped her think. As Nelli made occasional happy little sounds while gnawing on her prize, I wondered what she thought *about*.

"Well, yes, I *am* finished filming for the day," I said to Lucky. Which was why I was now fully covered in layers of warm winter clothing, with my face clean of Alicia's makeup. "But as I was leaving the set, Ted asked me if I'd meet him at his mother's store later to try on some outfits for a party scene that we're supposed to film later on."

To my relief, he hadn't wanted me to do the fitting at that moment, since he had a meeting to go to right after the shoot; so I hadn't had to cancel my plans to confer with Lucky and Max over dinner at the funeral home.

"How is the filming going?" Max asked me.

I waggled my hand. "So-so."

I started giving them a judiciously edited account of the day's events while I served myself some steamed Chinese broccoli. Then I succumbed to temptation and put a dumpling stuffed with succulent shredded duck on my plate.

After our eventful lunch on Doyers, which had concluded with Ted assuring a departing Lopez that we certainly would not attempt to film on location again without a permit, most of us had returned to the loft on Hester Street to shoot part of a different scene there, so the day wouldn't be completely wasted.

The loft, which was chilly and pretty bare-bones, had belonged to Benny Yee, and it served as Ted's production base. This was where I had auditioned for my role. Ted used some of the space to store all his film equipment. Another part of the loft was set aside for the actors to get into costume and makeup. The rest of the space was a film set decorated to look like a small apartment; this was where the movie's protagonist lived, and a number of scenes took place here.

As we were setting up for the afternoon shoot there, I'd learned that Ted had an additional problem, besides losing Benny as an investor. It turned out that Benny had not left his widow as well-fixed as everyone assumed, and Grace Yee needed to sell this loft in order to solve the financial problems created by Benny's recent business setbacks. These fiscal woes, she had explained privately to Ted, were why she couldn't honor Benny's memory by sinking more money into the movie which had been his last investment in life. Even for Benny's nephew, Grace just couldn't spare the cash—as her sons kept telling her.

She was sympathetic to Ted's situation and didn't plan to kick him out of the loft, but she was going to have to put the place on the market soon. She was just waiting to be advised of an auspicious date for that.

"Astrology is very important to Chinese people," Ted explained in a quick aside to me, when telling us about the possibility of losing the loft as our production base and primary set. "She wouldn't want to launch the sale on an unlucky day."

Fortune and luck, both good and bad, kept playing a big role in everyone's fate here, including mine.

Due to the economy, the loft might sit on the market for a long time. After all, although it was in a good location, it would probably need remodeling and updating to be useful to anyone besides an indie filmmaker or a tong underlord. (I was curious about what Benny had used the place for before loaning it to Ted, but I assumed I was better off not knowing.)

"Or this loft might sell within days to a buyer who wants us out of here by the closing date." Ted concluded with a shrug, "There's no way of knowing."

"What'll happen to the movie if we lose this space?" Bill asked anxiously. "I really need this film to succeed, Ted. My parents . . . you know."

I resisted the urge to give Bill a reality check. Even

if the film got finished, which wasn't a given, *success* was nowhere in this low-budget movie's future. Not with Ted's clumsy script and plodding direction.

"Don't worry, we'll find another space," said the ever-optimistic Ted. "Our fortunes are improving all the time. I've got a meeting later today with our new backer."

"We have a new backer?" I asked eagerly.

"Well, I *hope* he's our new backer," said Ted. "Fingers crossed."

Indeed.

Dressing, undressing, and sitting around waiting to work were uncomfortable in the frigid loft. So was touching each other, due to how cold our hands were. We wound up working on a love scene between Brian and Alicia today, during which my shirt kept getting hiked up (but stayed on); and every time Bill touched my bare skin, it was hard not to shriek.

Cynthia wasn't needed for this scene, since Mei wasn't in it, so she had gone home after lunch. Archie was with us on set, though, since Jianyu came to Brian in a vision while Alicia was trying to seduce him.

None of us had our lines down well for the scene, since we hadn't expected to shoot it today, so progress was slow and we had to do a lot of retakes. Which meant that I spent much of the afternoon repeatedly flinging myself at Bill, who responded with comedic uncertainty to Alicia's aggressive sexuality. The first few takes were a little uncomfortable between us, since we were scant acquaintances who'd never done more than shake hands before, and now I was in his arms and kissing him. But after we'd done this several times in a row while Ted asked me to tilt my head differently, the production assistant called out the lines we kept forgetting, and Archie was practicing moves nearby with his sword while waiting for his cue . . . the awkwardness faded, and Bill and I got pretty comfortable with each other.

Kissing a fellow actor in performance isn't like kissing someone in life. Your character may well have complex feelings about embracing the other person, but *you're* just doing your job. So unless your relationship with the other actor is making the situation complicated (which wasn't the case here), once you get over the initial embarrassment of intimately touching each other, doing a love scene isn't that much different than doing a close-contact fight scene or a dance routine together.

It's all physical acting, and in each instance, you have to rehearse together, develop trust and a comfort zone with each other, learn your mutual moves well enough to make the scene look spontaneous and natural, hit your marks, say your lines, and make sure your face can be seen when the director wants it seen. And whether you're on camera or on stage, the whole time you're touching and kissing each other while exchanging seductive dialogue and pretending to be turned on, lots of people are right there in the room watching you. When filming a love scene, the director may be within a foot of your embracing bodies, and the camera and microphone may be perilously close to hitting you in the head.

So although Bill was the first man who had touched me this way since Lopez had left my bedroom Christmas morning, there was no similarity whatsoever between the two experiences, and one didn't remind me of the other.

Anyhow, as I now told Max and Lucky, we'd gotten a very late start on filming today because of the Doyers Street mess, and we hadn't really learned our lines for the scene we wound up working on. (I didn't tell my two companions that the scene involved a lot of kissing and fondling.) So we didn't get much done today and would have to return to the same scene tomorrow.

"And at some point," I concluded, "we'll also have to go back to Doyers to film the scene we should have filmed today."

Max reached for a second helping of noodles as he said, "It was most thoughtful of Detective Lopez to offer to help expedite the necessary paperwork for the filming to proceed more smoothly."

"Thoughtful, my elbow," said Lucky. "He owed it to her."

I froze for a moment, feeling awkward as I realized he must know what all his colleagues who'd been busted at Bella Stella knew—that I'd had sex with Lopez (twice) after the arrests at Fenster's, and then he'd never called me.

Lucky added, "He's the reason she lost her last job, after all."

"That's right," I said with an emphatic nod, though I recognized that Detective Quinn had a point; I'd lost my job because I was working in a mob joint that got busted. Even Thack had said it was bound to happen eventually.

"Besides," Lucky added, "it's no secret that Detective Lopez has got a thing for Esther. Anyone can see it. So he probably feels bad about what he did to her. Maybe he even wishes he could go back and change what happened."

"Yes, I suppose so," said Max, oblivious to the subtext that I suspected I was hearing. "Helping her now was obviously the honorable thing to do."

"Hmph," I said, recalling that Quinn seemed to think Lopez was helping me in hopes of getting laid again.

"Yep. If he's bein' a stand-up guy now," said Lucky, "well, it's no more than he *should* do for a lady he's wronged that way he wronged our Esther."

Our eyes met for a moment, and I saw that he did indeed know. But he was, in his way, a gentleman of the old school, so he would never mention it. Not directly, anyhow—and probably not ever again, either.

So I smiled at him and said, "Being saddled with the job of liaising between Ted Yee and city bureaucracy might even be sufficient punishment. *I* sure wouldn't want to be in Lopez's shoes now."

"And speaking of Detective Lopez," Lucky said, though his tone suggested he was changing the subject, "it's kinda funny that he's poking around Chinatown because of the Ning family."

"Funny ha-ha or funny strange?" I asked.

"From where I'm sittin', funny coincidental." He added with a philosophical shrug, "Or maybe not. Uncle Six has got his fingers in so many pies, maybe it ain't that strange that Young Blue Eyes and I both wound up with our hooks stuck in him at the same time."

"Ah!" said Max, who had obviously followed Lucky's mixed metaphors better than I had. "While Detective Lopez is revisiting his former investigation of the younger Ning whom the elder Ning is now trying to get exonerated, you have uncovered relevant information about the Nings in the course of your inquiries into Benny Yee's affairs."

"Yep."

"Oh." I said in surprise to Lucky, "Do you mean you think Uncle Six wanted Benny dead?"

"Sure looks like it," he confirmed.

"I don't understand," I said. "They were both in the Five Brothers tong. Wouldn't that make them allies rather than enemies?"

"Well, I don't know about the Chinese, kid—John's an educated boy, so he could tell us—but Sicilians must have a hundred proverbs that warn you how dangerous your *friends* can be," said Lucky. "Sometimes they rat on you . . ."

Which was presumably what Victor Gambello was worried about these days, with so many of his "family" members being arrested.

". . . and sometimes they stab you in the back—which they're in a position to do because you trusted them. After all, giving someone an opportunity like that is a mistake a man doesn't make with his enemies."

Max asked with interest, "Are you saying you've learned that Benny Yee coveted Uncle Six's leadership position in the Five Brothers?"

"Bingo, Doc."

I said, "And I suppose a man like Uncle Six holds onto his position by being ruthless to challengers?"

"It's pretty much a requirement of the job," said Lucky.

"Then I would say he seems a viable candidate for our unknown adversary," said Max.

"But Uncle Six was so courteous at the wake," I argued. "Bowed before the coffin, spent a lot of time paying his respects to the relatives, stayed to mingle with visitors. John said his behavior is what restored the family's face after that scandalous scene between Benny's mistress and his wife."

"Hearing about that is what put him on my radar," said Lucky. "The Chens told me they were surprised by it, since everyone knew he didn't like Benny. So that got me to thinking that maybe he was the one who whacked the guy."

"Because he showed such respect for the departed?" I asked. "Don't you think he might have done that just because exercising benevolence toward a dead rival was good for *his* face?"

"Esther's point is well taken," said Max. "No doubt Uncle Six's behavior that evening enhanced his own social credit, not just the Yee family's. It was a shrewd choice, a way of confirming his unshakeable stature."

"Maybe," Lucky conceded. "But another possibility is that Six is one of those guys who get a kick out showing up at a funeral and acting like the dead guy was their favorite person, when they're really the one who sent him down for the dirt nap."

"Well, that's *creepy,*" I said disapprovingly.

"No argument there," said Lucky. "I mean, sure, sometimes you can't get out of attending the send-off of a guy you whacked. But that ain't no reason to be *oily* about it."

I couldn't think of a reply to that, so I stuffed my shredded duck dumpling into my mouth.

"A person who could murder Benny Yee and then show such solicitude to his widow at the wake . . ."

Max nodded. "That would certainly be in keeping with the cruelly ironic methodology of the murder—sending a death curse to a notoriously superstitious man."

I asked, "Do you think Uncle Six could be some sort of sorcerer?"

"Possibly," said Max. "Lucky, do you know if he has any previous connection with mystical events?"

Lucky shook his head. "As far as I can tell, he don't. I've talked with reliable sources about this. And Six is a high-profile guy, after all, meaning there's always a lotta chatter about him. So I think I'd have found something by now—at least a question mark—if he had a habit of conjuring mysterious mojo."

"In that case," said Max, "I am inclined to think that rather than possessing the sort of power used in this murder, he instead is a man with the resources to secure the assistance of a discreet person with the necessary skills."

"Definitely," said Lucky. "I know something about this guy's reputation. If he wants a thing to be done, it gets done. Maybe he saw someone with dark power and thought of a way to use it to get rid of an inconvenient upstart who was getting on his nerves." He added, "Or maybe he wanted to whack Benny in a way that would never point to him—or even be recognized as murder—and so he looked around for someone who could help him pull that off."

"Either way," I said, "it sounds like Uncle Six is someone who could have arranged the weird way Benny was killed."

"And he had motive," said Lucky. "In fact, he might've felt pushed to it. I hear that Benny was getting pretty aggressive with Ning by the time he died."

"That sounds reckless," I said, remembering the ruthlessness I had sensed in Uncle Six at Benny's wake.

"Or desperate," said Lucky. "Benny was having a run of bad luck lately, just like his widow told your movie director. One of his perfectly legitimate business interests went bust last month, and then the cops shut down a less-than-strictly-legal operation that was a good earner for him. Maybe if things had been going well, he'd have been more patient and bided his time. But with his luck turning sour and his business concerns bleeding money, he started getting pushy, demanding a bigger cut of things and trying to grab more power. And that didn't go over well with Joe Ning."

"No, I wouldn't think so," I said, finishing the food on my plate and resisting the urge to reach for seconds. I had a feeling that every extra bite would show up in whatever costumes Ted wanted to me to try on at his mother's store tonight. "Well, at least we have a viable suspect now. That's progress. Uncle Six is not a person I look forward to investigating, though."

"You should stay away from him," Lucky said firmly. "Leave this to me. At least until we know more. Got it?"

"Got it." I was not inclined to argue. After all, whatever we might suspect about Joe Ning, the only thing we actually knew for certain right now was that he was the sort of adversary whom Lucky knew how to handle—even while lying low in a funeral home. "I gather you're going to try to find out if Uncle Six has made friends lately with someone who has unusual talents?"

"That's the plan." He looked at Max. "How about you, Doc? Any information on the magic cookie front?"

"I have made progress in my research," said Max, having finished his meal, "and am ready to implement a partial solution to our problem."

Since Lucky seemed to be finished eating, too, I started closing the food containers as Max continued speaking.

"Using a physical object to deliver a death curse is a widespread phenomenon and longstanding tradition, of course," he said. "The specific method of conveyance being used in this instance—a fortune cookie—seems to be unprecedented, as far as I can ascertain, but apart from that, this appears to be a very conventional form of mystical murder. In a sense, it's a bit like dispatching someone with a firearm."

"I'd say it's *nothing* like that," said Lucky. "Killing someone with a cookie? That's just *wrong*."

"I think I see what you're saying," I said to Max. "There are all different kinds of guns and bullets, but there's a sense in which they're all the same. With every one of them, after all, you point the weapon, pull the trigger, and shoot the victim."

"Precisely," said Max. "There is obviously talent involved here—we witnessed in my laboratory a few nights ago how much sheer *power* was instilled in the curse that Benny received."

"And I won't be forgetting that experience anytime soon," I said truthfully.

"Yet there is also a certain . . . mundanity, if you will, to this person's practice of magic. In studying the matter, I have come to believe that our adversary is methodical, deceptive, and thorough, but not particularly creative or original. This may be a natural mindset, or it may be that the conjuror is relatively new to the practice of mystical arts and still learning the classics, so to speak."

Nelli made a cheery, high-pitched sound as she shifted her position on the floor by the door to get more comfortable, then resumed gnawing on her bone.

Max continued, "The conventionality of cursing someone with death via an ensorcelled object means that I have previous experience with related phenomena, and also that I have found substantial research material to rely on for some of the specifics of this particular method."

I rose to my feet and started putting the remains of our dinner into the little mini-fridge that Mr. Chen kept here for pack lunches and leftovers. "So how do we take the whammy off the next misfortune cookie that comes along?"

"I'm pleased to say that it's a simple matter of destroying the cookie via mystical means," Max replied. "I have already made the preparations in my laboratory, so that we can immediately dispose of any suspicious cookies that we encounter."

"Excellent," I said.

"There is a catch, however," Max warned.

"There always is," Lucky said on a sigh.

"All my research on similar conveyance methods strongly indicates—to the extent that I consider it a virtual certainty—that breaking open the cookie is what activates its dark magic. Until then, although extremely dangerous in terms of its *potential*, it does no damage."

"That's also in keeping with how we were told Benny died," I noted. "He was fine after receiving the cookie; it wasn't until he cracked it open that he died."

Max nodded. "In the act of breaking or cracking the cookie, the curse is immediately inflicted. And once engaged, I am sorry to say, it cannot be lifted, mitigated, or redirected." His expression was grave as he said, "Thus the victim is doomed. Inexorably cursed with death. Nothing can save him or her from that imminent fate. Based on the immediacy with which Benny Yee's death curse took effect, I postulate it's unlikely the victim will survive more than a few minutes after the cookie is cracked. Certainly not more than a few hours, anyhow."

"Well, *that's* grim," said Lucky.

We all looked at the fortune cookies which had come with our meal. They were still sitting on the big desk where we'd just had dinner.

"I may never eat another one of those things again," I said.

"These don't look like the one that killed Benny," Lucky pointed out.

"Even so . . ."

He nodded. "You're right, kid. I've lost my appetite for these things, after what Max just said."

"Obviously," said Max, "we must be vigilant. Rather than risk another murder, any suspect cookie should be seized immediately so that I can safely destroy it. But such seizure must be conducted with the utmost care. Any damage that the cookie sustains before I am able to nullify its dark power is likely to be fatal."

"You mean that even after the cookie is no longer

in the presence of the victim," I asked, "cracking it will still cause his death?"

"Or it may cause the death of the person carrying it," said Max. "It depends on the intention, the method, and the skill being exercised in the creation of the curse, and we don't have that information at this time."

"In other words," I said, really starting to *dread* the next cookie, "if Benny's secretary had gotten hungry and broken open the cookie herself, or if she had tripped and dropped it while giving it to him . . . We don't know which one of them would have died, but one of them would probably be toast?"

"Precisely." Max looked at both of us with concern. "So if you take possession of a potential misfortune cookie, you must be *very* careful."

"That does it," Lucky said darkly. "We *gotta* put this killer out of business. What if Benny had given that cookie to one of his grandkids, for chrissake? What then? Huh?"

"Oh, my God," I said, realizing the horrific extent of the Evil we were confronting. "Either the child might die as a result of breaking open his treat, or his grandfather might die right in front of him."

Max nodded. "Lucky is correct. We *must* find and stop this killer. Otherwise—"

He was interrupted by Nelli suddenly jumping to her feet and growling menacingly at the closed door.

We heard a footstep and realized someone was on the other side of it.

Lucky rose quickly, pulled a gun out of his waistband, and ordered me in a low voice, "Get under the desk and stay there. *Now.*"

13

風水

Feng shui

A system of geomancy for orienting and organizing buildings, structures, and spaces.

I was about to crawl under the desk, as instructed, when there was a knock on the door. Then a man's anxious voice called, "Alberto? Are you in there?"

"Oh, good God," Lucky said in exasperation, lowering his gun. "I'm getting *way* too jumpy."

"As am I." Max took a steadying breath. "I thought Nelli had detected a demonic being or menacing entity."

Nelli's tail wagged a little with uncertainty as she realized the new arrival was not a threat.

"Alberto?" called the voice, sounding alarmed.

"That's Mr. Chen, isn't it?" I said, heading for the door.

"The way our favorite familiar growled, Nathan probably thinks there's a demonic being in *here*." Lucky called, "Yeah, it's me, Nate. Everything's fine."

I shoved Nelli aside and opened the door for John's father. Since we hadn't really met, I introduced myself, then I apologized for our dog—whom he was eyeing with alarm. Nathan Chen was not as tall as his two sons, but he had the same trim build, good posture, and attractive features. His lined face was pleasant, his hair was mostly gray, and he looked about sixty.

"Nelli, calm down," I admonished.

Canines are among the most socially oriented animals on the planet, so they're very sensitive to etiquette. Nelli, by now, realized she had growled at someone who was a friend of her pack, so she was embarrassed and eager to rectify this blunder. But the grinning and panting apologies of a dog the size of a Shetland pony could be a little off-putting to a stranger unfamiliar with Nelli's goodhearted nature—especially if he was not a dog person, which John's father clearly was not.

As I pulled Nelli out of his way so he could enter the room, Mr. Chen's gaze fell on the gun in Lucky's hand.

"Is there bad news?" he asked sharply. "Are you in danger?"

"No, no," Lucky assured him, setting the gun down on the desk. "I'm just tense. Been cooped up for too long."

Mr. Chen nodded. "This isn't good for you, stuck inside here for two weeks. I think it's time to risk moving you. John's worked out a plan for . . ." He glanced at me and Max, then said, "Well, we can discuss the details later."

"I ain't ready to move yet," said Lucky. "We gotta solve this thing first. Then I'll get out of town."

"You're that convinced Benny was murdered? And that whoever killed him is a threat to others?" Mr. Chen asked.

As he answered, I could see that Lucky was thinking of the grandchildren to whom Benny Yee might so easily have given that deadly cookie. "Yeah. Me and the doc and the kid, we're gonna see this through, like we always do. And then I'll be ready to make a move."

"The doc and the kid?" Nathan repeated. "This is starting to sound like a Western."

"How do you do, sir? I'm Dr. Maximillian Zadok. You were so busy during Mr. Yee's wake that I did not have the pleasure of an introduction then." As he extended his hand in greeting, Max added, "I hope our canine companion didn't alarm you too much just now."

"She's a bit startling," was the tactful reply, "but I can see that she meant no harm."

They chatted for a couple of minutes, both civilized men with Old World manners. Max complimented Nathan Chen on his well-run business and his fine sons. Mr. Chen, in turn, expressed an intention (insincere, I assumed) to visit Max's West Village occult bookstore one of these days.

"What are you doing here, anyhow?" Lucky asked him. "I thought this was your game night."

"I think I'm coming down with a cold. So I left early and came back here to get some paperwork to do at home, in case I'm not well enough to come in tomorrow." He added to me and Max, "I don't want to sneeze and cough on the bereaved."

"Indeed, no," said Max.

I glanced at the clock on the wall and said, "Oops, I've got to go. I'm supposed to meet Ted at Lily's shop soon." I hadn't been there before, but I had the address, and it was an easy walk from here.

"Ah, Lily Yee?" Mr. Chen smiled fondly. "Please give her my regards."

"Of course."

"Shall I accompany you, Esther?" Max said. "If Lily is there, it might be an opportunity for me to pursue my inquiries."

"Good idea," Lucky said briskly. "And I'll pursue mine."

Observing the spring in Max's step as he gathered his things and started donning his heavy coat, I realized, without surprise, that he was looking forward to seeing Lily again. I hoped he would actually remember to pursue relevant inquiries when speaking to her . . . But I knew how hard it could be to hold a train of thought when you're fatally attracted to the person you're speaking with, so I vowed to refrain from quizzing him on the results of the conversation.

When Max picked up Nelli's pink leash, Lucky said, "Uh, Doc, maybe you could leave her here?"

"Here?" Max repeated.

"Here?" blurted Mr. Chen.

"I could use the company," Lucky said. "It gets pretty quiet in here at night."

"Ah. Yes," I said. "I guess it would." What with no one else in the building being *alive,* and all. "And a dog is a good companion."

"Also a good ally when confronting Evil," said Max. "Brave, stalwart, valiant, and true."

Nelli wagged her tail and drooled a little.

Max added to Lucky, "I am sure Nelli would be delighted to keep you company, my dear fellow. But, er, she does need to go outside from time to time, you know."

Lucky looked at Nathan Chen, who sighed and gave in.

"Remember?" he said to Lucky. "We almost never use it, but if you go down through the basement and then back up the stairs on the other side of the cellar, there's a door that leads to the alley that's behind

Kwong's Carry-Out. It's not scenic or fragrant, but it will probably serve your purpose."

"No CCTV cameras back there?" Lucky asked.

"No."

"That'll do, then."

"Well, then, Nelli," Max said to his familiar, "you'll be keeping Lucky company for a while."

Lucky said, "We should call John and ask him to drop off some dog chow on his way home tonight."

"He'll be out late," said his father. "He and Bill Wu are rehearsing tonight."

"Right, the lion dance." Lucky said, "Well, I'll be up late, too, so whenever he gets here is fine."

"Come on, Max," I urged. "Ted's expecting me soon." Punctuality is one of the key components of professionalism for actors, and I am religious about it.

Nelli seemed a little surprised not to accompany us when we left, but since she was very fond of Lucky, she made no objection. And she had her juicy bone, after all, which seemed to be her priority anyhow.

The brutal wind that had been whipping through Chinatown all day had finally died down, but it was bitterly cold tonight. Despite the chill, though, the streets of this neighborhood were as busy as ever. Red banners and bright gold good luck symbols hung in windows and around doorways, waiting to welcome the New Year the following week. Shoppers were examining produce on the market tables that were set up outside of small greengrocers. The restaurants we passed were all crowded with noisy diners, and the bright lights and bustling crowds imbued the cold night with energy and cheer.

Feeling refreshed by our lively surroundings, I realized how tedious it must be for Lucky to be cooped up in the funeral home all the time. I wondered if John, who was skilled with hair and makeup, could create a disguise for him—one that would conceal his identity well enough for him to get out and about, as long as he was careful. If nothing else, at least he could take Nelli for a walk each day, which would suit them both. I decided to mention it to John next time I saw him . . .

Which turned out to be five minutes later, since he was inside Yee & Sons Trading Company when we arrived there.

"What are you doing here?" I asked in surprise, smiling at him as Max and I entered the shop.

He smiled, too. "I wanted to talk to Ted, so I stopped by here on my way to go rehearse with Bill." John greeted Max, then said, "Dad called my cell a few minutes ago and told me you were on your way here. He says Dr. Zadok is leaving his trusty steed with us for a few days, and I have to go pick up some food for her."

"You'll need a *lot* of food," I warned him.

"I figured."

"Hello, Miss Yee, how nice to see you again." Max removed his furry cap as he greeted Susan, who was behind the cash register of the store. "This is still a family business, I see. Do you work here full-time?"

"I help out as much as I can," she said. "But I'm at school a lot."

"Susan's a grad student in architecture," said John.

I was a little surprised by how humble the shop was, since the Yees were a prominent family. Although clean and cheerful, it was a tiny storefront, and when I looked around at the stock, it was all just cheap souvenirs, the sort of tacky junk I would never waste my hard-earned money on. Susan was a student, and Ted was an impoverished indie filmmaker, so Lily and her offspring presumably relied on the income from the store. Did this place really support them?

"As an architect," Max asked Susan, "do you take an interest in *feng shui?* I notice the door is slightly tilted, and a mirror faces it. Are these deliberate choices, or happenstance?"

"If I'm not being tested on something or assigned it as a project, then I don't have time to take an interest in it," Susan said. "I have a heavy course load."

She certainly found time to harangue her brother in public, though, I thought.

"Ah." Max nodded politely. "No doubt your mother appreciates your help here."

"No doubt," said Susan, obviously not in a friendly mood tonight. I saw an open textbook behind the cash register, along with a notebook, a big cup of coffee, and some pens and highlighters, and I realized she probably wanted to get back to her studying.

So I asked, "Is Ted here? He's expecting me."

"Yeah, he's around. He said you'd be trying on some of the dresses we've got here. For his film." She rolled her eyes when she said the final word. Then she looked toward the back of the shop and bellowed at the top of her lungs, "Ted! Esther and John are here! *Ted! TED!*"

I winced at her volume.

There was a pause, and then we heard very faintly, from somewhere in the distance, "Send them up!"

"Up where?" I asked Susan.

She pointed to the back of the shop. "Go around the corner, past the shelves, make a left, go up the stairs there, make a sharp right, up more stairs, double back, and you'll find him."

"Oh, good," said John. "As long as it's simple."

She added, "Shout for Ted if you get lost."

"Is your mother here, by any chance?" asked Max.

"My mother?" she said in surprise. "Yeah, somewhere. She's doing inventory. I haven't seen her for a couple of hours. Maybe Ted knows where she is."

Susan sat down and started reading her textbook, which I took as a clear indication that she wanted us to go away now. So we did.

At the back of the shop, we went around the corner, into another room, and walked past a bunch of shelves featuring beautiful Chinese dolls, the kind the look like court ladies from an imperial dynasty. I was puzzled by why this merchandise, so much nicer than the stuff I'd already seen, wasn't in the front of the store—or even in the window. My perplexity deepened as we made a left and found ourselves in a section of the shop stocked with a fine array of religious carvings, statues, and little altars. This was quality stuff, a whole different level of merchandise than the cheap trinkets in the front of the store. I began to realize how deceptive the humble storefront was—and how capable this place probably was of supporting the Yee family, after all.

Looking around, John said, "I'm sure this stuff used to be in the front of the store. And the cheap stock that's there now used to be in the basement." He shrugged. "I suppose Mrs. Yee decided to shake things up a little."

Recalling the obsession that Fenster & Co. had with thieves, I said, "I wonder if the reshuffle had something to do with shoplifters? It's pretty easy to walk out of a store with something that's shelved only four feet from the door. Maybe Lily decided it was good business to use the front of the store for the cheapest stuff."

"Maybe so," said John.

It seemed a shame, though, given how much nicer

most of Lily's merchandise was than you'd guess upon looking in the window. A lot of people must walk right past this place who *would* come in and browse if they had any idea what nice stuff lay further inside, where passersby couldn't see it. Well, maybe Yee's had a reputation that ensured people came inside, anyhow.

"Oh! Wrong way, I guess," John said in surprise as we turned a corner and found a staircase that was going down rather than up. "I must've got turned around."

"Understandable," said Max. "I'm feeling rather disoriented."

"Let's double back and try going in the other direction," I suggested.

As we did so, John said, "They've really changed things a lot since the last time I was here. Everything's in a different place." He laughed wryly and added, "It seems like even the walls and stairs have moved."

"How long ago were you here?"

"Two or three years, I guess. I hadn't really seen Ted for a while before he asked me a few months ago if I'd work on his film. We lost touch when he was touring with the band, and ever since he got back, I'm always in class or in the lab."

"He was in a band?"

"Before he was a filmmaker, he was a bass player," said John. "That didn't really work out, though, and his mother had to send him money to get home from Kansas or someplace like that."

"And what did he do before the band?" I asked, suspecting that Ted may have been through several professions by now.

"He tried art school for a while, but . . . well, you know."

I had a feeling I did know. However, although I didn't think Ted had much talent, he did have a lot of enthusiasm for filmmaking, and he had invested tremendous commitment and energy in *ABC.* So maybe he'd stick with this career choice. It made no difference to me, though, just as long as he at least stuck with it until this film was finished or the money ran out—whichever came first. I wondered how Ted's meeting had gone this evening with his potential new backer.

We made a sharp right—and found ourselves facing a wall of carved masks, rather than a staircase.

"Ted?" I called, recalling Susan's advice. *"Ted!"*

"Up here!" he responded, his voice still pretty faint. "Find the stairs!"

"Find the stairs?" I muttered. "Well, thanks for *that* helpful tip."

"This place is astonishing," said Max. "One really can't tell from the street how big it is."

"*Enormous* is more like it," I said, looking down a very long aisle in hope of seeing some stairs.

"Oh, yeah, it's a big store," said John. "Well-known, too. I guess Yee's has been here for at least fifty years."

Although a fairly regular shopper in Chinatown, I had never been to Yee & Sons before. But I came to this neighborhood to buy food and practical goods at cheap prices, not art and souvenirs, so this wasn't the sort of place I usually went into.

As I turned down a shorter aisle, then went around another corner, still without seeing a staircase, I noticed that another reason this wasn't the sort of place I shopped was that most of the stock was well out of my price range. Some of it might even be out of Max's price range, I realized, as I eyed an elaborate antique couch from (according to its label) nineteenth-century Hong Kong which cost tens of thousands of dollars.

This whole section of the store was a crowded jumble of gorgeous traditional furniture, most of it very high-end stuff like that couch. Carved wooden screens, hand-painted porcelain vases big enough to hide Nelli in, chairs with elaborately embroidered cushions, heavy desks, large cabinets painted with classical Chinese scenes . . .

"Wow, this place is amazing," I murmured.

No one replied, and when I turned to look at my companions, I discovered I was alone.

"Max?" I called.

"Over here!" he called from somewhere on my left. "I didn't realize we had gotten separated!"

"John?" I called.

"Oh, there you are," he said behind me.

I turned around in surprise as he approached me. "I thought you were that way," I said, jerking a thumb behind me.

"And I thought you were that way." He nodded in the direction he had just come from. "Man, this place is really confusing, isn't it?"

I said, "I suppose the idea is, the harder it is to find your way back out once you're inside, the more likely you are to give in and buy something."

John smiled at that, then he glanced at his watch. "I need to meet Bill pretty soon, so we really need to find Ted."

"Ah-hah!" Max cried. We both turned to see him at the end of our aisle. "There you are."

Reunited, we all went in search of the stairs again—and this time we found them. I called Ted's name when we reached the next floor, and he answered. But when we went in the direction of his voice, we soon found that we seemed to be getting farther away from him, rather than closer.

"This place didn't used to be such a maze," John said in some exasperation. "It was always big, but I at least used to be able to find my way around."

We rounded another corner—and were surprised to bump into Lily Yee. Per her daughter's comment, she appeared to be taking inventory. Dressed in dark slacks and a pretty red blouse, with her black hair in a heavy bun at her nape again, she was carrying a clipboard and wearing a pair of reading glasses perched on her nose.

"John!" she said in surprise. "Ted didn't mention you were coming." Then she recognized his companions. "Hello, again! Max, how nice to see you."

"Hello, Lily." Max executed a gentlemanly little bow and beamed at her. "I'm pleased to see you looking so well."

"Oh, nonsense," she said with a smile. "I look a mess!"

It would take at least thirty minutes of makeup and hairstyling for me to look that much a "mess," so I said nothing.

"Are you looking for Ted, er . . ." She said to me, "I'm sorry, I've forgotten your name."

"This is Esther Diamond," said John. "She's taken over the role of Alicia in Ted's film."

"What? Oh." Her face fell. "*Oh.* I thought . . ." She sighed. "Well, never mind."

I recalled that, at Benny's wake, she had seemed to assume that Ted planned to meet me for a date, not an audition. Wishful thinking, but I could understand it. What hardworking widow with an unemployable grown son *wouldn't* hope to palm him off on another woman?

"You must be the actress who Ted said would be here tonight to try on some dresses," she said to me.

"Yes, but we're having trouble finding him."

"This place can be a bit of a maze," she said with a smile. "Come with me."

"Oh, good," I said to John. "We have an intrepid guide to take us upriver."

As I expected—since it was her place, after all—she led us unerringly to Ted, who was in a section of the store devoted to cheongsams, kimonos, and other clothing.

Ted, who was talking on his cell, waved to us and started wrapping up his call. "Well, I'm glad you won't need a second surgery on the leg. And I'll be in touch about a date to film in the apartment."

After he got off the phone, he greeted us all.

Then his mother asked him, "Did you finish unpacking those statues from the new shipment?"

"Huh? Oh, I forgot."

Lily's face went very still. A lesser woman, I sensed, would have scowled at him. Speaking evenly, she said, "Ted, I really want those on the floor tomorrow. With the New Year just over a week away—"

"Sure, I'll get to it, Mom."

"When?"

"Um . . ."

"And I still need you to clean out that back room, too."

"Uh-huh."

"And don't forget to take out the garbage tonight."

"Okay, Mom, don't worry."

"You keep saying that, Ted, but then you don't—" She looked at the rest of us and evidently decided not to criticize her son here and now. Instead, she said to him, "Please just make sure the things we've discussed get done by tomorrow."

"Right, Mom." He paused. "Um . . . what were those things again?"

With that look of resigned disappointment which I had seen before on Lily Yee's face when speaking to her son, she said, "I will write you a list."

"Okay," he said cheerfully. Ted was feckless, but good-natured.

"Now I shall leave you with your friends and return to working on the inventory."

"May I assist you?" Max offered.

"Oh, thank you, Max." She gave him a warm smile. "That is very thoughtful. And I would enjoy your company."

But although he seemed pleased by her response and he smiled back, I thought his expression seemed a little melancholy. Almost regretful. I wondered if he was thinking of another woman who had lived in another era, someone who had inhabited a world that must have been very different from this one. And I had a feeling he was recognizing in his heart, that organ which is such a slow learner, that despite the resemblance which drew him to her, Lily Yee was not Li Xiuying—whoever she had been.

I said to him, "I guess I'll send a search party after you when I'm ready to leave."

Max responded with a distracted nod, still gazing after Lily Yee with that melancholy expression as she turned to lead the way back to another section of her labyrinthine store.

14

忠

Loyalty

After Max and Lily parted company with us, John asked Ted, "Was that Mary on the phone? How is she?"

"They don't think they'll have to operate again," said Ted. "But she's looking at a long recuperation."

"Just how bad was the injury?" I asked.

"Bad," said John. "She slipped going down the stairs of her apartment building. Broke the leg in two places."

I winced. "What rotten luck."

"You said it." Ted nodded. "You never met anyone with worse luck than Mary."

"It was one thing after another," said John—which I remembered someone saying at lunch today, too. "First, she got mowed down by a runaway food cart on Broadway."

"What?" I blurted.

"Such a weird freak accident. Nothing broken, just superficial injuries," Ted said to me. "But she was so bruised and banged up, I postponed the start of the film for a week. She couldn't work on-camera in that condition."

"Then a few days after we started shooting," said John, "she got this virulent chronic rash. *Very* uncomfortable. I was afraid the makeup had caused it, even though the rest of the cast was fine."

"I still don't see how it could be the makeup, John. The only place you were using it was on her face, which was just about the only place Mary *didn't* have that rash."

"After that, she went into anaphylactic shock one day."

"Oh, my God," I said. "That could have killed her."

John asked Ted, "Did they ever figure out what caused it?"

"I don't know," said Ted. "I don't think I've asked about it since she broke her leg."

"Man, it really *was* one thing after another, wasn't it?" I said in amazement. "That poor woman."

"It was like she was cursed," Ted said.

"Cursed?" I repeated with sudden dread.

"But the surgery on her leg went well and it

sounds like she'll be all right," he added. "Well, as long as nothing *else* happens to her for a while."

I took a breath to steady myself. When Ted said *curse,* he was just using a figure of speech—a very apt one, given Mary's run of bad luck. Max had said the death curse would work quickly and couldn't be mitigated; and, obviously, Mary wasn't dead. She also didn't have anything to do with Joe Ning. Or with Benny Yee, apart from being in his nephew's film.

"Are you all right?" John asked me. "You look a little . . . I don't know."

"Oh, I'm fine," I assured him. "Mary's story is just really upsetting, you know?"

"In that case," said Ted, a big grin starting to spread across his face, "let me take your mind off it with some good news! My new backer has stepped up to the plate. We can keep filming after Uncle Benny's investment runs out!"

"Hey! That's great!" In the spirit of the moment, I gave Ted a big hug. "I'm *so* glad."

"Great news, Ted. Congratulations!" John shook his hand, patted his back, then turned to give me a hug.

I was so pleased I'd be working for a while longer, and so grateful to John for introducing me to Ted, I squeezed hard.

When we let go, he murmured, "You smell nice."

I laughed. "I think that's crab in spicy sauce. Or maybe Nelli."

"It's definitely not Nelli," he said with a smile. "I remember what she smells like."

"Who's Nelli?" Ted asked.

"Never mind," said John. "So who's your new backer?"

"I can't really say." Ted made a vague gesture. "He wants to be a silent partner. For the time being, anyhow. At least until we get more details worked out."

"But he's investing enough money for us to finish the film?" I prodded.

"That's one of the details we have to work out," said Ted. "Exactly how much money he's putting in. He wants to see a budget and, well, I don't really have one. Well, not like a detailed, formal one. Most of it is in my head."

Somehow this didn't surprise me. And since there seemed to be a *hole* in Ted's head . . .

"Still, it's good news," I said, determined to look on the bright side. For a while longer, I could keep eating and continue saving toward next month's rent, and I was acting instead of waiting tables or office temping. So it was all good.

"I have good news, too," said John. "Since you're not sure how much of the, um, budget your new backer will cover, I think I've got a plan for raising additional money."

"Really?" Ted was suddenly alert. (Indie filmmakers are *always* alert when someone says they might be able to raise money.)

"Since I'm pretty much carrying my lab partner through this term, he owes me a big favor," said John. "The upshot is that his girlfriend, who does something in NYU's film school, says she can help us host an investor event. She's done this before, and it worked, so she knows the ropes."

John explained that Ted would need to prepare a short sample reel from the movie—a full scene or two, plus a short montage of some other scenes and shots. Then he'd rent a hall and invite a few dozen venture capitalists to come to view the reel. Among them, there should be a few people who'd be willing to invest in the movie. John's NYU acquaintance would help us stage the whole evening for maximum effect and best results.

"Oh, I know what to use! I've got some great footage of a speech that Jianyu makes to Brian about Confucian values. Archie delivers the whole monologue while working with his nunchaku." Ted demonstrated by waving an imaginary version of the flailing weapon all around his head. "It's really cool."

"Archie doing his moves might work better in the montage," said John. "He does look impressive doing his thing."

I shrewdly sensed that John might not be a big fan of Jianyu's tedious speeches.

"Hmm." Ted thought it over.

"Anyhow, I think you should definitely use one of

Esther's scenes. I know it's mostly a Chinese story, but I think it'll get investors interested when they see how good she is in the movie," John said. "And you'd need to prepare some comments about the film, Ted. A short introduction, talking about the themes and the story, its meaning and message, why it will appeal to audiences. You know the sort of thing."

Ted nodded and recited, "*ABC* is a coming-of-age story about a first-generation American-born Chinese guy torn between his attraction to Western culture and its emphasis on the individual, as represented by Alicia, and traditional Chinese culture, with its emphasis on family, duty, and the importance of face, as represented by Mei."

"Well, you've got time to work on the speech," John said tactfully. "You'll also need to prepare a package to hand out. It should include a written summary of the film—"

"A treatment," I supplied.

"Oh, right, that was the word." John nodded. "And you'll have to provide the attendees with a copy of the budget—so, um, it's just as well you'll be working on that for your silent backer."

"Oh, right . . . A budget . . ."

"After we show the film clip, there could be a question-and-answer session with the actors. The investors would probably like to see the cast."

"We could come in costume," I suggested. "Archie could do a martial arts routine. Cynthia and Brian could talk about their characters. And I . . . um . . ." I could fight off hypothermia in one of Alicia's costumes.

"You can charm the investors," said John. "Just be yourself and say funny things, the way you do."

Without being immodest, I had to agree that being myself would be more charming than being Alicia.

I said, "So it sounds like this event would cost time and money, but it could really pay off if done well, Ted."

"We'd need to supply refreshments, too, obviously." John added to me with a smile, "You can't host anything in Chinatown without providing food."

"In that case," I said, "count on me being there."

"We should make sure we invite a lot of Chinese and ABC investors," said Ted enthusiastically. "After all, this is *their* story."

Who knew? Maybe they'd see it that way, too, and sink money into Ted's flaccid script. At any rate, it was a good idea, and I said so to John.

Ted agreed and gave him a hearty handshake, thanking him for making the initial contact that generated this idea. John offered to introduce Ted to his lab partner's girlfriend as soon as possible, to get the ball rolling.

"Man, the morning started off so bad, and now just look at where we are tonight!" Ted said happily.

"I've secured a new backer. John's contact can help us find more investors. And your detective friend, Esther, will help us get our location permits. Our luck is really changing!"

As if to punctuate that statement, his cell phone rang.

"Detective friend?" John said to me while Ted looked at his phone to see who his caller was.

"Oh, *no,*" Ted said wearily. "It's Susan."

His sister probably couldn't leave the front of the store untended, and phoning him certainly made more sense than bellowing a conversation through the multi-floor maze of this building.

"She has *really* been on my back lately," Ted grumbled, with the first sign of irritability I'd ever seen in him. The phone went on ringing, with Ted obviously reluctant to answer it.

"I've noticed," said John.

So had I.

"Why don't I help more in the store? Don't I realize Mom wants me to take it over someday? Blah, blah, blah." Ted shook his head. "A shopkeeper? Come *on.* Don't they get it? That's not who I *am.*"

The phone rang again.

"And Susan keeps saying she's sure I'll wind up quitting the movie, anyhow, so why not give up now and stop 'wasting' everyone's time and money?" Ted said resentfully, "Why can't she just give me a break and back off?"

John said, "While I was downstairs waiting for Esther to get here, I told Susan about my NYU contact and my idea for the investors party. I thought it would get her to lighten up. You know, the idea that we could get some real money for this project. But . . ."

"She didn't seem noticeably light when I got here," I said.

"No." John shrugged. "Well, Susan's always been pretty intense."

"Not exactly tactful, either," I noted.

John said, "It's best just to let her roll off your back, if you can."

We looked at Ted, whose phone kept ringing. After a lifetime of trying to let Susan roll off *his* back, he obviously still felt her weight there.

"You'd better answer," John said to him. "She knows where you live, after all."

Ted nodded, sighed, and took the call. "Yeah, Susan, what is it?" He listened for a moment, then said, "I *am* going to help Mom with that, but right now I'm in the middle of . . . No, it's *not* . . . I . . . You . . ." Ted rolled his eyes and gave up trying to speak. He turned away from us and started pacing as his sister reamed him a new one over the phone.

"So you have a detective friend?" John asked me again.

"I know a guy in the NYPD," I said vaguely. "He . . . I guess you could say he owed me. So he's going to help us."

"A cop, then?"

"Yep. Those are the people who usually become NYPD detectives. Cops."

I was watching Ted, who looked liked he might need a stiff drink by the time his sister got through with him. I could understand Susan's (and Lily's) irritation with Ted. I really could. But it nonetheless seemed to me that his sister was way too harsh with him—and too invested in how his daily life was (or wasn't) working out. I wondered if it was because of the strong bonds within a Chinese-American family? Or perhaps because their father was dead, and Susan was trying to fill that void?

Or maybe, I thought, Susan was just an interfering bitch who liked to pick on her little brother—who wasn't any good at fighting back. I had an older sister, and we didn't get along that well—though we were certainly never as bad as *this*—so I knew something about sibling tension and friction. I'd always stood up to my bossy older sister, which was why she knew where the line was and seldom crossed it. Ted had apparently never drawn that line for *his* bossy older sister, and as a result, even in adulthood, she was riding roughshod all over him.

Given what I had seen of the family, I didn't think it seemed healthy for these two to keep living under the same roof together. They were adults. Maybe it was high time for Lily to shove them both out of nest . . . though I had a feeling that wasn't how things were done around here.

"So is he . . ." John cleared his throat. "Um, I mean, would he be the same cop who . . ."

I looked at John now, realizing he seemed uncomfortable about something. "Hmm?"

"I'm just wondering . . ."

"Wondering what?" I looked back at our companion. "Poor Ted. I know he's—well, an airhead. But does Susan have to keep laying it on so thick? What's her problem, for chrissake?"

"Oh, family, duty, and the importance of face, blah, blah, blah," said John, which made me laugh.

"Well, it's really none of my business." I reminded myself of that by saying it. After a moment, I added, "Sorry, were you asking me something?"

"Um, yeah . . ." He looked uncomfortable again, but pressed on. "Is this cop the same guy who . . . I mean, well, Uncle Lucky said you went through a bad breakup recently."

"He said that?" I blurted in surprise.

"Well, no. Being Uncle Lucky, what he said was more like, this no-good bum done ya wrong, and a girl like you deserves better than some two-faced cop."

"He talks about my personal life to you?"

John blinked at how sharp my voice was. I was thinking about my fight with Lopez at Bella Stella, in which we—well, mostly *I*—had revealed very private things in a very public way. I had no doubt that someone had eventually repeated the juiciest details to Lucky after being released on bail, but it had never occurred to me that *he* would repeat the story to someone.

"No, no, Esther, we weren't gossiping." John paused. "Well, actually, I guess we were. I mean, *I* was. Not Uncle Lucky. I mean . . ." He took a deep breath. "Let me start over. I asked Lucky if you're seeing anyone, and he said, no, but you might be feeling fragile because you've just had a bad breakup with a cop who didn't treat you right."

"Oh. Okay. I see." I calmed down, understanding the situation better now. And then I felt a little amused as I pictured Lucky reluctantly explaining my love life to his honorary nephew. "I doubt he said *fragile*."

"No, it was more colorful than that. But very respectful," John assured me. "He really cares about you. In his tough-guy way."

"I know," I said fondly. "I really care about him, too. Which is kind of a weird position to be in."

"Tell me about it," John said wryly. "I've never known a more law-abiding man than my father, Esther. He wouldn't *jaywalk*." He continued in a low voice, so that there was no chance of Ted overhearing, "But now he's concealing a fugitive. And he would have been *offended* if this notorious Mafia *capo* hadn't come to us for help when he was in such serious trouble." John smiled as he concluded, "That's the effect my uncle has on people who get close to him. Even knowing what we know about him."

I smiled, too. John had pretty well nailed it. Then I remembered my idea for liberating Lucky, so to speak, by providing him with a disguise. I suggested it now to John.

"It's a good idea," he said. "I can probably come up with something. And he'd sure be glad to get out of the building for a little while now and then. He's starting to bounce off the walls. I think that's why he's so fixated on Benny's death."

There was a lot to say about that, of course . . . but I decided to let Lucky tell it to John. He had time on his hands, after all. And, really, I thought it should be up to Lucky, anyhow, to decide how much he wanted any of the Chens to know about this business. Given how dangerous we now knew a misfortune cookie was, Lucky might well want John to stay in his NYU lab rather than help hunt down the next accursed cookie.

"Anyhow, Uncle Lucky only told me about you and that cop because I asked. And he didn't say much." After a moment, John prodded, "So the cop who's helping out Ted now . . . is it the same guy?"

"Same guy." But I didn't want to talk about Lopez. It was too complicated. Too raw. Too tender. Too *something*. So I said, "Hey, aren't you going to be late meeting Bill?"

"Oh, my God, I forgot! *Bill.*" He looked at his watch. "Damn, I'm already late. I'd better call and tell him I'm on my way." John looked around. "If I can find my way out of here. We should have left a trail of breadcrumbs."

I pointed behind him. "I know we came from that way . . . I think." Now I wasn't sure. I felt disoriented again.

"I've got go. I'll see you soon, Esther." John waved at Ted, who didn't see, and then headed out.

I looked around, wondering which dresses Ted wanted me to try on. I gazed longingly for a minute at a beautiful emerald-green kimono with gold, violet, and indigo embroidery. I certainly couldn't afford something like this, but Alicia could. It was so gorgeous, I let myself fantasize for a few moments about wearing it . . . then I moved on with a resigned sigh. During my first couple of days on the set, I had argued with Ted about his costume choices for Alicia, but I gave up after that. As much as I disliked her outfits, I was coming to realize they suited her shallow, one-dimensional, sex-obsessed character, so I might as well go with the flow.

And *speaking* of being obsessed with sex . . . my phone rang, and when I looked at the LCD screen, I saw that Lopez was calling. My heart gave an unwelcome but undeniable leap.

Maybe he was finally calling to apologize and explain. I wondered if Detective Quinn had advised him to adopt the alien abduction story when pleading with me for forgiveness. I was by now just so glad he was phoning me, I admitted to myself with a conflicted mixture of self-disgust and relief, that I might be flexible about his explanation (i.e. something less extreme than dismemberment or abduction *might* be acceptable), as long as he was humble and remorseful enough in his apologies.

"Hello?" I said into my phone.

"Oh, good, I'm glad I got you," he said, his familiar voice flooding my whole system. I remembered him whispering against my skin as we made love, murmuring into my ear as I drifted off to sleep, talking softly with me at dawn as he dressed for work . . .

"Can you talk?" he asked.

"Yes," I said, seduced all over again by those memories. "Of course."

In my head, I ran his lines.

Seeing you today made me realize I would do anything to get you back. To be with you again. To make it all up to you.

That was good. He could start there and then segue into how sorry he was, how he'd rather die than ever hurt me like that again.

"I'm meeting my old partner first thing in the morning," said Lopez. "The guy who's in department's movie unit now."

"What?"

"And reading this thing, I've got a bunch of questions. Because I know *he's* going to have a bunch of questions."

"What?" I said sharply.

"I'm talking about Ted's script," he clarified. "*ABC.*"

"What?"

"Um . . ."

There was a pause.

So I filled it. "You're calling me about Ted's script?" I said in outraged disbelief.

"Yes. That's right." Lopez sounded relieved, as if we were getting on track now. "And the thing is—"

"Why are you calling *me* about this?" I demanded shrilly.

"Because I can't get a hold of Ted. Every time I call him, I get his voicemail. I just tried him again."

I glanced across the floor, to where Ted was still pacing and talking with his sister, trying to placate her and convince her of . . . whatever.

Lopez continued, "And I really need to get some answers about this script before my meeting tomorrow morning."

"What?"

"There are a couple scenes here that *seem* to be set in a city location, but the script doesn't specify—"

"What?"

"Um . . ."

There was a pause.

I was beside myself. After weeks of not calling

me—not after hours of steamy sex, not after I left a message asking him to call me, not even after he'd *arrested* me . . . *This* was why he finally picked up a goddamn phone and dialed my number?

To talk about *Ted's script?*

"Are you okay?" Lopez asked hesitantly. "You sound a little . . ." He cleared his throat. "Are you okay?"

I wanted to *kill* him. I wished he were here right now so I could commit a heinous crime of passion—for which any sane jury in the land would surely acquit me!

"I can't *believe* you!" I raged.

"What?"

"What did I ever see in you?"

"Huh?"

"You're calling me about *Ted's script?*"

"Well . . . yeah."

"What's the *matter* with you?" I demanded. "What could you possibly be thinking?"

"There's nothing the matt . . . I'm thinking the script . . . I mean, I thought . . ." He sounded absolutely lost. "Wait. Hang on. I thought you *wanted* me to help you. Didn't you? Or has that changed since lunchtime?"

"Don't use that tone with me," I snapped.

"I'm not using a *tone*, I'm just trying to under . . ." He took a breath and tried again. "Do you want me *not* to help now? Did something happen?"

"Oh, my God," I said wearily, sitting down on a cushioned stool, suddenly drained of energy. "I am such a fool."

"Esther?" When I didn't he respond, he prodded, "Esther, what's going on? Where are you?"

"I'm trapped inside Yee's Trading Company," I said, feeling exhausted. "Don't send help. You'll never find me."

"What?"

"You're calling about the script. About the locations."

"Yes." He asked hesitantly, "Is that all right?"

"I'm an idiot," I muttered. "I'm pathetic, and I'm an idiot."

"Are you *drunk?*" he asked, sounding puzzled.

"That's a good idea," I said vaguely. "Maybe I should try it."

"Huh?"

"Oh, good grief." I sighed, shaking my head.

Lopez had said he would help with the movie, and so he was helping. That was the kind of guy he was. He did what he said he would do.

With one notable exception.

The one I couldn't get over. The one I wanted to *kill* him for. The one that was turning me into a crazy person.

I sighed. "Look, you should talk to Ted about this, not me. I'm not sure what he's got in mind for each scene."

"I tried to talk to Ted, but—"

"He's right here with me," I said, feeling ready to go home and have a long hot soak in the tub, followed by an early night in bed. Alone. Again. "Ted's talking to his sister right now. It's a phone call I think he'd welcome any excuse to end. So I'll tell him to get rid of her so you can talk to him. Okay?"

"Okay, good. Thanks. Because this meeting tomorrow will be a waste of time if I don't have the answers I'll need."

"Call him in five minutes," I instructed.

"Will do. And, um . . . I mean . . . This is what you want, right?" When I didn't answer, he said, sounding as tired as I felt, "I'm trying to do what you want, Esther. But I don't know what . . . Sometimes you . . . I can't . . ." He sighed and said, "I'm just trying to make it right."

Of course. He was a man.

He had come to my home, had his way with me, left, never called, arrested me, *still* didn't call . . . and *this* was his way of trying to make it right.

Of course.

"Are you there?" he asked.

Yin, yang, Mars, Venus, men, women . . .

"Esther?"

"We've got a new backer," I said, "so we're going forward with filming. Thanks for your help. We appreciate it."

"You're welcome. I *want* to help you."

"It's the honorable thing to do," I murmured.

"Well . . . if you say so."

"And you'd like to get laid again."

"Whoa," he said in surprise, "that kind of came out of nowhere."

"Am I wrong?"

"Of course you're not wrong." He said quietly, "But I'm not going to ask for payment in kind."

"Not if you value your life."

"Well, yeah," he replied, and I could hear the smile in his voice. "I know who I'm dealing with, after all."

"And now it sounds like you need to deal with Ted."

"Not *that* way. He's not my type."

"Ted!" I called. *"Ted."* I caught his eye and pointed to my phone. "Detective Lopez says he's been trying to reach you. It's important. Get off the phone right now so he can call you, okay?"

"Oh, excellent!" Ted gave me a thumbs-up. "Gotta go, Susan. Detective Lopez has news for me!"

I had a feeling their conversation would take a while. Which was fine, since I decided I was by now in no mood to try on slutty dresses. I'd tell Ted to concentrate on Lopez tonight, and I'd go home. Choosing a costume from the store's stock could wait a few days, since the scene where Alicia would wear a Chinese-style outfit wasn't in the coming week's shooting schedule.

"Mission accomplished?" Lopez asked me.

"Yeah, Ted's off the phone now," I said, watching the director disconnect his sister. "And I'd like to find my way out of this place before dawn, so I'd better set off on my expedition now. Especially since I need to find Max, first."

"You're with Max?" he asked, his tone carefully neutral. Max had often been a subject of discord between us, and I guess Lopez was trying to avoid more conflict at the moment. "Is he involved in the film, too?"

"Yes, I'm with Max. No, he's not involved in *ABC.* And I'm not answering any more questions tonight, officer."

"Just *one* more question. Please? So I'll know."

"All right, *one.* What is it?"

"Are you speaking to me?" he asked. "Seriously. I really don't know, and . . . Well, I'd like to know. Just for informational purposes."

"Am I speaking to you?"

"Yes."

I thought about it for a moment.

"At this point, I don't even know," I said honestly. "I just don't know."

15

緣分

Yuanfen

Fate, mutual destiny; the force that brings two lovers together or binds two people in a relationship.

"Oh, *yeah.* This is the one. *This* is the dress," said Danny Teng, *dai lo* of the Red Daggers. "She should wear this in the movie."

His reptilian gaze slid over me as I stood before a mirror in Yee & Sons Trading Company while wearing a short, tight, sleeveless, Chinese-style polyester dress. It was mostly black, with one red panel. Although the neckline was perfectly respectable, the side-slits in the skirt went up so high that I kept worrying that Danny could see my underpants.

Then again, maybe my half-naked feeling was just due to the way he was undressing me with his eyes.

With my hair hastily piled atop my head and a pair of black go-go boots completing this ensemble, I studied my reflection for a moment, then said to Ted, "I look like a Eurasian hooker."

"You look *hot,*" said Danny.

"Does *he* really get a say in this?" I said in disgust to Ted.

"Huh?" Ted, who had been studying my outfit, blinked and asked me to repeat the question. Then he responded mildly, "Oh. No. This is a directorial decision, Danny."

"Hey, just giving my opinion as a red-blooded male," said Danny, relaxing in a chair with his feet up and his hands folded behind his head. "But if the reporter lady wants to keep trying on more dresses, no problem here."

For the past week—ever since Ted had announced he had a new backer—Danny had spent time on the set with us every single day. Sometimes he was there for over an hour; sometimes, to everyone's relief, he left within twenty minutes. But at some point each day, he showed up and hung out for a while, making a nuisance of himself by smirking at the men and ogling me and Cynthia. And Ted wouldn't get rid of him. Our director just asked us to tolerate Danny's occasional presence and left it at that, offering no explanation for this rude, distracting thug hanging around our set each day.

At first, I had assumed Ted must owe Danny

money, and Danny had come to collect. But by the second day, I realized the truth: Danny Teng must be Ted's new "silent" backer, and he was monitoring his investment.

Oh, *great.*

Danny sure didn't *look* like a guy with money to invest, but I supposed that was probably normal in his line of work. I mean, being well-groomed probably wouldn't fit in well with a Red Dagger's daily tasks of extortion, assault, and loan-sharking. Danny's sleazy appearance was much better suited to credibility when conducting that sort of business.

And Ted, I now realized, was an even bigger idiot that I had supposed. No wonder Susan was always so angry at him!

After all, it only took a very short acquaintance with Danny Teng to realize he would slit someone's throat without a second thought just for getting on his nerves. So what would he do to Ted if the film lost money? Or didn't get finished? Or turned out to be lousy (as seemed not unlikely)?

We were all concerned about the situation, but Ted just vaguely kept assuring us that everything would be fine and there was no reason to worry. Since I *was* worried, though, I was pushing John about the investors' event he had proposed. John, who shared my concerns about Ted's (and everyone else's) safety while Danny Teng was involved in the film, had by now introduced Ted to his NYU film contact. But until Ted took some of the necessary steps, such as preparing a budget and a sample reel, there wasn't much for anyone else to do besides nag. Which didn't really work on Ted; if it did, after all, then Susan or his mother would have gotten somewhere with him by now.

We had so far endured more than a week of Danny's daily visits to the set, and it looked like things would be this way for a while.

Being none too bright, Danny wasn't quite able to process the information that I was an actress, not a reporter—as he had assumed at Benny's wake. So now he vaguely seemed to think I was an investigative journalist who was performing in Ted's film in my copious spare time. I didn't try to clear up this misunderstanding, since it sometimes meant I could get rid of Danny by asking him for personal quotes about his life of crime for my "newspaper."

This evening, alas, Ted and I had Danny all to ourselves. Earlier in the day, we had been filming on Hester Street with the regular crew and several cast members. But since tomorrow was the firecracker festival, the first day of the Chinese New Year, this was a busy time for everyone in the production except me. It was sort of like Christmas Eve was for gentiles, I supposed—and me, once again, spared the frantic bustle by virtue of being Jewish. (So at least there's some advantage, once in a while, in being one of the Chosen People.) Ted had halted work shortly before dark and let everyone else go.

John and Bill went off for their final practice before tomorrow's big day of dancing in the streets in their elaborate lion costume, surrounded by firecrackers and dense crowds. Others went off to do their final grocery shopping for the holiday, prepare a family feast, or finish cleaning and decorating their homes in time to welcome in the New Year.

And Ted and I walked over to his mother's store, accompanied by Danny, to choose Alicia's costume for the scene in which she would show up at a family event dressed in an inappropriately tiny cheongsam (so I was probably destined to wear this chilly dress for that scene, since it certainly suited the script), in a doomed attempt to prove to her Chinese-American boyfriend how "ethnic" she could be. Or something. By contrast, Mei would be dressed with simple elegance and good taste, behaving with modest dignity and grace while Alicia got progressively drunker, louder, and ruder.

Although it was a pretty silly scene, with Alicia being more socially tone-deaf than a rock (or, to give another example, than Danny Teng), I was starting to look forward to doing it. One of the fun things about acting is the chance to do things you'd never get to do in reality (such as fight to the death with a rapier, rule England, or win an international chess tournament) and to behave in ways that you'd never dream of behaving in your own life—and to do it without consequences, either. Alicia would humiliate herself and lose her boyfriend for behaving like a gauche, drunken idiot in that scene; but I'd have fun being outrageously rude and clueless, get paid for it, and maybe go out for a pleasant meal with my colleagues afterward.

Looking at my reflection again now, I asked Ted, "So this is the dress you like best?"

Ted walked around me, a frown of concentration on his face and his hand on his chin, studying me as if I were an abstract sculpture. While waiting for his verdict, I ignored the icky kissing noises that Danny was making. Finally Ted said, "Yeah. I think it looks good on Alicia, and it'll look good on camera. Are you okay with it, Esther?"

"I guess so. But I'm a little worried about how high these side slits go."

"Hmm." Ted examined one of them. "We could have about an inch of it sewn together, if that would make you more comfortable."

Ignoring Danny's protests, I said, "That would work."

To my relief, Danny's cell phone rang, taking his attention off me. He answered the call while Ted said to me, "How does it feel apart from the side—"

"Holy fuck!" Danny shouted, leaping to his feet.

We both flinched and looked at him.

"No *fucking* way!" Danny screamed.

I grabbed Ted's arm and started slowly backing away from Danny, heading for a long aisle down which we could escape this area. I found Lily's store as disorienting as I had last time, but I didn't care if I got lost now—I just cared about getting away from Danny. He was obviously a dangerous man to be around when something made him angry—and it was clear that something had just *enraged* him.

Danny switched to Chinese and was talking rapidly now.

"My Cantonese isn't that good," Ted said, "but I think he's saying, 'Don't talk to anyone. Don't go anywhere.' "

"I don't care what he's saying," I whispered. "Let's get out of here before he takes it out on us, whatever 'it' is."

"Now he's saying he'll be right there," Ted whispered to me as I continued slowly tugging him toward that long aisle nearby. "He says he's leaving right away."

Oh, thank God, I thought.

"You two! Don't move!"

We froze when Danny pointed at us. He had ended his call and was shoving his phone into his pocket, his movements angry and clumsy. His eyes were wild and his face was flushed. Something *big* had obviously happened.

I had no intention of asking what it was. I didn't

want to know. Given his mood, I just wanted him to leave.

"I gotta go," Danny said roughly. "How the *fuck* do I get out of here? This place is like a puzzle!"

"Oh. Well, uh . . ." Ted scratched his head. "You go back down that aisle behind you, turn left, then keep walking until you come to—"

"Just fucking show me!" Danny shouted. "Now! Take me to the goddamn front door!"

"Okay," said Ted. "Okay. I'll show you. Calm down and I'll—" He flinched when Danny started screaming at him in Chinese. I had a feeling the gist of it was, *Don't tell me to calm down*, probably accompanied by some choice epithets.

"Okay. Sorry," said Ted. "Esther, you stay here. I'll be back in a few minutes."

I nodded and said nothing, not wanting to attract Danny's attention by speaking. I held my breath until he and Ted disappeared from view, then let it out in a rush and sank into a chair, wondering what had happened to set Danny off like that.

After my nerves stopped vibrating, I considered changing back into my own clothes, but decided I'd wait for Ted to return. He seemed satisfied with this costume, but I was pretty tired of changing clothes by now; so in case he wanted to take one more look at this dress before settling on it, I decided to leave it on until I was sure we were done here. And since I was a little chilly, I slipped on my coat while I waited.

I checked the time and was surprised to discover how late it was. No wonder I was feeling hungry. I decided I'd pick up some food and go to Max's place after I left here. Now that I had deposited some of my modest movie salary into my bank account, it seemed like it should be my turn to buy dinner. And I wanted to confer with Manhattan's resident mage.

I was starting to think we'd been wrong about Evil's voracious appetite on this occasion. If there had been any mystical murders in Chinatown since Benny Yee's death more than two weeks ago, we hadn't heard about them; and between the three of us, we'd been doing our best to follow events closely in this neighborhood. But no one connected to Uncle Six or Benny Yee had died, and there seemed to be no local gossip about mysterious mojo, death curses, or fresh corpses found clutching broken gourmet cookies.

Maybe we had overlooked the fact that killing Benny Yee was just business to someone like Uncle Six. If he had found a clever way to do it, a mystical means that wouldn't be detected as murder, it didn't necessarily mean that such a cool-headed man was going to go off the deep end and start sending misfortune cookies to other enemies, too. If Benny had been a high-profile problem for him, then maybe Uncle Six had just wanted a one-time low-profile solution, a method he didn't intend to use twice.

And since Lucky refused to leave town until we

were sure no more cookies would hit the street, so to speak, I thought it was time to rethink our strategy. The Chens loved Lucky, but he was starting to drive them crazy after three weeks as their resident fugitive. They were getting pretty tired of Nelli, too, who was still keeping Lucky company more than a week after Max and I had left her there. Thanks to the disguise John had fashioned for the old mobster, Lucky and Nelli could go outside once or twice a day, but they still had to be careful. The rest of the time, the inactivity and uncertainty of his situation was making Lucky pretty stir-crazy, three weeks on.

There had only been one more Gambello arrest this past week, and that one had occurred out of town. Detectives Lopez and Quinn had driven to Saranac Lake, a town five or six hours upstate by car, to work with local authorities there to apprehend their suspect, so they'd been out of town for a few days. Before leaving, though, Lopez had made good on his promise to help Ted, and the slow process of getting the necessary location permits was now underway.

There was no question of doing a location shoot during the firecracker festival, though. Ted should have applied months ago if he wanted to do that. But it looked like most of the other locations would be approved, thanks to Lopez's help—though not as fast as Ted had hoped. The wheels of bureaucracy turned slowly, even with grease.

Growing bored, I checked the time again, and was surprised by how long I had been waiting. Realizing Ted must have forgotten about me—and that I probably should have expected it, knowing him—I decided to leave. I grabbed my purse and headed for the stairs, trying to remember the directions that Ted had started giving to Danny before the *dai lo* had insisted that the director show him the way.

After several turns, twists, and switchbacks, though, I was lost and had no idea where I was. That was when I realized that I was also still in my costume. No longer chilly after I'd donned my coat, I'd been comfortable enough to forget I wasn't wearing my street clothes.

I wondered if I should just resign myself to wearing Alicia's party dress for the rest of the night and keep looking for an exit. I'd be chilly once I got outside, but at least I wouldn't waste additional time wandering around here. Trying to find the clothing section and the dressing room again could turn this into a long evening.

"Oh, great, Esther," I muttered. "Just *great.*"

"Hello? Is someone there?" called a male voice—one that sounded familiar.

"Hello?" I called back, trying to figure out where he was. "Who's there?"

"Esther? Is that you?"

"Yes," I called. "Lopez?"

"Yeah. I think I'm lost," he said. "Well, no, I'm *definitely* lost."

It sounded like he was somewhere in the area on my left, beyond the tall painted privacy screens and hanging textiles that surrounded me. "Stay where you are," I called. "Keep talking. I think I can find you if you hold still."

"This place is like a mystery wrapped up in a maze and concealed in a rabbit warren," he said. "I'm not even sure what floor we're on."

"I think we're on the third floor," I called. "So you're back in town now, huh?"

"Yeah, we got back from Saskatchewan last night."

"I thought it was Saranac Lake."

"That place *feels* like Saskatchewan. I've never been so cold in my whole li—Oh! There you are." He smiled at me as I popped my head around a corner and found him. "Did you bring provisions? I'm not confident about finding our way out of here before the spring thaw."

"I'm going to call Ted and tell him to come rescue us. He was supposed to come back upstairs and never did. Probably forgot about me."

"Probably," said Lopez, who obviously knew him by now.

But when I tried Ted, I got his voicemail. "Oh, for God's sake. He's not answering."

"He's good at that." As the flaps of my coat swung

open, Lopez said, "I don't know why you're risking pneumonia on a night like this, but that dress looks great on you."

"I came here for a costume fitting."

"Oh, of course." His gaze roamed over me, and the store suddenly didn't feel chilly anymore. "Are you *sure* you're not playing a hooker?"

"No, just an exhibitionist." I put my phone back in my purse. "So why are you wandering around here?"

"I was supposed to meet Ted. His mother told me he'd be up here with you. I had no idea what I was getting into when I said, 'Okay, I'll just go upstairs and find them.'"

"Fools rush in," I said.

"And if Ted's not up here with you, and he's still not answering his phone . . . I'd bet real money that he's forgotten I was coming here tonight."

"I have a feeling you're right," I said. "He didn't mention it."

"*Great.* Well, I'm too busy to waste time trying to track him down. So I'm ready to get out of here."

"So am I," I said. "I don't suppose you remember how you got to this spot?"

"Um . . ." He led me to the other end of this aisle, then stopped and frowned in puzzlement. "I could have sworn I came this way . . . But this is definitely not the stuff I walked past before. I'd remember seeing a few hundred old telephones, radios, and analog TVs. Does anyone *buy* this stuff?"

"I don't know. I didn't even know that there was stock like this on this floor."

"Well, if we just keep following along the wall," Lopez said, "sooner or later, we're bound to come to an exit door or some stairs."

"You say that with the confidence of someone who hasn't spent much time in this place."

As we passed bookcases filled with about five hundred copies of Chairman Mao's Little Red Book, he said, "Weird. Well, if we get stuck here for a long time, at least we'll have some light reading material to help pass the hours."

"Hey, look—stairs!"

We descended these, but when we got to the next floor, we couldn't find a way down to the main floor. I called out a few times, hoping Lily (or *someone*—anyone!) would hear me, but there was no response. "I sure hope she hasn't closed up shop for the night."

"Probably not, the lights are still on. But if we wind up trapped here overnight, I sure hope there's something to eat."

"Me, too."

"You're hungry?"

"Starving. I haven't had . . . Hang on." I looked around and said, "I've been here before. I remember this couch." It was the elaborate nineteenth-century piece from Hong Kong that I had noticed on my first visit.

"Jesus, at that price, it would be hard to forget," Lopez said, looking at the tag. "It is made of *gold* or something?"

"I think if we keep going this way, we can get back down to the main floor."

"So if you're hungry," he said, following me in that direction, "how about I buy you dinner when we get out of here?"

I stopped so abruptly that he bumped into me. I staggered a little, and he caught me by the shoulders. I jerked away from him, saying, "Don't *touch* me!"

His removed his hands immediately and backed away. "Sorry, sorry."

"You've lost touching privileges," I snapped.

"Am I supposed to just let you fall down?"

"Oh, like *that* would be the worst thing you've done to me!"

"I *told* you why I arrested you," he said. "Why I *had* to be the one who arrested—"

"That's not what I'm talking about!"

He blinked. "*Oh.* You mean *that.*"

"Yes, *that,*" I said. "How could you think I'd go out for dinner with you tonight after you—"

"Had sex with you and then didn't call," he said wearily.

"Yes!"

There was a long, tense silence between us.

"Okay. Here it is," he said. "And you won't like it."

"I really, really believe that."

"I didn't know it was a week. I wasn't thinking about time. I was . . . preoccupied."

I waited, but he didn't say anything else. "That's *it?* That's *all* you've got to say?"

"No . . ." He ran a hand over his face, then sat down on a chair that probably cost more than he earned in a year.

"Don't sit *there,*" I said in alarm. "You might—"

"A chair that costs that much should be able to support a person for a few minutes," he said irritably. "And I'm kind of tired. No, *really* tired. I can't even remember the last time I wasn't exhausted."

"Fatigue is not going to get you out of—"

"I know. I'm just saying." He blew out his breath, a weary gesture that made the dark hair hanging over his forehead flutter a little. "It's been . . . a bad few weeks. Right now, I can't think of a single person in my life who isn't mad at me."

"Yeah, well, you've given some of us really good reasons to be mad at you."

"True enough."

He did sound exhausted. But I didn't care.

"Do you have any idea how humiliated I've felt? And how . . . how . . ." Okay, if we were going to have an honest talk, I might as well say it. "How hurt?"

He looked at me, his expression softening. I realized his blue eyes were bloodshot again. "I was mostly getting *angry* from you. But now that you mention it . . . Yeah, I can guess. It must have hurt." Holding my gaze, he said, "I'm sorry, Esther. I'm really sorry. I screwed up."

Just like that.

They were the words I'd been waiting weeks to hear. Not eloquent and flowery, as I'd imagined his apology on a few occasions. But stark and sincere. And, as apologies go, sufficient.

It kind of took the fight out of me.

I sat down on a chair that definitely cost more than *I* made in a year.

After a long moment of absorbing his apology in silence, and realizing that hearing it had helped, I nonetheless knew that I still needed an explanation.

I said, "I don't suppose . . ."

"What?" he asked.

". . . that you were abducted by space aliens?"

He gave a puff of laughter. "No. Sorry. Is that what you were hoping?"

"It would have been an acceptable explanation. That, or being dismembered by marauding bandits. Or maybe having your tongue cut out by—"

"I get the picture," he said. "Ouch."

"I just kept trying to think of . . . *why*."

"My reason's not as good as any of your theories," he said. "Or as colorful."

"Well?" I prodded.

"It's so complicated, I don't even remember where it . . ." He gave himself a shake. "Yeah. Wait. I do. When I got to work that morning. Christmas Day. After I left your apartment. I was still floating on cloud nine. Didn't even mind when Napoli gave me a hard time for being late. All I could think about was . . . well, *you.* Us. That night. I was sleep-deprived and flooded with good hormones and *really* relaxed, and I thought . . ."

"What?"

"That it would be smooth sailing for us from now on. You and me. Because, of course, one night of great sex completely fixes *everything* between two people." He shook his head. "God, I'm an idiot."

"You know, it helps a lot of if you use a telephone at some point after the sex," I pointed out.

He decided to ignore that and press on. "Anyhow, then reality intruded. The way it does. I was supposed to be writing up my report about Fenster's. That's why I'd gone to your place that night. To find out what the *hell* you were doing in the middle of that mess, in the middle of the night, with Max, his neurotic dog, a Gambello *capo,* and a bunch of really confused elves and reindeer." He paused, maybe hoping I'd jump in and explain—or maybe just bemused all over again by that image. "So that morning, I still didn't know what to say in my report, and I didn't really want to think about it. Not right after we'd . . .

I just didn't want to think about *you* and a police report in the same space that morning. You know?"

"I appreciate that."

"So I set it aside. And since it was Christmas Day, there wasn't much else to do besides paperwork. So I decided to start sifting through the mountain of stuff we'd been collecting on the Gambellos during the Fenster investigation. Someone had to do it, after all, and it was a good way to avoid worrying about out how to keep you out of a police report—*again.*"

And that was when he found it. While sleepily leafing through scattered pieces of evidence that had been collected in the past week or two because OCCB was looking in the wrong place for the Fenster hijackers, he found solid evidence that Bella Stella was laundering money—and he could connect various members of the Gambello crew to it, as well as Stella herself.

"I was jazzed at first. Barely *awake,*" he said, "but pretty excited. OCCB had known—or had assumed—for years that Stella's place was a laundry for the Gambellos. But we'd never had any proof. And suddenly, there it was. Right in front of me. Before lunch on Christmas Day, when I'd only been poking around in that pile because I didn't want to write a report that was going to mess with my love life."

Speaking of which . . . Then he remembered that I worked for Stella—and that I considered her a friend. Above all, he recalled that I was broke, down on my luck, out of work after Christmas Eve, feeling low, and *counting* on working at Bella Stella after the holidays.

"And that's when I really lost the plot." Lopez's voice was heavy with self-recrimination. "I knew what I should do—what I was *supposed* to do . . . But I stalled. And then . . ." I could see that this was hard for him to say to me. Hard for him to remember or admit—even to himself. "I buried the evidence."

"You did *what?*" I blurted.

"I still can't believe I did it. All I could think about was . . . Look, I'm not putting this on you, Esther. I'm *not*. It's all on me. No one else. But all I could think about was what it would mean to you. How upset you'd be. Stella in jail, your job gone, no income . . . And so I did the worst thing I've ever done."

"Lopez . . ." I shook my head, having no idea what to say.

Whatever I had been expecting, it wasn't *this*. I knew he had fudged some reports here and there to protect me, to keep my name out of things—and that his conscience troubled him over that. Troubled him a lot, in fact.

So if anyone *else* had told me that Lopez had deliberately buried evidence against the Gambellos . . . I just wouldn't believe it. No way.

I stared at him in stunned amazement.

I knew it wasn't my fault. I hadn't known about

it, and I certainly hoped I wouldn't have *asked* him to do it . . . But when I recalled how angry and upset I had indeed been when he shut down Stella's that night, I couldn't pretend that this really was all on him. I knew he'd concealed that evidence for me. And I knew he must have despised himself for it—and must have been wrestling with some pretty complicated feeling about me, too, as a result of that.

He continued, "I was so wrapped up in that . . . that whole *thing* all day, I didn't even check my phone for the first time until I was on my way out to Nyack that night to see my family."

By then, I recalled, Max's festive Christmas gathering at the bookstore was winding down, and I was starting to wonder why Lopez hadn't called me yet. It was the beginning of my long, steep slide into tail-chasing craziness.

"That's when I got your message," he said. "The one you left me after you woke up. I wanted to talk to you, but I *didn't* want to. You know? I didn't want to tell you what I had done. I didn't want to lie to you. And I couldn't think about anything else. So I figured I'd call you later, when I wasn't such a basket case."

By the time he got to his parents' house that night for a late Christmas dinner, his exhaustion, his tension, and—above all—his shame had put him in such a rotten mood that he had quarreled badly with his mother, his father, and both of his brothers.

"None of whom are speaking to me yet," he said. "Though my mom still calls regularly to *tell* me she's not talking to me."

Lopez went straight back to the city early the next morning, leaving his family fuming. He returned to work, though he was supposed to be on leave, because he *had* to fix what he had done. He couldn't live with it. So he retrieved the evidence he'd hidden. Then he did the next stupid thing, he said, in an impressive line-up of idiotic moves. He shifted the evidence so that someone *else* at OCCB would find it.

"I figured we'd still get the right result," he said, "but it wouldn't be *my* fault that you lost your job and your friend went to prison."

However, no one else spotted the evidence he tried to slide subtly under their noses. This made him so exasperated and guilt-ridden that he quarreled with a number of his colleagues, none of whom knew why he was being such a temperamental ass.

So Lopez finally realized he had to man up, "find" the evidence, and bring it to light.

"There was no other way. I couldn't face myself, you, my family, my colleagues, my priest—*anyone*—until I did what I should have done from the start. My sworn duty. My goddamn *job*. What I'm *supposed* to do."

He was still worried about how I'd react, though. So he decided the best way to handle the problem would be to raid Bella Stella immediately, since I had told him that I wouldn't be working there until after the holidays. That was why he started pushing and prodding impatiently for a quick bust, which further irritated all his colleagues and his boss.

"*Everyone* was ready to kill me by then. I don't why they didn't just drop me off a cliff one night and cover their tracks," he said. "And New Year's Eve was an idiotic night to run a big operation, of course. But we couldn't do it before that, because of the way I'd messed around with the evidence for days. And I wouldn't let them wait until after that, because I didn't want you involved in the bust—and I knew you'd be working after the holidays."

Now, as if finding someone else to blame for his woes, he glared at me. "How was I to know that a shift had opened up and you'd be working there that night? Not just working, but *dancing on tabletops*—"

"Oh, would you let that go, already?"

"—while I was going through *hell* because of you. Because of the way I felt about . . . because I didn't want you to . . ." He made a disgusted sound. "Well, no, mostly because I'm an idiot."

"At least that's one thing we can agree on," I said mildly.

"So I was caught totally flatfooted when you started saying, in front of *all* of Bella Stella, Esther—"

"Oh, how did you *think* I would react to seeing you in those circumstances, after you hadn't even—"

"I know, I know. Never mind. But when you said

that I'd gone a whole week without calling you . . . It was news to me. I was so squirrelly, I hadn't clocked that at all. I had no idea it had been a week since we'd . . ." He shrugged. "I was thinking about you constantly and worrying about all kinds of stuff. But not about *that*—about how long since the last time we'd talked."

"We *didn't* talk that night," I said. "You had your way with me and then left."

"We talked a *little.*" After a moment, he said, "Anyhow, that's it, Esther. Everything. All of it. Well, until I *arrested* you."

"You did get me out of jail, though." I wasn't angry anymore. I was stunned, sad, amazed, sympathetic, and worried, but not angry. I *was* still a little irritated, though. "Not to harp on this, Lopez, but you should have called. Everything that was going on, all the stuff you've described . . . It didn't occur you to that you should *tell* me at some point?"

"I was going to tell you," he said defensively. "I was going to get it all sorted out and taken care, clear the decks, shut down Stella's . . . and then call you."

"Then?" I repeated. "*After—*"

"Yeah. *After.* I was going to explain everything to you calmly, as a done deal, when it was all over. And that's also when I'd break the news that you'd have to find a new job."

"*That* was your plan?"

"It was."

"That was a bad plan."

"Yes, I have since figured that out," he said sourly. "But by the time I found you working at Stella's that night—where you *weren't supposed to be*—I'd been so busy torturing myself and everyone around me, I had no idea that a whole week had passed since we'd slept together. So is there *any* possibility you could let go of that particular grievance now?"

After my stony silence had filled the cavernous interior of Yee & Sons Trading Company for a few long, awkward moments, Lopez muttered, "I just said the wrong thing again, didn't I?"

"There are times," I said, "when I really cannot believe what a *guy* you can be."

"Yeah, well, if it gives you any satisfaction," he said morosely, "you've got a lot of company right now."

I looked at him for a long moment. Then I rose to my feet, walked over to him, took his face in my hands, and kissed him.

He was so startled he froze for a moment—then relaxed and started kissing me back. And it was exactly the way I remembered his kisses—dark and sweet, seductive and dizzying . . . I sank into him, into the dark heat of his mouth, the strength of his arms, the flutter of his breath on my cheek, and the tickle of his hair brushing my skin as we shifted to get closer to each other.

I had been starving for him since the moment I

woke up in am empty bed on Christmas Day. And now I feasted.

After a few minutes of making up this way—because sometimes we really were just so much better at this than at talking to each other—we paused to breathe. I gulped in air, resting my forehead against his as I leaned on his shoulders, my legs shaky and my heart pounding joyfully. His arms were tight around me and his legs straddled me as he leaned back a little in his extravagantly expensive chair to meet my gaze. He looked dazed, inquisitive, aroused—and a little wary, as if not sure we were done arguing.

"Men." I looked down into his wide-eyed gaze and shook my head. "Honestly."

"This isn't a trick question," he whispered, pulling me closer again. "Are you speaking to me now?"

"Maybe," I murmured against his mouth. "If you buy me dinner."

He smiled. "I'd like that."

"Not Chinese food, though," I whispered, our arms still around each other as we nuzzled and teased a little. "It's all I've eaten lately."

"Hmm. Well, um . . . I know a good Cuban place that's not far from here. In the East Village."

"That sounds good." Then I remembered where we were and laughed. "But first we have to escape from Yee's Madhouse."

"Oh, right." He let me untangle myself from him,

then he looked around as he rose to his feet. "Maybe if we—"

"Hello?" a woman's voice called. "Detective? Are you still here?"

"Lily!" I cried, recognizing her voice. "Yes, he's here! So am I. We're having trouble finding the way out."

"Ah! I think I know where you are. Don't move, please." When she appeared about half a minute later, she said, "I didn't know you were still here, Esther. But when I was getting ready to close the store, I realized I had not seen the detective leave yet. Here, let me show you out."

"Thank you," I said, feeling disinclined ever to come back here again. Not without a compass and a big ball of twine, anyhow.

Once back down on the main floor, we said goodnight to Lily, who seemed to be alone in the store, and went out the front exit. As soon as the icy air enveloped me, I remembered that I was in Alicia's skimpy costume and huddled deeper inside my coat, shivering a little.

Lopez put his arm around me and pulled me close, trying to keep me warm. "I drove a police car here—one with a heater that actually works, go figure. Come on."

"Oh, good," I said. "But are you supposed to use a police car on a date?"

"No, so I'm counting on you not to rat on me." He

guided me to his car, then halted a couple of feet away from it when his phone rang.

As he reached into his pocket for his cell, I said, "That's not your mother, is it?" The ringtone was different.

"No, it's Andy—Detective Quinn. He's not even supposed to be on duty right now, so I don't know why he'd be calling."

"And you have to take his call," I said with resignation.

"Sorry." He held the phone up to his ear. "Lopez."

As a gust of wind blew down the street and crept under my coat, I stepped away from him and went around to the passenger side of the car, waiting to be let in.

"What?" Lopez said, looking stunned. "You're *sure?* When?"

My heart sank. I knew that look, that tone. We wouldn't be having Cuban food—or anything else—together tonight.

"Yeah, of course. I'll be right there," he said, exactly as I had known he would.

After he ended the call, he looked at me across the roof of the police car. "I'm really sorry . . ."

"I know."

"I have to go." He came around to my side of the car, gave me a quick kiss, then said, "I'll call you."

I gave him a look.

"I'll *call* you," he said firmly.

I nodded. When he started walking away, though, I frowned. "Aren't you forgetting something, detective?"

He turned around to look at me. "Huh?"

"Your car," I pointed out.

"Oh. No, I'm just going a couple of blocks."

I realized something must have happened on his Chinatown case. I nodded and waved him off, smiling as I watched him walk away with a spring in his step, the bright lights shining on his black hair. Then I looked down into the car, thinking with regret that it would have been nice to go home in a heated vehicle. And get into bed with a heated man . . .

And that was when I saw it.

Sitting on the passenger seat—so that I might easily have crushed it if I had gotten into the car without looking—was a large, prettily wrapped, chocolate-drizzled fortune cookie.

16

死

Die, dead, death, condemned to die

As soon as Max saw the decorative fortune cookie in my hands, he understood why I had come to the bookstore at night, without warning, shivering in my slutty red dress and go-go boots.

(Well, okay, maybe my costume puzzled him; but he instantly comprehended the rest of the situation.)

My hands were shaking with nerves. Which made even me *more* nervous, lest I drop the cookie and wind up inadvertently killing Lopez or myself—take your pick.

I was glad Nelli was at the funeral home with Lucky, rather than here. Her usual friendly greeting would have put Lopez's life at risk. Or mine.

"M—M—Max," I said, my teeth chattering as he

opened the door of the shop for me, so that I could enter while securely holding this *thing* with both my hands. "Coo—coo-coo—"

"A misfortune cookie. Yes, I see it. Come inside!" After he closed the door behind me, he said, "Where did you . . . Er, perhaps you should hand it over to me, Esther."

I was still shaking like a leaf in the wind. My fingers were curled convulsively around the cellophane wrapper that contained the cookie, squeezing the slippery material so hard I was losing feeling in my hands. I was so terrified of dropping the thing, which I had brought here by taxi (also a terrifying experience) that I couldn't seem to relax my grip.

"Lo—Lo—Lo . . ."

"Lo mein? Lower Manhattan? Lone cookie?"

"Lop . . . ez . . ."

Max's blue eyes widened. "This cookie was intended for Detective Lopez?"

I nodded. I took a few panting breaths, trying to steady my nerves and make my teeth stop chattering. "Found in his car."

"Esther," Max said firmly, "you're overwrought. You need to give me the cookie."

"Someone's trying to kill him, Max!" I wailed.

"Esther," he said sharply, "*give me the cookie.*"

I surprised myself with a hiccup . . . then took a long, slow, deep breath and forced myself to release the cookie to Max.

He took it from me gently, carried it slowly through the shop, and set it down on the large old walnut table where he often studied his musty tomes or did his bookkeeping.

"Well done," he said. "Well done, indeed, Esther. I can only imagine how emotionally fraught your journey here was."

"Destroy it," I said vehemently. "Destroy it *right now,* Max. Someone is trying to kill Lopez!"

"Yes, we must dispose immediately of the cookie. Then we can confer."

When he picked up a cocktail shaker, I snapped, "For God's sake, Max, this is no time to mix a drink! Lopez's life is at stake!"

"No, no, this is the means of disposal," he said soothingly.

I blinked. "A cocktail shaker?"

"It's made of silver and it contains liquid. Those are the two requirements of the vessel I need for this ritual."

"Oh. I see."

I sat down quite suddenly. It was unfortunate that there was no chair beneath me.

"Esther!"

"I'm all right," I said, lying there winded, sprawled on the floor. "A little bruised, but . . . I think I'm going to stay here for a moment. While you . . . you know . . . *destroy that cookie.*"

Upon seeing the cookie in Lopez's car, all I could

think was, *Someone's trying to kill him! Someone's trying to kill him!*

And right when *I* had finally decided *not to* kill him, too.

Nothing mattered but saving his life. Without hesitation, I had picked up a heavy iron doorstop I found sitting outside a darkened shop door, smashed one of the windows of Lopez's car, and seized the cookie.

His car alarm was shrieking as I walked away. Moving carefully, with the cookie held carefully in both hands, I went in search of a taxi. I only realized now, in the safety of Max's place, how lucky it was that no one had grabbed or tackled me. Chinatown was so crowded, there must have been witnesses to my smash and grab.

I sat on the floor now, huddled in my coat, recovering from the cold night but still shaking with emotion as I realized how close Lopez had just come to death. My God, what if I had gotten in the car? What if I had sat on that cookie?

Or what if we hadn't made up and decided to go to dinner together? What if he had driven off alone, with his death curse sitting on the seat beside him, waiting to be activated? I would never have known, until after it was too late . . .

Even though my stomach was empty, nausea welled up inside me and I felt like I might be sick.

I started taking slow, even, deep breaths, trying to pull myself together.

Max was chanting in a language I didn't recognize as he raised the silver vessel over his head. The misfortune cookie sat on the table, inert, ordinary looking . . . and so deadly that I was almost afraid to look at it, now that I had turned it over to Max.

Destroy it, destroy it, destroy it . . .

Lopez's survival was determined entirely by what happened to this garish little confection. I couldn't *stand* the tension.

Max set down the cocktail shaker and stood there for a moment in silence with his head bowed. Then he lifted off the top, carefully picked up the fortune cookie (which was still in its cellophane wrapper), and dropped it into the silver receptacle. He put the lid back on and then stood there staring at the shaker.

"Now what?"

"We wait for the elixir inside the vessel to take effect and—Ah!"

Thick, white, putrid smoke started seeping out from beneath the shaker's lid.

White, the color of death.

"Max?" I clambered to my feet, prepared to flee.

"Don't be alarmed," he said. "This is quite normal."

"Yeah, *right.*"

The shaker started trembling, subtly at first, and then with rapidly growing violence, until it was soon shaking as fiercely if rocked by a major earthquake. The sour-smelling white smoke was by now billowing out in roiling clouds, escaping from beneath the vessel's rattling lid and accompanied by a menacing hissing sound that made my hackles rise. After doing this for what seemed like a long time, but was probably only about thirty seconds, the shaker gave a little hop, landed back on the table with a muffled thud, and went completely still and silent. The smoke that filled the room began dissipating, though it still stank.

As I stared at the quiescent cocktail shaker, I realized I was panting with anxiety. Max's posture was alert and his expression taut, but he looked focused and intent rather than worried or puzzled.

After a long moment, he reached for the shaker, removed the lid, and pulled a slimy, dripping object out of it. I stared at it for a moment with a frown . . . until I realized what it was.

"The cellophane wrapper?"

He nodded. "The only part of that confection that was neutral rather than evil."

"*Whoa.*" I needed to sit down again, but this time I made sure I found a chair first. "Some part of me hoped . . . you know."

"That this cookie was a merely a harmless treat which you had, in your anxiety, erroneously perceived as a threat?" He showed me the interior of the shaker. Nothing remained but the elixir. The mystical potion had completely eradicated the cookie and the death curse it contained. "That was an understandable hope, Esther. But as you can see . . . the cookie conjuror has tried to kill again."

"Evil is voracious," I said, "and feeds on its own appetite."

"I wish it were not always so," Max said gravely. "And yet, it always is."

I pulled out my cell phone, fully focused now on stopping the killer before he took another crack at Lopez—who was probably still in Chinatown right now, a vulnerable target.

Lucky answered his phone by saying, "Hey, kid, I was about to call you. I just found out—"

I interrupted him and cut to the chase. "Uncle Six is the murderer, and he's trying to kill Detective Lopez."

"Huh?"

I met Max's eyes as I gave the old hit man a summary of what had happened tonight, and I concluded, "So the killer must be Uncle Six! Or, at least, he's the mastermind behind the conjuror."

"No, we got that one wrong," said Lucky. "I just found out—"

"Of *course* it's Six," I insisted. "We know he wanted Benny dead. He's bound to want Lopez dead, too. After all, Lopez is the cop who put his brother in prison three years ago and who's going back over the case now to make sure his brother *stays* in prison."

"It's a good theory," said Lucky, "but it don't work. I just found out—"

"Lucky, the killer just tried to whack Lopez!" I said shrilly. "We've *got* to stop Uncle Six! Now! To-night!"

"I can tell you're upset, but you gotta calm down and listen to me," Lucky said firmly. "Six is dead."

"We don't have time to *calm down*. We have to . . . to . . ." I blinked. "What did you just say?"

"Uncle Six is dead," Lucky said.

I shot out of my chair. *"What?"*

"What's happened?" Max asked, startled into jumping out of his chair, too.

Lucky said, "Joe Ning was found dead today. Sometime after dark. The Chens will be handling the funeral."

"Uncle Six is dead?" I asked. "You're sure?"

"He's dead?" Max asked. "Is there a cookie in the vicinity?"

I said to Lucky, "Max is asking—"

"Yeah, I knew what the doc would ask," Lucky said. "So I made sure *I* asked. That's why it's taken me time to get word to you. I was finding out—"

"And?" I prodded impatiently.

"Uncle Six received a gourmet fortune cookie a couple of days ago. A gift. His housekeeper thinks there was a card with it, but no one really knows. The old guy was a diabetic, not supposed to touch sweets. But you know, the will is weak . . . So today he cracked it open. Only got to eat about half of it before he died, poor bastard." After a moment,

Lucky added, "I guess no one mentioned to him exactly how Benny died—about two seconds after breakin' open a fortune cookie just like that one, I mean."

Who would have mentioned it, after all? The few people who knew about it supposed that that Benny's own superstitious reaction to the nasty fortune inside the cookie had made him fatally clumsy that day.

"Only you saw the possible significance in what happened to Benny," I said, recalling that Lucky had exhibited sensitivity on previous occasions too, to mystical danger. "You and Max."

"How exactly did Mr. Ning die after cracking the cookie?" Max asked.

"Freak accident," Lucky replied when I relayed that question. "They think he tripped. Maybe had a dizzy spell after eating the cookie—a reaction to the sugar he wasn't supposed to eat."

"Tripped where?"

"The balcony of his apartment," said Lucky. "Fell six stories straight down. Hit the street below with a really messy splat."

I winced.

"No one else got hurt, though," Lucky added.

I suddenly realized *that's* what had made Danny Teng go ballistic at Yee & Sons earlier tonight. He was receiving news of Uncle Six's death. And he took it badly. Given the kind of business they were in, he probably assumed Uncle Six had been murdered.

That was the case, of course—but not in a way that Danny could recognize, let alone avenge.

I slumped into my chair, realizing what this meant. "Oh, Lucky, this is *awful.*"

"Yeah, our killer's turning up the temperature, and we still gotta find him and take away his rolling pin," he said. "But don't shed any tears over Uncle Six, kid. A quick exit kinda goes with the life he chose. And it's not as if he was a friend of ours."

"No, I don't mean Six's death," I said. "I mean we're starting all over now, with a cold engine. We've got no idea who's trying to kill Lopez!"

There was a silence, then a low whistle. "Someone's trying to whack a *cop,*" he said as it sank in.

"Could it be Paul Ning, the brother who's in prison?" I asked.

"Nah. Joe had all the juice. Paul's an empty shirt. Also penniless, thanks to a gambling habit he ain't got the skill to support. Paul won't even be able to keep his lawyer now that Joe is dead. So Lopez probably ain't even among Paul's problems anymore, now that his brother's been whacked. He's lost his protection."

My heart was thudding with dread. "Then if this isn't about the Nings . . . Why is someone trying to kill Lopez?"

My voice broke, surprising me, and I struggled not to burst into tears.

Max gently took the phone away from me and conferred with Lucky for a few minutes, while I struggled to regain my self-control. Max ended the call a few minutes later, saying we'd be in touch again tomorrow.

I was calmer now, though filled with anxiety. "I should have remembered that Lucky's got no reason to care what happens to Lopez. He's in hiding because of Lopez, after all."

"I believe that Lucky would be the first to say that his problems with Detective Lopez are strictly business, whereas Evil is highly personal—and must be confronted," Max said soothingly. "I can also assure you that it has occurred to Lucky, as it has to me, that if Detective Lopez had offered you a lift, rather than leaving on foot to investigate—I believe we may assume—Uncle Six's death . . . Then you might indeed have sat on the cookie by accident. And since we don't know how precise or skilled these death curses are, only that they are quite powerful . . . You might have been the next victim. Alternately, if you had never seen that cookie, who is to say that Detective Lopez would not have given it, for example, to his mother? Or to some other innocent?"

I put my hands on my emotion-flushed cheeks, feeling a little dizzy again as I considered the geometrically expanding possibilities for death and destruction contained in the misfortune cookies. "I hadn't even thought of that! I was just so panic-stricken to realize *he* was in danger."

"Perfectly understandable, since you are fond of him," said Max. "But Lucky, who is *not* fond of Detective Lopez, more readily perceived the extended ramifications of your story."

I sighed in despair. "What are we going to do, Max?"

"For now, I urge you to go home and get some sleep."

"What?"

"There's been a new murder and an attempted murder. As we feared, the killer is augmenting his attacks, now that cursing his victims with death has proved to be such a convenient solution to his problems. Therefore, it behooves us all to be alert and effective. You seem overwrought and fatigued, so I strongly recommend rest."

"But how I possibly *rest* when—"

"Your young man is safe tonight," Max assured me. "Remember, from the killer's perspective, the attack on Detective Lopez is in motion now, and the murderer is awaiting results—unaware that we have confiscated and neutralized the murder weapon. He will not attempt another strike until he realizes the first one has failed, and that seems likely to take some time. Uncle Six, after all, did not immediately activate the curse; it took a matter of days. The murderer presumably anticipates that possibility with this methodology. In fact . . ." He seemed to lose his train of thought, and he wound up staring off into space for a few long moments. "Hmm."

"Max?"

"It's very subtle, isn't it?" he murmured. "If not for Lucky's keen instincts, murder would never even have been suspected."

I was looking at his gentle, bearded face, but not sure what I saw in his distracted expression and slightly unfocused gaze.

"The beauty . . . the patience . . . the indirectness . . ." He nodded and murmured, "Yes. Subtlety."

"Max?" I prodded. "Something has occurred to you, hasn't it?"

He blinked and looked at me, as if surprised to discover me sitting right in front of him. Then he said briskly, "I must do some research. And perhaps an experiment. And you, my dear, must go home and get some rest. We'll speak again tomorrow. Shall I call a taxi for you?"

I realized that he wanted to do the kind of work he did best when alone and undisturbed, and also that he was right about my needing rest. I could barely hold a thought or form a coherent sentence by now. I was so wrung out, I really *wouldn't* be of any use to Lopez—or anyone else—if I didn't get some rest.

I went home, squandering more money on cab fare rather than brave the subways and icy streets in my state of anxious fatigue and Alicia's tiny dress. I didn't expect to hear from Lopez tonight, partly because it was pretty late by now, and partly because he was probably working. Even if the NYPD thought Joe Ning's death was accidental, they presumably still had to investigate when a tong boss took a dive off a sixth-floor balcony. And although it wouldn't be Lopez's case, he would take an interest in it because of his own Ning investigation—which meant he'd probably want to be at the crime scene tonight, along with a bunch of other cops.

And I was glad of that. Because I found it comforting to picture him surrounded by many cops tonight while they worked the crime scene and canvassed witnesses.

With that soothing image of him, I was actually able to get a good night's sleep, despite having thought when I crawled into bed that there was no way my jittery nerves would let me slumber. In fact, I was still dead to the world when my phone rang the next morning, startling me awake.

Hoping my caller was Lopez, I reached for my cell on the bedside table and answered without opening my eyes. "Hello?"

"Oh, did I wake you, Esther? Sorry. I thought you'd be up by now."

The voice was familiar, but not the tone. "Ted?" I said groggily. "Is that you?"

"Yeah." He gave a dispirited sigh.

Accustomed to his (often groundless) optimism

and enthusiasm, I was surprised by how low he sounded. "Is something wrong, Ted?"

"Things aren't looking good, Esther. I'm not going to tell the cast and crew for a few days, since I don't want to spoil the holiday for them. But since this isn't *your* holiday . . ."

"Yes?" I prodded, remembering that Chinese New Year's started today.

"I just wanted to let you know that, well, you might want to start looking for another job. I don't think the film's going to be able to go forward."

That got me to open my eyes and sit up. "What? Why? Ted, what's happened?"

"I've lost my backer," he said sadly. "God, that's two in a row. In the same month! Can you *believe* my luck?"

"What do you mean, you've lost your backer?"

"He died last night."

For a moment, I wondered if Danny Teng had gotten himself killed while out looking for trouble in the wake of Uncle Six's swan dive off a balcony . . . and then it hit me.

"Uncle Six was your new backer?"

Of course.

"Oh, I guess you heard about what happened?" Ted said morosely.

Danny was Joe Ning's enforcer, his lackey, despite his boast to me at Benny's wake that he worked for himself. He'd been on our set each day at the behest of his boss, Uncle Six, who was the one who was investing in the movie and wanted an eye kept on it.

I also realized now why Ted had never returned to my costume fitting last night.

"When you were helping Danny get out of the store, he told you, didn't he?" I said. "That Uncle Six had just died."

"I couldn't believe it," said Ted. "I went with him to the Nings' place, sure he must be wrong. *Hoping* he was wrong. But, no, Uncle Six was dead." After a moment, Ted added, "It'll have to be a closed-casket service, of course."

After a fall like that, I supposed so.

I asked, "Did you have a contract with Uncle Six? Anything like that?"

"No," said Ted. "He didn't really work that way."

"Oh. I guess not," I said.

Maybe the film would have been some sort of money-laundering scheme for the tong boss . . . But, actually, I suspected it was instead a perfectly legitimate business interest. A matter of face. Of stature. As one of the most powerful men in his community, it was Joe Ning's rightful place to support a young ABC filmmaker who was employing Chinatown talent and telling a story about the life of dreams and ambition, sacrifice and hardship, guts and true grit that people lived in the narrow, overcrowded streets of their famous and infamous neighborhood.

And although I didn't think much of Ted's writing or direction, I could understand what this film meant to him. In a way, I could even imagine what it might have meant to Benny Yee and Uncle Six.

"I'm really sorry to hear about this, Ted," I said sincerely. "But what about John's idea for getting new investors?"

"Maybe . . . I don't know, Esther . . . I need to step back and take a break. Think things through, you know? Maybe when your luck keeps turning so sour, it means you're chasing the wrong fate." He added, "After everything that's happened, I really feel like this movie is cursed."

Luck . . . fate. . . . cursed . . .

Something was taking shape in my mind. Pieces of the puzzle were tumbling together, a jumble of stuff that *almost* made sense . . .

And then Ted said the thing that showed me the pattern.

"Can you do me a favor and tell your friend—Detective Lopez, I mean—that I don't think I'll be needing those location permits, after all?"

"Lopez," I said, my blood running cold.

"Please tell him I really appreciate his help."

Lopez, helping with the film, to try to make things right with me.

Ted continued, "But I'd hate for him to do any more for me at this point."

Benny and Uncle Six, putting up the money for the film.

"Not when I'm not even sure," Ted said, "whether we'll be going forward."

Luck . . . fate . . . cursed . . .

Those three men had all received a misfortune cookie.

"Oh, my *God,*" I murmured breathlessly, feeling the chill down to my bone marrow now.

We had been looking in the wrong direction. This wasn't about the criminal underworld, a power struggle in the Five Brothers, or an attempt to liberate a tong boss' homicidal younger brother from the prison where Lopez had helped put him.

Benny Yee, Joe Ning aka Uncle Six, and Detective Connor Lopez . . .

The *film* was what those three men had in common!

They had all helped Ted realize his dream by keeping the troubled production rolling forward, against the odds and despite multiple setbacks.

"When you just keep having the worst luck over and over," said Ted, "there must be something inauspicious about your project."

"The worst luck . . ." I repeated slowly, remembering something else now.

"I guess I sound very Chinese today," he added wryly.

"That's what everyone keeps saying about her," I murmured, thinking aloud. "Mary had the worst luck. It was just one thing after another . . ."

"I know," said Ted. "By now, I almost feel like I brought it on her by casting her in the film."

"Maybe you did," I mused.

"Pardon?"

"It was as if she was cursed," I said slowly.

"Um, I hope nothing bad has happened to *you*, Esther?" he said anxiously. "You sound a little strange."

"Ted, I need Mary's phone number," I said briskly. "It's important."

17

危機

Crisis, critical moment

"It was a small box of gourmet fortune cookies. A gift from Lily Yee," I told Max, relieved that he was taking my news much better than I had expected. "Mary Fox thought Ted's mother was trying to make her feel welcome, since she was the only person in the cast or crew who wasn't Chinese."

"Ah, I think I see," Max said gravely, his expression sad but resigned. By the time I had arrived at the bookstore to share my information, a couple of hours after Ted's call had awoken me, Max had already come to some sobering conclusions of his own. He continued, "Because Mary wasn't Chinese, she was the only one whom Lily could count on *not* to recognize the Chinese symbols in the fortunes that lay within those cookies?"

"That's what I think," I confirmed. "Even someone like John, who wasn't any good at his Chinese lessons, can read at least a hundred characters. Out of the entire cast and crew, Mary was the only person who Lily could be positive would never recognize any of the Chinese symbols for bad luck, injury, illness, and harm that must have been written on those fortunes."

And, indeed, she did not. The actress, who enjoyed an occasional treat, kept breaking open those fortune cookies, with no idea that *they* were the cause of her various problems. And I didn't tell her the truth when pumping her for information by phone this morning, under the chatty guise of wanting to wish her well and get her insights into Alicia. Fortunately, she had eaten the last of the cookies only minutes before breaking her leg, so no more mystical misfortune would be inflicted on the poor woman. Mary was safe now.

"When I *think* of what Lily put Mary through, Max . . ." I shook my head in appalled revulsion.

Chinese New Year celebrations were underway in Chinatown. With various streets closed off for the festivities and traffic so heavy on the thoroughfares, Max and I had abandoned our taxi from the West Village before we reached Canal Street. It would be faster to walk the rest of the way. So we were proceeding to Yee & Sons Trading Company on foot, bundled up against the weather. It was sunny out, a good day for a colorful celebration, but cold.

"Mary's a trooper, though. A real pro," I said with admiration. "She kept coming to work despite the rash, the anaphylactic shock, being run over by a food cart. It must have driven Lily crazy that her curses were working, yet the actress didn't quit and production kept rolling forward."

As we reached Canal Street and waited for the light to change so we could cross, I continued, "I think that must be why Lily started in on Benny next. If she was going to take the risk of cursing someone else with bad luck, someone who actually might *recognize* some of the symbols she used, then it needed to be worth the risk. If she got rid of Ted's backer, then the project would collapse. So it must have seemed worth chancing."

Benny was raised in the US and probably no scholar, but he was very superstitious. Maybe Lily had played on that. If you convince a man who believes in bad luck that he's cursed with it, perhaps it becomes a self-fulfilling prophecy. Had Benny's business losses and misfortune in the final weeks of his life been Lily's doing? I suspected they must be, since Benny's losses ensured that Grace Yee couldn't continue supporting the film after her husband's death and had to sell the loft where Ted's production was based.

I also thought I knew who had told Grace Yee about her late husband's affair with his secretary. Lily probably hadn't expected the hysterical scene at the wake. I thought she must have intended to distract Grace from the subject of the death curse . . . which Grace had found suspect enough to take home with her before she gave it to John.

"I think Lily wanted Ted to get more serious about working in the store and someday taking it over," I said as Max and I crossed Canal Street, along with dozens of other pedestrians. "He dropped out of art school. He needed her to rescue him when his band went bust. Enough was enough, from her perspective. And *now* he was devoting all his time and energy to filmmaking. Whether or not his mother realized how lame his script was, she must have known how disorganized the production was and how bad Ted was at running things."

I recalled Susan's noisy hostility to Ted in a public restaurant after Officer Novak shut down our illegal filming in Doyers Street. It was probably far from being Ted's first absurdly careless screw-up on this production, and it obviously drove his family crazy.

"Even so . . ." I shook my head. "Escalating to *murder* just to try to halt Ted's film? It's crazy."

"Also evil," Max said.

"Does Lily seem that unbalanced to you?"

"I don't know her well, Esther. And I must confess that my judgment has been clouded by her resemblance to a woman I admired very much," he said with mingled sorrow and self-recrimination.

"Li Xiuying."

Max seemed surprised that I remembered the name. "Yes. And Li Xiuying would be . . ." He smiled a little wryly. ". . . critical of my foolishness, rather than flattered or sentimental, if she knew that my memories of her had interfered with my efficacy when lives were at stake."

I recalled that John's father also seemed to have a soft spot for Lily; and I remembered how warmly she had greeted Uncle Six at Benny's wake despite obviously not having been pleased to see him arrive. "Lily Yee isn't just a woman who physically resembles someone you admired, Max. She's also one who uses her beauty and her charm with experienced skill."

Even Mary Fox, with whom I had spoken this morning, thought Ted's mother was "the sweetest lady," though I now knew Lily Yee had inflicted just about everything but plague and boils on her.

I could hear Chinese music coming from the park, blaring through loudspeakers. In the narrow streets and lanes around us, I heard the rhythmic pounding of drums and cymbals—the traditional accompaniment to the lion dancers, who were roaming the neighborhood now. As we left Canal and turned down a side street, we came upon one such company. An immense orange lion was bobbing, bounding, and leaping around gracefully outside of a tofu shop, demanding his due. People were gathered around watching, while the musicians who traveled with the lion played the hypnotic percussion music for his performance. The two men who wore the costume—one as the head, one as the body—worked so well together, it was easy to forget that the prancing, beautiful creature was a two-man puppet rather than an enchanted four-legged beast. Its massive, dragon-like head was decorated with gold, red, and white fringe, and it was batting its long eyelashes flirtatiously at the various spectators and passersby on this street—including me and Max; but we were too preoccupied to appreciate the performance. As we approached, a smiling shopkeeper came outside and offered the lion a red envelope of lucky money and half a head of cabbage.

"Lily is also a more *daring* woman than I would have guessed," I said to Max after we were far enough away from the musicians that we could hear each other's voices again.

Like the rest of Chinatown, this street was very crowded today. I took Max's arm so we wouldn't get separated as we made our way through the dense throng of people.

Lowering my voice so we wouldn't be overheard, I continued, "She's tried to murder a cop, and she's killed two tong bosses. It's not really what you expect of a softspoken widow who runs a retail shop."

"No, it's not," he agreed. "Lily may not be acting alone. In any case, it's the shop that should have alerted me sooner. The disorientation that everyone experiences in the store. It was a cue that mystical energy was at work there, but due to . . . to my compromised judgment, I didn't recognize it."

After calling Mary this morning and getting confirmation of my new theory that this whole murderous mess was about sabotaging Ted Yee's film, I had put on heavy layers of sensible winter clothing and raced over to Max's to try to convince him that Lily Yee was our villain. I had expected to encounter considerable resistance, given the interest he had shown in her. Instead, I was surprised to find that he had formed a similar theory since last night, albeit via a different path of investigation.

He had realized last night that the misfortune cookies were the product of a subtle and devious personality whose motives we had entirely overlooked in our pursuit of more obvious ones elsewhere. Combined with his uneasiness about Lily's confusing emporium, he had stayed up late researching his suspicions and experimenting with a potential solution.

"I believe the store is mystically warded," Max said as we turned another corner, getting closer to Yee & Sons. "In its natural state, it is indeed a large establishment, but probably rational and orderly in its layout. The effects of mystically manipulating *feng shui* elements are what make it such a puzzling place in which everyone gets confused and lost. Except for members of the Yee family, who are presumably protected from the effect with a countermeasure. Probably something quite simple, such as a charm or blessing bestowed at periodic intervals, perhaps under the guise of a family ritual that Ted, who seems to be innocent in all this, considers benign."

"Well, your theory would explain why an airhead like Ted can always find his way around that place while habitually competent people like John and Lopez can't even find the second floor," I said. "But why would Lily turn her own store into such a maze, Max?"

"To conceal what's going on there," he said grimly. "The creation of fatal curses. The disorientation is a side effect of this concealment, not a goal in itself. In fact, I postulate that it is an *unwelcome* side effect, since it is noticeable and inconvenient—but a side effect which its creator is apparently not experienced or skilled enough to mitigate or eliminate."

"The effect is recent. I know that much," I said. "She hasn't been doing this forever. John said the store didn't used to be like that—so confusing, so hard to navigate. Which means that cursing people with death probably isn't a lifelong habit. It's something she turned to recently—after Ted, instead of settling down to run the store now, decided to make movies."

And rather than let her grown son live his own life—or just kick him out of her house if she disapproved of his pursuits—Lily had inflicted illness and accidents on a lead actress in his film, imposed financial problems on Benny before murdering him, killed Ted's next backer, too, and tried to murder Lopez for helping expedite Ted's filming permits.

If we found any misfortune cookies at Yee & Sons today, I'd be very tempted to shove them down Lily's throat.

"Here we are." As we reached the front door of Yee's Trading Company, I looked at Max with concern. "Are you sure you're ready for this?"

Max smiled sadly and gave my arm a reassuring squeeze. "She is not Li Xiuying. She never was. I merely . . . danced with a ghost for an evening or two."

"Oh, Max . . . Li Xiuying must have been quite a woman."

"She was remarkable," he said wistfully. Then he cleared his throat. "But she has been gone a long time, and there are people here and now who need our protection—as she would certainly remind me. So, come," he said firmly. "We must put an end to this dreadful business."

"Yes."

When we entered the shop, though, rather than immediately launch into a confrontation with Lily, who was standing near the cash register, we just stared in bemused surprise.

Apparently the Yee family had turned a corner of some sort since I had spoken with Ted this morning.

Lily stood there with her long black hair tumbled down her back, rather than in a tidy bun. Her beautiful face, free of makeup today, was ravaged with emotion and streaked with tears. And Ted, always so easy-going and cheerful, was now shouting at her in anger.

When he saw us, he cried, "Esther! You would not *believe* what my family has been doing!"

"Inflicting terrible curses on anyone who tries to help you make this movie?" I guessed.

Lily shrieked in horror, covered her face with her hands, and sank to her knees, sobbing copiously. Which wasn't really the reaction I had been expecting.

Ted's jaw hung open as he stared as me. "You *know?*"

"We figured it out a little while ago." Since Ted wasn't exactly the sharpest knife in the drawer, I asked, "How did *you* find out?"

Over his mother's wailing sobs, which he ignored, Ted said, "After I talked with you, I was ready to tell Mom my decision. That I'm going to quit making the film." With an exasperated look at his sobbing mother, he said, "*She* thought that meant I'd work full-time in the store now and eventually take it over. But I explained that will *never* happen. Never!" He looked at Lily and shouted, "Get that through your head, once and for all!"

"After all I have done!" she shrieked.

Ted said to us, "I'm thinking of going into graphic novels. I've always loved comic books, and it would be a great format for *ABC.* In fact, I think I could get a whole series out of Brian's search for identity! See, I'd change the story so that—"

"And your mother reacted badly?" I asked loudly.

"My mother reacted like a *lunatic,*" Ted said with a long-suffering look, starting to calm down a little now that he was talking to someone who was *not* his mother. "Oh, my *God,* Esther, the things Mom did to Mary. Unbelievable! I think we should give Mary this whole damn store by way of apology."

Max asked, "Where are the misfortune cookies made?"

"Huh?"

"The curses," Max clarified. "Where is the work done?"

"Oh. I don't know. We didn't get that far." He looked at his mother. "Mom?"

Lily wiped her runny nose with her sleeve. Breathing hard, still on her knees, she thought it over for a moment, then nodded. "Yes. The workshop should be destroyed. She will kill again."

"She?" I said.

"Susan." Max looked at Lily. "It was Susan who augmented the attacks, wasn't it?"

"I urged patience," Lily sobbed. "There was no need to *kill*. The white girl was out of the movie. Benny was losing money everywhere and couldn't keep funding the film. We only needed to wait . . . But Susan is too American."

"I *beg* your pardon?" I said, offended.

"For her, everything must be now, now, now."

"Oh, that's not because she's American, you manipulative, curse-inflicting witch," I snapped. "It's because she's a homicidal maniac!" Then I blinked in surprise and looked at Max. "It's Susan, then?"

"It's *both* of them," Ted said in disgust. "Mom, I am *so* leaving home. For good, this time."

Max said, "Lily had the gift and taught it to her daughter—who has, I believe, a very great talent?"

Lily nodded and then let out another keening wail, rocking back and forth on her knees.

"You suspected this?" I said to Max.

"Not until you told me about poor Mary Fox on the way here," he said. "That's when I realized the approach to sabotaging Ted's film had changed a great deal, though the methodology had remained the same. I suspected a devious, amoral mother may have started the plot, and then been superseded by a very talented and murderous daughter."

"Susan killed Benny and Uncle Six?" Then I realized something else. "Susan tried to kill Lopez!"

"She wanted to kill John, too," said Ted in outrage. "Because he came up with a plan to help me get investors."

"She was beside herself about that," Lily said, wiping her eyes. "The loss of face, the shame—Ted publicly begging strangers for money for his 'piece of crap' movie. It was even worse, Susan said, than taking money from gangsters like Benny and Uncle Six."

"So she planned to kill *John?*" I said in horror.

"Where is the cookie?" Max said urgently. "She must have made one for John."

"I destroyed it this morning," Lily said. "John is a good boy. I told her she couldn't do this. I wouldn't allow it." Lily's face crumpled again. "We fought terribly. She has gone *insane*. I cannot control her."

"Did she make another cookie after that?"

"No, there was no time."

"Oh, thank God," I said.

"But she will try again. She will never stop. I see that now. The workshop," Lily said to Max, taking deep gulps of air. "It must be destroyed. The whole thing. And the wards must be eliminated."

"Susan established the wards, didn't she?" said Max.

"Yes."

"Of course," he said. "A talented sorceress of Chinese heritage, studying architecture in the mundane world. What would be more natural than for her to experiment with the most esoteric aspects of *feng shui* in order to conceal the powerful fatal magics being created in this building?"

So Susan had lied about not being interested in *feng shui.* I realized now that Max had suspected something of the sort—though he had been distracted by the ghost of Li Xiuying in the face of Lily Yee.

I turned to help Max as he started struggling out of the old daypack he had donned over his heavy coat. Once the pack was removed, he reached inside it and pulled out . . .

"A hammer?" I said. "What are you going to do with a hammer?" It seemed a rather mundane thing for Max, of all people, to carry around.

"Susan is very powerful," he said. "Very talented. But not original or creative. And she's inexperienced. I believe that destroying the wards which have made this building such a peculiar place to visit will be almost childishly simple."

He walked over to the mirror that faced the door. Although he had commented on it during our first visit here, I'd barely noticed it. It was just an ordinary red-framed mirror hanging on the wall. It faced the door and, like that structure, was tilted at a slight angle.

Max said a few words in Chinese—I had no idea whether he was speaking Mandarin or Cantonese—then smashed the mirror with his hammer.

The whole building seemed to inhale, quiver, and then scream. As the floor beneath my feet heaved and gave way, I fell down. Ted shouted and flew across the room, as if thrown by a giant unseen hand. Mystical wind whipped through the store, blowing Lily's long hair wildly around her head. Max, who somehow stayed upright, continued smashing the mirror with his hammer. Then he began pulverizing the broken pieces that lay on the heaving floor. From my prone position, I saw Ted fly back in the other direction, screaming in panic, his eyes wide with shocked fear.

When I heard a horrible screeching behind me, I rolled over, expecting to see the building collapsing on top of me or something. Instead, I saw the slightly tilted doorway straighten itself out, realigning until it was perfectly perpendicular to the floor, undulating and shuddering with the effort. As soon as it finished this transformation and went still . . . All the heaving, shrieking, screeching, and blowing stopped.

I lay there on the solid, unmoving floor, breathing heavily. Ted promptly fell on top of me, as if dropped by the unseen hand that had been flinging him around the room. He apologized to me, sounding winded, then rolled away.

"Is everyone all right?" Max asked, breathing hard. "I realized only after the event commenced that I should have warned you there would be some dramatic effects."

"Oh, y'*think*?" I said.

"Whoa!" said Ted. "That was like a religious experience!"

Still breathing hard in reaction, I sat up and looked around. The store looked different now. Not unrecognizable—the style of the building and basic décor were the same. But everything was lined up in a visibly more rational pattern now. I could see the back of the store, a flight of stairs, neatly-aligned shelves, straight walls . . . Although I had no interest in venturing upstairs here ever again, I had a feeling that if I did so, the layout would be perfectly self-explanatory now, rather than a mystifying maze from which it seemed impossible to escape.

Max looked at Lily. "The workshop?"

"Downstairs," she said. "I will show you."

"What about John?" said Ted. "Someone's got to help him!"

I looked at Lily. "I thought you said you destroyed the cookie that Susan created to kill John?"

"I did, but Susan is . . . *demented,*" Lily said in a tragic tone. "Determined to kill him. To stop him from helping Ted."

"And?" I prodded, worried about John.

Ted said, "She got a gun from Danny Teng. She's planning to *shoot* John."

Lily added, "She's out looking for him right now."

I glared at Lily. "You realize, don't you, that you've raised a ruthless, obsessive killer?"

"And a bitch," Ted grumbled.

"She is too American," Lily said again, which made me want to slap her.

"We must divide forces!" Max declared. "Lily and I shall destroy the workshop and eliminate all remaining mystical influences from this edifice."

I nodded. "Ted and I will stop Susan from shooting John."

"Whoa. We *will?*"

"I will stop Susan from shooting John," I amended.

"Well, I could try to *help* . . ."

I asked, "What does John's lion look like, and where is it?"

The Yees didn't know. But, of course, I knew someone who could tell me. When I called John's "Uncle Lucky," he instructed me to head for Doyers Street.

"John's probably there right now. Look for a big red lion," said Lucky. "You can't miss it. Huge ears with gold tassels. And John's red sneakers. Nelli and I will meet you there!"

18

舞獅

Lion Dance

"I'm going to Doyers Street," I said to Max. I tried not to think about the fact that the street was also known as the Bloody Angle. "Ted, you try calling Bill and John. See if you can warn them!"

I dashed out of the shop and started running down the street, shoving my way through the holiday crowd. As I pictured Susan pointing a gun at John, I realized this was the sort of mundane problem that the police could handle better than anyone else. So I slowed down to a trot as I pulled my phone out of my pocket and called Lopez.

"Esther?" he said when he answered. "Is that you?"

"Yes. This is an emer—"

"A smash and grab?" he said. "Are you *insane?*"

"What?"

"After I left last night," he said. "You smashed in the window of my car—a *police car,* I might add—and stole my fortune cookie?"

"Oh! Right. *That.*"

"Yes, *that,*" he snapped.

"How did you find out?"

"They didn't make me a detective for my pretty face, Esther," he said tersely. "There were witnesses. I found them. Easily."

"Oh."

"That's it?" he said incredulously. " 'Oh?' "

"Look, I can explain, but not right now."

"I should have stayed away altogether. I don't know what I was thinking, coming back for more," he said. "Okay, I *do* know. Sex. Well, partly, anyhow. But this is the limit, Esther. Seriously. This is warped, even for *you.*"

"Even for *me?* What does *that* . . . No, never mind." I was still barreling through the crowd and shoving my way past people. "We can't talk about that right now."

"I don't think we should talk anymore at *all.* I must have been out of my mind to think we could—"

"This is an emergency!" I shouted at him. "Susan Yee has got a gun, and she's planning to shoot John Chen!"

"What?"

"On Doyers Street! Right now. John's in a red lion costume! Susan Yee has got a gun and is hunting for him! Send help!"

He could tell I was serious. "Doyers Street. Got it. I'm calling it in right now."

He ended the call. I shoved my phone into my pocket and ran as fast as I could, heading for the Bloody Angle, not bothering to apologize as I pushed people out of my way.

To my relief, as soon as I turned into the little street, I saw an enormous, beautiful, magical-looking, bright red creature in front of the little restaurant where I and the *ABC* cast had eaten lunch not long ago. The lion was performing a graceful, athletic dance for the crowd gathered here. Everyone was smiling, and many people were bobbing up and down a little in time to the percussion music that accompanied the dance . . .

But one pretty, petite woman in the crowd with a chic haircut was making her way toward the lion, her face grim with purpose, her eyes burning with deadly intent.

"John! She's got a gun! *John!* Susan's got a gun!"

I was running straight at them, shouting as loudly as I could. But the music was drowning me out and the dense crowd slowed me down.

On the other side of the sharp curve that defined Doyers, I could hear police sirens.

Oh, thank God!

They were coming up from the Bowery—and they evidently drove through the traffic barrier that had been established for today, heading straight for us.

The intrusion of police cars and wailing sirens on this scene startled everyone. People were turning around to look at the flashing lights and at the cops pouring out of the cars. The musicians stopped playing, wondering what was going on.

"John!" I screamed, and I could tell by the way the lion flinched that he heard me this time. My heart pounding, I burst through the crowd and screamed, "Susan's got a gun!"

"*Esther!* Get back!"

I recognized Lopez's voice and realized he must be in one of the police cars that was disgorging cops as I dived toward the red lion, practically bodysurfing over the crowd.

"*Nooooo!*" It was a woman's scream, shrill and enraged—Susan, I realized.

The red lion froze for a moment, then start undulating, as if struggling to shapeshift; apparently John and Bill were trying to get out of their costume.

I realized in the next instant that Susan was pointing her gun at *me* now. At point-blank range.

"Kid!" That was Lucky's voice, somewhere off to my right.

Nelli was barking.

"Esther!" Lopez shouted. "Get *down!*"

"Noooo!" Susan's eyes—insane, wild, wrathful.

I stared at the barrel of the gun.

You really should have planned this better, Esther.

I was about to be shot instead of John. Not really my intention in coming here.

"Esther!" Lopez shouted. *"Esther!"*

An enormous jet of flame shot from the mouth of the red lion toward Susan. It was like a horizontal waterfall of fire, pouring straight at her.

She screamed in startled fear, staggered backward, and dropped the gun. Although not in danger from the flame, which was nowhere near me, I staggered sideways to get further away from it.

As soon as Susan leaped out of the path of the fire, a man with curly blond hair and a big beard launched himself at her, taking her down in a flying tackle while bellowing loudly. Then Nelli was right behind him, barking ferociously.

Sobbing and shrieking, Susan struggled and tried to reach for the gun she had dropped, which lay nearby.

The bearded blond man kicked it away. "Don't even think about it, sister!"

Nelli was still barking.

"Lucky?" I said to the blond man.

"You all right, kid?" he called.

"Esther!" Lopez was there, his hands on my shoulders. "Are you all right? Are you okay?"

"Oh. Um . . ." Safe now, I felt slightly dazed. "I'm fine."

He shook me. "What were you thinking? *Never* step in front of a gun! Never!" Then he hugged me fiercely.

Uniformed cops were pulling Lucky off of Susan Yee. Not exactly the most balanced of women, she struggled like a wild thing, ranting and raving, shrieking and howling. When she flung out an arm, her fist connected with Lucky's face. He cried out and staggered backward.

"Oh, no!" I cried, pulling myself out of Lopez's bruising embrace. "Are you all right?"

"Fine. *Ow.* Fine." Lucky pulled off his fake beard and tenderly felt his jaw. "That girl coulda been a boxer."

"Officer Novak!" I said in surprise, recognizing one of the cops who were trying to get the frightened crowd under control.

"Miss Diamond." He nodded to me and grinned. "You movie people lead such exciting lives!"

"I think my heart stopped," Lopez said irritably. "And when did they start putting flamethrowers in the lions around here?"

"Esther! Are you all right?" asked the lion, its mouth now darkly singed from its fiery attack on Susan.

"I'm fine, John. A little shaken up, but fine."

"Uncle Lucky!" The lion trotted across the street.

"You got here fast," I said to Lopez.

"I was just around the corner." He grabbed me

again for another fierce hug and said against my hair, "What were you *thinking?*"

"I wasn't thinking," I admitted. "I just didn't want John to get shot. It really didn't occur to me until she pointed the gun at *me* that she might shoot anyone else. After all, she was obsessed with the idea of killing John."

"Why? I mean, who *is* John? Why does Ted's sister want to kill him?"

"It's such a long story." I shook my head. "Maybe later."

I realized that after weeks of being cold, I was sweating now. I unbuttoned my coat as I went over to Lucky and John.

John had removed his lion head, and he and Bill were looking at the enormous thing in perplexity.

"What the hell happened with that thing?" Lucky asked as he removed his wig. I saw that he was sweating, too.

"I don't know," said John, frowning as he stuck his head inside the lion's mouth, apparently looking for whatever had caused that burst of fire. *"Weird."*

Lopez joined him. "You mean that wasn't on purpose?"

John shook his head. "I don't even know what 'that' was."

Lucky said, "It saved Esther's life, though."

I looked at Lopez and remembered what Max had said.

Extreme stress triggers these interesting events. His emotions and his focus become powerful enough for him to affect matter and energy, though it's not conscious and he doesn't realize it's happening.

He'd obviously been pretty damn stressed by seeing Susan about to shoot me. I'd been pretty stressed by it, too.

So I thought *I* knew why a lifesaving burst of fire had poured from the creature's mouth, aimed straight for Susan. Even though everyone else, including Lopez, was mystified by the event as they poked and prodded John's singed lion costume.

Lucky said to me, "Is my face swelling?"

"Huh? Oh." I looked at his jaw. "Maybe a little. We should get some ice."

Lopez looked away from the lion to glance at us. He registered Lucky's presence with surprise. "Hello, Lucky."

We froze.

Shit.

Lopez looked at the hairy disguise that was now in Lucky's hand. "Do I even want to know why you were wearing a wig?"

Nelli, who recognized Lopez, greeted him with friendly good cheer.

"Oh, good," he said. "It's Max's neurotic dog. Where's Max?"

"Busy," I said. "Not here."

Lucky sighed in defeat. "You'd better take Nelli,

kid." He gave me her leash, then turned to Lopez. "It don't seem fair that this happened when I only came out here to save my nephew's life."

"And he saved me, too," I added, hoping this would help.

"Uncle Lucky?" John said, looking worried.

"But whaddya gonna do? You got me, detective." He stretched out his wrists toward Lopez to be cuffed. "And I ain't saying a thing until I see my lawyer."

Lopez looked down at Lucky's outstretched arms, then back at his face. "I must have missed a chapter. What are we doing?"

John and I looked at him.

He looked at us.

I finally said, "You're not going to arrest him?"

Lopez asked Lucky, "Did you do something illegal here today that I didn't see?"

Lucky lowered his hands. "You're not bringin' me in?"

"For what?"

Looking a little annoyed now, Lucky said, "You've arrested half the family!"

"Yeah, and I'm hoping to arrest a few more," Lopez said. "But I don't have a warrant for you."

"What?" John blurted.

"What?" I said.

"Either you're smarter than you look," Lopez said to the old mobster, "or you're as lucky as they say. Because we can't get anything on you. You're free to go."

"I'm what?"

"Of course, if you want to confess some crimes, I'd be happy to take you in," Lopez offered.

"No, no. That's fine. I'm happy to be a free man, detective."

Lopez shrugged and then turned away from us to speak to Officer Novak.

John started laughing. "Oh, my *God.*"

"Shut up," Lucky said darkly to him.

I was laughing, too.

"Three weeks trapped in a Chinese funeral home," I murmured to Lucky. "And the cops weren't even looking for you."

"If the two of you ever tell *anyone* . . ." he muttered.

John and I just kept laughing.

"Hmph." Lucky took Nelli's leash from me and stomped away, the picture of offended dignity.

As the milling crowd began to thin out a bit, I saw Detective Quinn over by the police cars. He was talking on his phone.

"Esther, I don't even know what to say." John turned to me. "I think you saved my life today."

"Does that make you indebted to me for a thousand years?" I asked with a smile. "Or do you have to save *my* life now?"

Lopez finished speaking with Officer Novak and caught my eye. He made a gesture indicating he wanted me to join him.

Here we go, I thought. I'd have to explain about last night's smash and grab.

"I was thinking more along the lines of inviting you to dinner," John said. "You know, to thank you. And to . . . well, maybe just to have dinner together?"

Lopez raised his brows at me, impatient to talk.

"I mean, can I call you?" John asked.

"Huh? Oh, sure," I said. "Will you excuse me, John?"

I wasn't looking forward to this, but I'd better get it over with.

"You're sure you're okay?" Lopez asked in a low voice when I reached his side. "You scared me to death today."

"I'm fine." This had happened before. At Fenster's, in fact. So I said, "It turns out that the second time a deranged killer points a gun at you, you get over it faster than the first time. I'm already feeling more like my usual self. Weird, huh?"

"Everything about this was weird," he said, looking again at the singed red lion head. "But none of it as weird—"

"Here we go."

"—as you breaking into my car last night to steal a *cookie*. What the hell was that about?"

"I was hungry," I tried.

"Esther."

"Where did you get that cookie?" I asked.

"Someone sent it to me at work."

"Who?"

"Not sure. The card got lost."

"I see."

I was *very* glad Susan was going to prison. (Well, I assumed she was. Apart from pointing a loaded gun at me and John today, she was also still screaming and fighting, over by the squad cars, as the police were trying to book her. I didn't think she was going to turn out to be a very convincing defendant.

"Earth to Esther," Lopez said impatiently.

"What? Oh." I said, "I'm really sorry about the car."

"It can be repaired. I'm not sure this can."

"This?"

"Us. Esther . . . what were you *doing?*"

I decided just to tell him. "I was saving your life. The cookie contained a mystical death curse."

After a few seconds of silence, he said, "That's it? That's your story?"

"Yes."

"Well, doesn't *that* just figure?" he said in disgust. "I have no idea what to do with you."

"Maybe there are some things we should try to talk—"

Nelli burst into a hysterical torrent of barking—a furious, frightening, menacing sound. I turned to look at her, startled by the racket—and saw Lucky restraining her while she bared her fangs at Detective Quinn, who was simply passing by. He gave her a wide berth, looking as startled as anyone would look in those circumstances.

Although Lucky had a firm hand on her collar, he wasn't reprimanding Nelli. He was looking down at her with a puzzled frown. She was growling and barking, her eyes fixed fiercely on Quinn, her fangs dripping, her hair standing on end. Even after the detective was well past her, her gaze remained glued to him, fierce, menacing, warning him to watch out. Her whole body was puffed up, aggressive, and ready for action.

"Oh, for fuck's sake, Esther," Lopez said. "You cannot have a dog that size who behaves that way. Especially not in the city! Max needs to get rid of her. I mean it."

I was still looking at Nelli. Then my gaze shifted to Lucky. He looked up and met my eyes. He jerked his chin, indicating we should leave.

"We'll get her out of here," I said absently to Lopez. "Sorry."

"Esther, I'm serious. That dog is dangerous. And you and I aren't done talking about what you did last night, either. Esther! Are you listening to me?"

"Bye," I said. "I've gotta go."

When I reached Lucky's side, I asked, "What the hell happened? What set her off?"

"I don't know," Lucky said in a low voice. "All

that guy did was walk past us. Didn't even look this way. But she went berserk as soon as she sensed him. And look her even now. She can't take her eyes off him."

I looked at Quinn, who was at least fifty yards away now, talking with a cop at the other end of the street. He looked completely normal—as he had looked each time I'd encountered him.

"Nelli?" I said, bemused by the familiar's behavior. "Nelli?"

But she ignored me, her gaze fixed on Quinn, her posture menacing, a faint growl rumbling in her throat each time he moved.

"Max says she can sense demonic entities and mystical beings," Lucky pointed out. "And we seen her react to dangerous things before."

"But Quinn just seems like a normal guy," I protested.

"To you, maybe. But not to our favorite familiar—a mystical being herself, who entered this dimension to fight Evil." Lucky asked, "Who is that guy, anyway?"

"Lopez's new partner," I said with a dawning feeling of dread.

"In that case," Lucky said, "I think we'd better go talk to Max."

I watched Lopez walk over to Quinn, who grinned at him and said something. Lopez shook his head, and the two of them stood talking.

Nelli growled again, clearly upset to see someone she liked standing that close to Quinn.

"Yeah," I said, wondering what Nelli sensed about Lopez's new partner that alarmed her so. "We *do* need to go find Max."

Author's Note

Tiger

People born in the Year of the Tiger, as I was, are said to be courageous, honest, lucky, rebellious, arrogant, unpredictable, and resilient. I can live with that description.

The idea for Lily Yee's store came from a shop that I entered just to get out of the rain when visiting Vancouver's Chinatown several years ago. Much like the shop in this novel, it was a small, generic storefront that blossomed into an extensive maze of rooms full of wonders and oddities. My enchantment with that place led me to start thinking about a story that would take Esther Diamond to New York's Chinatown.

The idea for the misfortune cookies was the result

of editor Betsy Wollheim mercilessly rejecting one mediocre title after another for Esther's Chinatown adventure, until I came up with *The Misfortune Cookie*. Initially relieved that She Who Must Be Obeyed had *finally* approved a title for the book . . . I then realized I needed to come up with a plot for it. (It's always something.)

In researching this book, I paid multiple visits to New York's Chinatown (and I took Betsy along with me for several hours on a particularly frigid day, so I got my revenge). Following the lion dancers around was probably the most fun I had, out of many wonderful experiences there. Some of the most informative hours I spent in Chinatown were with Susan Rosenbaum, the Enthusiastic Gourmet, who offers fascinating food tours of the neighborhood. But tasting dried cuttlefish is not an experience I ever intend to repeat.

For readers interested in delving further into Chinatown, some of my most enjoyable background reading included: Jennifer 8. Lee's engaging *The Fortune Cookie Chronicles: Adventures in the World of Chinese Food*; Patrick Radden Keefe's *The Snakehead: An Epic Tale of the Chinatown Underworld and the American Dream*, which I found unputdownable; and the beautifully photographed *Chinatown, New York: Portraits, Recipes, and Memories* by Ann Volkwein and Vegar Abelsnes.

My thanks to Dan Dos Santos, the brilliant artist

for the Esther Diamond series, who has raised the bar still higher with this dynamite cover. Thanks also to the tremendous co-publishers at DAW Books, Sheila Gilbert and Betsy Wollheim, to managing editor Joshua Starr (who puts up with a *lot*), and to the rest of the wonderful team at DAW Books.

Finally, I must emphasize that this book is a work of fiction and does not seriously seek to question, challenge, or undermine the inherent and indisputable goodness of all cookies everywhere. Indeed, throughout the writing of *The Misfortune Cookie*, I relied heavily, as I so often do, on the Elizabeth Beverly Theory of Plotting (Liz is a prolific novelist and a friend of mine): There is no plot problem that cookies cannot solve.

Anyhow, I hope you've enjoyed *The Misfortune Cookie* so much that you immediately succumb to an uncontrollable impulse to go eat in a Chinese restaurant. Which is probably where Esther Diamond will be until she, her friends, and her nemeses return for their next misadventure—which book title will be announced on my website after I come up with one that She Who Must Be Obeyed approves . . .

—Laura Resnick